Flight

OF THE

Raven

MYSTERIES OF SPARROW ISLAND™

Flight
OF THE
Raven

ELLEN HARRIS

GuidepostsBooks®

New York, New York

Flight of the Raven

ISBN-13: 978-0-8249-4712-5
ISBN-10: 0-8249-4712-6

Published by GuidepostsBooks
16 East 34th Street
New York, New York 10016
www.guidepostsbooks.com

Distributed by Ideals Publications, a Guideposts company
535 Metroplex Drive, Suite 250
Nashville, Tennessee 37211

GuidepostsBooks, *Ideals* and *Mysteries of Sparrow Island* are registered trademarks of Guideposts, Carmel, New York.

The characters and events in this book are fictional, and any resemblance to actual persons or events is coincidental.

Acknowledgments
Every attempt has been made to credit the sources of copyrighted material used in this book. If any such acknowledgment has been inadvertently omitted or miscredited, receipt of such information would be appreciated.

All Scripture quotations are taken from The Holy Bible, New International Version. Copyright © 1973, 1978, 1984 International Bible Society. Used by permission of Zondervan Bible Publishers.

Library of Congress Cataloging-in-Publication Data

Harris, Ellen.
  Flight of the Raven / Ellen Harris.
    p. cm. -- (Mysteries of Sparrow Island)
  ISBN-13: 978-0-8249-4712-5
  1. Aircraft accidents--Fiction. 2. Missing persons--Fiction. I. Title.
  PS3608.A7828F55 2007
  813'.6--dc22

                          2006021347

Cover illustration by Chris Hopkins
Designed by Marisa Jackson

Printed and bound in the United States of America

10 9 8 7 6 5 4 3 2 1

*For Alpha Goodson Harris and
Eleanor ("Nanner") Harris Bonner,
women who lived their faith.*

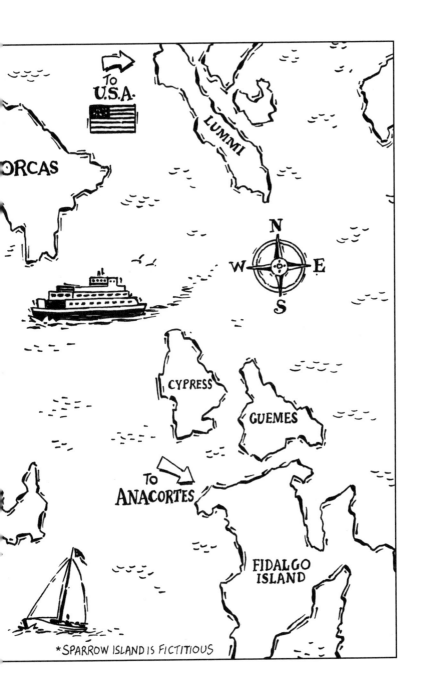

TO U.S.A.

LUMMI

ORCAS

N
W   E
S

CYPRESS

GUEMES

TO ANACORTES

FIDALGO ISLAND

*SPARROW ISLAND IS FICTITIOUS

Chapter One

Do you think they'll make it?" Bobby asked. He picked up the binoculars from the railing of the observation platform and trained them on the wooden box filled with branches and twigs that sat on the edge of the bluff.

"I think we've done our part for these particular birds," Abby told him, pushing a thumbtack into the last laminated poster on the observation platform's easel. "The rest is in better hands than ours."

Abby knew the answer wouldn't satisfy Bobby for long. He was an unusual ten-year-old. Like Abby, he had a curious mind, and a powerful need to fill in the specifics. More questions were sure to follow.

Abby shed her jacket, draping it over the back of the bench seat. The sunny September Wednesday afternoon had gifted them with summer temperatures. And the quarter-mile walk from The Nature Museum to the observation platform on the conservatory grounds had warmed her up considerably. Bobby's eagerness to see the birds had set a brisk pace.

"Can we put the puppets up out here so people can see them on Saturday?" he asked, his hazel eyes still clouded with worry.

"That's a good idea, Bobby," Abby told him. "But not until then. We don't want the falcons spotting the puppets and getting confused, you know. They still think of them as Mom and Dad."

Bobby grinned and Abby was happy to see the worry lines in his forehead disappear, at least for the time being. "Well, in a way they are, right?" he asked.

Abby nodded and smiled back at the boy. Bobby was proud of his part in constructing the puppets that had served as surrogate parents for the three peregrine falcons they had hand-raised at the Sparrow Island Nature Conservatory. And truth be known, so was Abby. This was the first time in her long career as an ornithologist that Abby Stanton had been given the opportunity to work closely with these birds of prey.

"They've sure grown up fast, haven't they?" Bobby asked, and Abby had to stifle a laugh. He sounded like a wistful parent himself.

Abby thought back to the day a few short weeks ago when a hiker had come in to tell her about the orphaned falcons. He'd stopped on the trail to take some photographs, and as he stood concentrating on focusing his camera, he'd heard the chicks. He'd stayed around, hoping for a chance to photograph the adults feeding them. The birds would be easy to spot with their gray bodies and pale breasts, and their distinctive black caps and mustache. But after a long wait, he'd finally noticed the feathers and other remains on the ground, along with a few tufts of red fur, and realized the adults weren't likely to be coming back. He surmised—correctly, Abby thought—that the adults had been killed while defending the nest from one of their few natural predators, a red fox. He knew the three young birds would not make it without help.

And now she shielded her eyes and looked up into the sky. One of the falcons had caught an updraft and was wheeling on the wing. The warm air hit the cliffs and was pushed up—the sun-baked rock creating thermals where the birds could soar effortlessly. Abby smiled contentedly. The bird's wings were outstretched and motionless as it floated high above in slow, lazy circles.

"This isn't really a release, is it?" Bobby asked as he stretched the banner he and Abby had made across the front of the platform. "Maybe we should have called it a graduation."

"You're right," Abby said. "It's not a release. The birds haven't been captive for some time now. The only thing holding them here is a sense of home, a feeling of belonging to a place," she said. *But that's a strong pull*, she thought, one she understood more than ever now that she had returned home to Sparrow Island.

The birds had started off inside the workroom at the conservatory building being fed by puppet parents to keep them from imprinting their human caregivers. They had then been "hacked out," or artificially reared. The nestlings were placed in a box high on a cliff some distance from the observation platform. Their human caregivers had fed them from atop the cliff until they could fly out and hunt on their own, which they'd been doing for a few days now. Though they hadn't gone off to find their own way in the world just yet, the time was coming, and the folks on Sparrow Island wanted an opportunity to give them a proper send-off.

Abby turned back to the platform and squinted. Only a few more items to put up in the display cabinet and they'd be done. Saturday's unveiling of the viewing platform would be the first official function to be held out here. The platform had been completed just last week with the addition of the handrails, again with ample help from community volunteers.

The platform was raised on stilts to facilitate better viewing of the bird habitats. It featured several shallow glass-fronted cases that displayed information about the conservatory and educational materials on the various birds that could be seen in season.

In front of the platform were benches so bird lovers could sit and watch for birds. When funding permitted, there would be several stanchions with spotting scopes, but for now it was BYOB—bring your own binoculars.

"Bobby, how about if on Saturday you do the part of the presentation that tells how we made the puppets and fed the nestlings in the beginning?" Abby asked.

Bobby's face lit up. He had spent hours studying the coloring and markings of the adult peregrines and helping Abby fashion puppets from burlap, felt, feathers and cork until they were reasonable facsimiles of Mama and Papa Falcon.

"Yeah, I'd love to. Should I tell about how people were all trying to do their best falcon imitations when it was their turn to feed?" he asked with a giggle.

"What do you think?" Abby asked. "Should we make up some award certificates for the best falcon imitations?"

"That would be pretty funny," Bobby said.

Getting the special permit required to hand-raise the nestlings had been a bureaucratic tangle, but Abby had become accustomed to dealing with red tape in her years as a research scientist at Cornell back in upstate New York. This was just one of many skills that had made Hugo Baron, the curator of the Sparrow Island Nature Conservatory, so eager to hire her in the first place.

Abby had been flattered, but she'd initially turned down his offer. Although she'd liked what Hugo had done with the land and how he had added The Nature Museum to the grounds—where children and adults could learn about the natural world—she was on the island for another reason. She'd returned to take care of her sister Mary after a car accident had left Mary's legs paralyzed. The plan had been that Abby would look after Mary during her recovery, oversee the necessary modifications to Mary's house, then return to her work and her life in New York when her leave was exhausted.

When she thought back to that time, it brought to mind a poster one of her colleagues in the lab had kept tacked to his bulletin board. It featured a bluebird looking out from a nest she'd built in a rural mailbox. Underneath, it read: *Life is what happens when you're making other plans.*

"Are Mr. and Mrs. Stanton coming on Saturday?" Bobby asked. "Mr. Stanton helped build the hacking box. And Mrs. Stanton helped feed the birds when they were really little. I'll bet they want to say good-bye."

"You bet they will," Abby said. "Yes, Mom and Dad are planning to be here. You know my dad is the one who got me interested in birds. He used to take me out birding when I was a little girl."

"You're lucky," Bobby said.

"Yes, yes I am," Abby said, taking in a great lungful of air scented with loamy earth, evergreen and the briny smell of the sea.

Abby thought back to the tragic event that had called her home, and how bit by bit she had begun to imagine what life would be like if she stayed—permanently. Her relationship with Mary had grown closer than it had been since they were girls. Mary, widowed for ten years, lived alone and needed her sister in a way she never had before. Abby was grateful, too, to be able to spend time with her parents on Stanton Farm. They were, after all, getting on in years and time was growing more precious.

As the days had passed, Abby began to feel that perhaps returning to the island was part of God's plan for her life. One night while Abby was sitting outside in the stillness of nature, she believed she heard God speak to her, counseling her on whether to stay on Sparrow Island or return to her life in New

York. She came to the realization that there was a time for everything in life, and it was now time for her to return home. Afterward she'd felt a peace that had been missing in her hectic life for a very long time.

And Hugo had been nothing if not persistent in his attempts to get her to come to work for him. In the end, he had fashioned a job with duties so well suited to Abby's talents, and hours so tailored to accommodate her desire to help Mary, she had to say yes.

"Is Mary coming?" Bobby asked. "I think her wheelchair could make it down the path, and the ramp for the observation platform is done now."

"Yes, I think Mary plans to come," Abby said. "Getting around is much easier for her now that she has the van. What a wonderful gift that has been."

"People here are nice," Bobby said, his tone matter-of-fact.

Yes, Abby thought. *People here are nice.* Now that she had made the move and was committed to staying, Abby was working on finding her place as a mature woman back in the home of her childhood.

Sparrow Island was an idyllic place, not only due to its scenic beauty, but also because of the people who populated the island. Some of them Abby had known for years. More recent arrivals she was just getting to know as she settled back into the community.

Like young Bobby McDonald at the rail watching out for his falcons. Bobby's mother was a teacher and needed child care

for Bobby on the days when she had after-school duties, so
Abby had come up with the idea of making him a junior docent
at the conservatory. The arrangement had worked out well,
though Abby was usually pleasantly exhausted from his questions by the end of the day.

Abby had never spent much time around children. For
most of her adult life she'd worked in her laboratory or outdoors doing fieldwork and attending conferences and sympo-
siums. She had, of course, always loved Mary's children,
Nancy and Zack. She had reveled in the role of aunt, but
truthfully, she'd never had the opportunity to spend much
time with them when they were growing up. After all, she had
lived and worked on the opposite coast and visits were few
and far between. And, more to the point, she'd never thought
of herself as being particularly good with children.

But then again, Bobby McDonald was an exceptional
child and he shared her endless curiosity about all things in
nature. She found she was seeing many things anew as she
shared his joy of discovery. It might be a cliché, but it didn't
make it any less true—seeing the world through the eyes of a
child was giving her a whole new perspective.

Bobby came around to look at the posters. "Do we have it
in here that the falcons can get up to two hundred miles an
hour when they're power-diving after their prey?" he asked.
"Because that's a really interesting fact."

"Yes, we do. Right here in this section," Abby told him,
pointing out the text underneath a beautiful watercolor illus-

tration of a peregrine in flight that one of the artists from the island had painted especially to commemorate Saturday's bon voyage celebration.

Bobby gave a satisfied nod and traced his fingers over the poster. When he had finished reading the passage he returned to his post, scanning the sky for any sign of the other two falcons.

Abby looked up to again admire the lone, soaring specimen. Then she noticed something else sharing the sky with the bird, and she instinctively stood up straight and grabbed the binoculars dangling around her neck. A plane—a small seaplane from what she could tell at this distance—seemed to be headed toward the water, its nose dipped at an angle sure to cause it to flip and cartwheel across the surface on contact. Abby tensed, but as she found it in her sights she saw the plane pull back up and gain altitude, leveling out again. *Must be a new pilot practicing an approach*, she thought. Even pilots experienced with landings on terra firma sometimes had difficulty learning the complexities of water landings. Dry land provided a certain constancy, but the sea surface was different day to day and, sometimes, hour to hour.

Abby studied the plane for a moment. Seaplanes, or floatplanes as people in the San Juans called them, were peculiar looking, with large pontoons affixed where the landing wheels would be on a regular plane. They looked like overgrown skis and gave the plane a cumbersome appearance, but they were a standard form of transportation in the islands. They could deliver a person right to a dock with relative ease, but it was imperative to have an experienced pilot.

The plane flew level for a bit, but just as Abby put her binoculars down, its wings began seesawing and it dropped altitude once more. The angle was less sharp, but the nose was still tipped too far down, and Abby gasped involuntarily as she shielded her eyes against the afternoon sun. The plane dropped lower, its wings still waggling, then its nose pulled up sharply and it started to climb.

"What do you see?" Bobby asked. "Is one of the other falcons back?"

"No, no, Bobby. It's just the one still. I was looking at that plane. I wondered if maybe the pilot was in trouble. But it looks like it's okay now. It's flying level again."

"Maybe they saw some orcas and are trying to get down lower to have a better look. They do that sometimes. Even though they shouldn't," he added disapprovingly. "Or maybe it's a student pilot."

He stood beside Abby. "I want to be a pilot someday," he said, first studying to see where Abby was looking, then bringing his binoculars to his eyes.

"It's just over there," Abby said, adjusting his angle slightly. "I think it's okay now. It's gone behind those trees." She tilted her head and listened and was reassured by the faint but steady thrum of the engine.

"I'm sure you'd be a good pilot, Bobby," she said. "Maybe when you get your license you can take me up for a ride, eh?"

"You bet," Bobby answered, still scanning. "I'm going to be a natural scientist, but maybe I'll study aeronautics too. Do you know what that is?"

Abby did indeed. She had studied aeronautics all her adult life, in what she liked to think was its authentic, divinely designed form. But she didn't have the heart to burst Bobby's bubble, so she replied, "Why don't you tell me what you've learned about it, Bobby?"

He proceeded to do so for the next five minutes, with hardly a breath drawn, all the while trying to catch sight of the plane through an opening in the trees.

Abby made the proper responses, but she was concentrating most of her attention on listening for the plane's engine to reassure herself it wasn't in any danger. It was now distant and indistinct, but still sounded normal. Satisfied that the plane was okay, she tuned back in to Bobby's recitation.

"Well, that's why I was interested in that plane," Abby told him after listening to what he'd studied about wing shapes, lift and thrust. "It seemed to be defying some of those precepts of flight. But your idea was a good guess. Maybe it's a beginner pilot, or at least someone inexperienced with water landings. Sometimes that takes a while to learn, I understand."

"Not like Shadrach, Meshach and Abednego. They can land on a dime anywhere they please, and it hardly took them any time at all to learn how." Bobby pointed to the sky, his smile wide.

He had been the one to give the falcons their names during

their first week at the conservatory when it looked like the chicks might not make it. He was hoping, Abby guessed, to imbue them with the strength of the three who had been cast into the fiery furnace and had emerged unscathed.

All three birds survived that early struggle, and soon it had been time for them to be hacked out. At that stage, Bobby's concern had been that the birds would never fly, having no adult birds to teach them. But the instinct was strong, and the birds, one by one, triumphed in their fledgling bouts with gravity. All three were now successfully hunting on their own, though Abby was still keeping a close eye out to be certain they were adapting successfully.

The release ceremony on Saturday would be a true community celebration. The volunteers had come to feel invested in the health and welfare of what were now known by all as the Sparrow Island Falcons. Abby sincerely hoped Shadrach, Meshach and Abednego would at least put in an appearance.

The chances were good that, if the birds made it through the first year, they'd return to nest somewhere nearby. She picked up her binoculars again and started to do a bit of avian real estate brokering, surveying the cliff for likely spots the birds might choose for nesting.

"This looks absolutely splendid," Hugo Baron said as he came up the steps, startling Abby.

He studied the items in the cabinet then gestured around the platform at the rest of the display, stroking his white mustache as he often did when he was deep in thought.

"You've done a magnificent job young man," he said to Bobby, bowing from the waist in a formal gesture. "And you too, of course, Abby, for whatever small part you may have played in it," he added teasingly.

"Are our falcons out and about today?" he asked, drawing his own binoculars to his eyes and pointing them toward the cliff.

"One of them is anyway," Abby said, indicating a point farther up in the sky. "We haven't caught sight of the other two yet, but that's a good thing. It probably means they're out hunting."

"Splendid," Hugo said again. "They are magnificent birds, aren't they? Have you spotted another one over there?" he asked, this time addressing Bobby.

"No sir," Bobby answered. "We were looking at a plane that was flying kind of wobbly off over that way."

Hugo looked to Abby. "Our best theory is that it was someone practicing water landings. Someone who definitely needs the practice, I might add," Abby said as she started to gather up the stapler and other supplies to take back to her office.

"Where did you see it?" Hugo asked.

"Just off to the southeast there," Abby said, pointing in the general direction. "It disappeared behind the trees." She pointed to a spot where an oblong rough of meadow gave over to a stand of windswept firs. "Headed toward that cluster of islands."

"Why, there's nothing much out there. Those islands are uninhabited. Maybe your theory is right. Someone might choose that out-of-the-way place to practice landings. But you say the plane was all right, you think? Not in any trouble?" Hugo asked.

"I think it was okay, from what I could see and hear. It looked like it was back on an even flight, and I could still hear the engine. It sounded steady."

Hugo scanned the horizon. "I don't care for floatplanes myself. Small planes of any stripe for that matter," he said, straightening to his full height and letting the binoculars drop. "Give me watercraft, rail—even a camel caravan—but spare me the little planes."

"But you've been everywhere in the world," Bobby exclaimed. "You must have flown in lots of small planes."

"Oh, quite right you are, young man," Hugo said. "I certainly have. Because that's what I have to do to get where I want to go. That doesn't mean I'm entirely comfortable with them. But you know, son, there's a lesson there. If we only did the things we're comfortable with, we'd accomplish little in life. Sometimes we have to stretch."

Bobby looked to Abby, a questioning look on his face. "Think about the falcons when we first got them, Bobby," she said. "All the literature told us it would be a lot of hard work and that the odds weren't good that we'd be able to save them. I'm sure that made you feel uncomfortable about taking care of them. I know it did me. But we went ahead and did it anyway, and now aren't you glad?"

Bobby grinned. "I see," he told her. "Like eating your

vegetables. You might not exactly like it while it's going on, but it's good for you when it's over."

Hugo let out a big, full laugh. "That's certainly one analogy."

Abby sometimes wondered if Hugo missed his world travels, but if he did, he gave no indication of it. He had come to Sparrow Island in the late 1970s, four years after his wife died of malaria while they were on a trek in Africa. He and Abby's parents had become good friends over the years, and now Abby considered him her friend as well as her boss.

They all started the walk back to The Nature Museum. "You know, Bobby and I are both of a different mind than you about planes," she told Hugo. "I love to fly, *especially* in small planes. It lets me see things the way the birds see them—and gives me a chance to experience the exhilaration of flight. In all my travels my favorite vision is that of the San Juans from a floatplane. From up there they look like jewels—emeralds sprinkled out on a blue velvet cloth."

"You'll get no argument from me on that last score," Hugo said as he walked along. He gave a grand sweep of his arm. "These islands are jewels—in every way. Such beauty. Such a rich tapestry of cultures and peoples. Such history. What do you think compelled me to establish the conservatory and build the museum here?"

"I don't know, but I'm sure glad you did," Bobby said. He trotted alongside them, pausing now and again to examine a rock or an insect. "The museum's going to be so cool when it's done."

"Yes, I'm hoping it will indeed be *cool*," Hugo said, smiling down at the boy, "but I hope it will never be finished. I want it to become better year after year. And I appreciate all your hard work toward that end." He clapped his hands together lightly. "But this workday is about over for all of us. Your mother called," he said turning to Abby, "and asked me to remind you that you and Mary are due at the farm for dinner tonight."

Abby put her hand to her forehead. "I'd almost forgotten. I guess I got a bit absorbed." She glanced at her watch. "I'm going to have to hurry along or we'll be late."

"That won't do," Hugo said, reaching for the bag. "You mustn't be late for one of Ellen Stanton's wonderful meals. Let me take these things and you two scoot along."

Abby handed the bag over, and she and Bobby went off across the parking lot, waving good-bye to Hugo, who disappeared inside the museum's front door with a little salute. The errant plane was all but forgotten.

Chapter Two

As the van turned off Primrose Lane and onto the long driveway for Stanton Farm, Abby saw that her father's farmhand Sam Arbogast had been working on the lavender beds. Her father had started growing lavender three years ago after he had successfully used it for his insomnia, and each year the patch had grown a little larger. Mary had been thrilled when he added this organically grown crop as Stanton Farm's latest enterprise. She made prodigious use of the fragrant flowers at her shop.

Their father had decided this past summer to follow the lead of other lavender farms on San Juan Island and set aside a Pick-Your-Own section and allow folks to visit the farm during the July Lavender Festival. The earnings had been welcome, but what George Stanton had valued more was the opportunity to evangelize about organic farming and to visit with the people who came to the farm.

Abby could still see, in her mind's eye, the rows of lavender in full bloom as they waved in the summer breeze. Both the view and the aroma had been heady.

Mary drove the van up the driveway alongside the Stanton Farm homestead. It led to the ramp at the front of the house.

Despite their best efforts, she and Mary were arriving fifteen minutes late to help with dinner preparations. Abby's car was in the shop today, so Mary had let her borrow her van. Abby had planned to pick up Mary at Island Blooms, Mary's flower shop, so they could go over to the Stanton Farm together. But first Abby had to deliver Bobby to his mother at the Green Harbor Public School, then she'd rushed to Island Blooms, only to find Mary putting the finishing touches on an arrangement for the head table for tonight's PTA banquet at the school. Mary'd had to finish and hand the centerpiece off to her manager Candace for delivery before they could leave. The delay meant they'd had to come straight to the farm.

Abby expected Mary to be upset by this development. Sergeant Henry Cobb was coming for dinner, and Mary would normally have wanted to make it home to freshen up and change her clothes—and perhaps pay a bit of attention to styling her silver hair, which was now in the slightest bit of disarray. But Mary seemed not to care that she had to settle for fluffing her hair with her hands and applying a swipe of lipstick before starting the van and heading over. Of course, Mary could get away with doing that and still look great.

Abby, on the other hand, could only hope to minimize her dishevelment. Her boots were muddy from walking out to the observation platform, and her short brown hair was windblown. She had known she'd be working most of the day outdoors, so she'd opted for jeans, a turtleneck and a Cornell sweatshirt when she dressed this morning. She was relieved when she searched her backpack and found a cardigan folded up at the bottom.

"Thank goodness," she muttered when she found a pair of loafers slid up under the seat of the van. She changed her shoes, pulling a couple of burrs off her sock, while Mary activated the lift that lowered her wheelchair to ground level. Abby peeled off her sweatshirt, tucked in her turtleneck and shrugged on the sweater. She finger-combed her hair and checked herself in the side mirror.

"Do I look decent?" she asked Mary.

"We both look presentable," Mary said, "and tonight that's the best we can hope for. It's more important that we be here to help Mom than how we look anyway."

"You're right," Abby said, tilting her head to look at her sister, trying to read her mood. "Are you okay, Mary?" she asked. "You don't seem quite yourself."

"Oh, I'm fine," Mary said, but Abby noticed she didn't look her in the eye. "Just tired I guess."

"Are you sure?"

"Oh, Abby, I just have a lot on my mind," she said, but then she looked up into Abby's face and something seemed to give way. "Abby, I've been thinking a lot lately. About Henry. You know I just don't think I'm doing the right thing by continuing to go out with him. I don't think it's fair to him."

"What do you mean?" Abby asked, distressed to see the look of deep sadness on Mary's face.

"I mean he deserves to go on with his life. To do all the things I can't do anymore."

"But Mary," Abby said, "Henry adores you. I don't believe he thinks he's sacrificing a thing."

"Well, he is," Mary said flatly. "And I know Henry. He's an honorable man. He'd never break it off with me. Not under these circumstances. I'm going to have to tell him I don't want to see him anymore. It's for his own good."

Abby squatted down beside the chair so she could look Mary square in the face. "Mary, I'm not trying to tell you what to do. But I want you to think about this—pray about this. Take some time and think it over carefully."

"But the longer it goes on, the harder it will be," Mary protested.

"Mary, if you go through with this, it's going to be hard anytime you do it. Have you really prayerfully considered all the ramifications of this decision?"

"I just think, for Henry's sake, it's the best thing—"

"That wasn't my question, Mary," Abby cut in. "Just promise me you'll give it some time before you do anything you'll regret."

"Yes, okay, I will," Mary said. She looked over at Abby and smiled, but the smile didn't go all the way to her eyes, which were missing their usual sparkle.

Abby had been happy to learn that her sister had been going out with Sergeant Henry Cobb of the San Juan County Sheriff's Office. The two had known each other only vaguely for many years. During all those years Mary had been a married woman, and Abby was sure Henry thought of her only as the nice, fun lady who ran the flower shop.

About a year ago, Mary had mentioned to Abby on the phone that Henry had come in to order flowers for the wife of one of his deputies who'd just had a baby boy. He wanted something special so he came in personally to pick something out. Abby could tell by the way Mary reported this that some new interest had sparked between them.

After that Abby noticed that Mary mentioned Henry's ever-more-frequent visits to her shop whenever he was on Sparrow Island. And soon they were going out to dinner, a movie or the occasional social outing.

Then came the accident. It had changed things. From what Abby could see, Henry was still as interested in Mary as ever, but was having a difficult time convincing her that his attentions were not driven by pity, but by a genuine desire to be in her company.

Abby liked Henry. And she could see that he clearly cared for Mary; Abby knew full well that Mary was very fond of him. This was not the time for Mary to be pushing people away, just when she was making such good progress in reclaiming her life. But the usually fun-loving Mary had grown a bit more moody since the accident, and more likely to question other people's motivations.

Abby pushed Mary's wheelchair up the ramp and opened the door for her, then let Mary take over.

Inside they each gave their mother a quick kiss on the cheek then donned aprons from the hook inside the pantry door and asked for their work assignments.

"Mary, you can make the salad, and Abby, you can butter the rolls and get them ready to put in to brown, please," Ellen Stanton replied, never missing a beat as she whipped up the filling for the lemon meringue pie she was making. It was one of Henry Cobb's favorites—one among many of Ellen Stanton's tasty dishes.

Mary maneuvered her wheelchair into the space between the table and the refrigerator. She turned her body to try to get the door open, but couldn't get the wheel to clear.

"Here, let me get the vegetables out for you, Mary," Abby said, urging Mary to wheel herself back over to her workspace at the butcher block table their father had ingeniously rigged to adjust from counter height to table height at the turn of a lever.

Both Abby and Ellen Stanton were trying hard to allow Mary to be as independent as possible. It was hard to resist the urge to help when they saw her struggle with everyday tasks, but Mary had made it clear that although she appreciated their love and support, she wanted to learn to do for herself. Both women were very proud of Mary's determination and tried to abide by her wishes, but it wasn't always easy.

"Thank you, Abby," Mary said. "Just this one time I'll let you, but only because that's such a tight space." She started to select green and yellow peppers from the assortment Abby put out on the table, part of the last crop from the bounty of the Stantons' enormous organic garden.

"You'll never guess what," Mary told them as they worked. "I got a call from Zack this morning. He may be coming in for a visit this weekend."

"That's wonderful," Ellen said, the warmth of a grandmother's love evident in her voice. "It seems like it's been such a long time since we've seen him. How's he doing?"

"Oh, he's happier than he's been in quite a long time. I can hear it in his voice," Mary answered, cutting the top off a plump bell pepper. As Abby bent over to reach for the butter, the fresh sweet smell of the pepper mingled with that of the succulent roast Ellen had just pulled from the oven to baste. Abby picked up the first thin green slice that came off Mary's paring knife and bit into it, realizing how hungry she was. Lunch had been a hurried sandwich at her desk, and she'd had a busy afternoon.

"Zack's music must be going well," Abby said, delighted at the prospect of seeing her itinerant musician nephew. "He's always happiest when his music is flowing freely. Where is the band playing now?"

"They've been in Chicago for a few weeks. Apparently, there are several jazz venues there whose owners have really taken a liking to him and the guys."

"We'll have a big dinner right here on Sunday," Ellen said, mentally planning another menu even as she prepared tonight's.

"Let's not get ahead of ourselves, Mom," Mary answered.

"He said he *might* be able to get away, not that he'd be here for sure. He wanted to check in to see what my plans were before he tried to arrange it. He said he'd call back tonight. Weekends are usually his busiest times, but apparently their bass player is the best man at a friend's wedding. They weren't able to find a satisfactory substitute for him so they didn't book any dates."

Men's voices drifted in from the backyard. "There's your father," Ellen said. "He's been out with Sam to look at that leak in the barn's roof. Sam thinks he'll be able to fix it before winter sets in, thank goodness."

"Sam's been a godsend, hasn't he?" Abby asked.

"He truly has," Ellen answered, sliding the roast back into the oven. "I don't know what we'd do without him."

Abby heard Sam say good-bye to her father and her ears registered the thud of his truck door closing, but still her father didn't come into the house. A moment later she heard a new male voice and saw Mary look up sharply as she recognized Henry Cobb's greeting. Her face registered a whole series of conflicting emotions, and Abby reached over briefly to pat her hand.

"Oh my, Henry's early," Mary said, snatching at the strings of her apron. "I must look a sight."

"You look lovely, dear," her mother told her. "You always look lovely."

And though that sentiment was spoken by Mary's mother—who might not be considered entirely objective—

Abby had to agree. At the age of fifty-eight, Mary was still a striking woman. She had classic features, a beautiful clear complexion and dazzling blue eyes. And even though Mary had never seemed aware of how beautiful she was, she was always concerned about presenting herself well and being well-groomed, more it seemed out of respect to the person she'd be seeing than because of self-conscious preening.

Abby heard the men come clamoring across the back porch. Their progress paused briefly and Abby heard footwear fall in two muffled thumps, probably her father taking off his boots. She couldn't hear exactly what Henry and her father were saying, but something in their voices didn't sound like they were engaged in idle chatter.

Henry came in and stood in the doorway of the kitchen, twisting the brim of his campaign hat in his hand. He was wearing his uniform of dark green pants, a desert tan shirt and green tie, with his green sheriff's department jacket over it. Abby sensed all his energies coiled like a spring. He smiled briefly at Mary, then gave Ellen an apologetic look. "Mrs. Stanton, I'm so sorry, but I just came by to tell you I'm not going to be able to stay for dinner tonight," he said, his delivery rapid.

"Oh?" Ellen said. "I'm sorry too. Not bad news, I hope."

Mary wheeled her chair closer to Henry.

"I don't know yet," Henry told her and Mary. "We've had a plane go down somewhere over the islands to the south and I'm headed out in one of the patrol boats to search."

"Oh heavens," Mary said. "Is anyone hurt?"

"That's the thing," Henry answered. "We don't know much of anything yet. From all we've learned there were at least two people aboard, but we haven't gotten any distress calls from them. We're doing an aerial search, but now with it almost full dark, unless there's fire from the wreckage or a signal fire, that won't be much help."

"What kind of plane was it Henry?" Abby asked, her own senses now on high alert.

"It was a floatplane, white with an orange stripe. From the description, sounds like maybe a Cessna 180," he said, gesturing with his hat as he edged toward the door. "A fisherman off Decatur saw it and thought there was something irregular about the way it was flying, but once it went behind the trees he lost track of it."

"I think I saw it too, Henry," Abby told him, "at the conservatory just before I left." She glanced at her watch. "A little less than two hours ago. I'm sure it was the same plane. The one I saw was behaving strangely too."

Henry stopped moving, and she recounted what she and Bobby had observed using her hands to try to describe the plane's tilt and angle. "We guessed it might have been a new pilot or one just learning to make water landings," she said.

"That's what the fisherman thought too. There were glassy water conditions this afternoon. But a couple of pleasure boaters spotted it and thought it sounded like maybe it was having engine trouble. We can't get a bead on where exactly it went down and no one's reported an expected flight overdue.

Do you think if I go out and get the map you could show me where you saw it last?"

"I might be able to do better than that, Henry," she said. "You know I've spent all my life watching birds in flight. For what it's worth, I think maybe I could get a general heading and trajectory for you based on what I saw."

"Great." Henry glanced at his watch. "Let me go grab the map. I really need to get a move on. I'm shorthanded right now, of all times. I've got one deputy out sick and another that really *should* be out. He's got a horrible cold, maybe the flu. But, he's hanging in there for me at the station. Neither of them is in any condition to go out on the search. And I need my last man standing to look out for anything else that might happen in our spread-out jurisdiction while I'm out looking for the plane."

"Why don't I just go out with you, Henry?" Abby asked. "I promise I won't slow you down and I can go over the map with you while we're underway."

"Oh, I don't know . . ."

"Abby knows how to take care of herself, Henry," George Stanton said. "And she's worked with search and rescue before, back in New York. She'd be a help to you."

"Yes, but I couldn't ask you to do that. You're needed here," Henry said. His face was turned to Abby, but he cast a sidelong glance in Mary's direction.

"Don't you worry a minute on my account," Mary said. "I'll be just fine. Mom and Dad will be here and when I'm ready to go home I can call Janet or Margaret if that will make you feel better. As long as you're sure it's safe, take Abby along. There may be people out there injured and needing all the help they can get."

Abby caught the haunted look that passed briefly over her sister's face, but Mary immediately regained her composure.

"She's right," Abby said decisively, pulling her apron off. "We're wasting time here." She knew Mary was reliving the accident. Any mention of tragedy brought it all back for her. Abby hadn't been able to be there for her sister in that dark hour, but maybe she could be there for someone else tonight.

"Okay, then," Henry said. "I won't refuse the help. Truth is, I'm in kind of a bind. Mary, you're sure you'll be okay?"

"Yes, yes, of course," Mary said, making a shooing motion. "Now you two get going, and for goodness sake, be careful."

"Mrs. Stanton, my apologies again," Henry said, tipping his hat and settling it back on his head. "I hope you'll give me a rain check on dinner."

"You're welcome at Stanton Farm anytime, Henry. God be with you both."

Mary wheeled to the door behind them and reached up to catch Abby's hand. She pulled her back in briefly and whispered to her softly. "Please don't say anything to Henry about what we talked about. You're right, I need time to think about it."

"Of course I won't," Abby said. "It's not my place."

"And be careful," Mary added. "*Very* careful."

Outside, Abby quickly changed back into her hiking boots and grabbed her heavy jacket and backpack from the van. The sense of urgency was rising in her and triggering memories of the first search she'd ever been involved in. Several years back when she was doing field research in upstate New York, a small girl had wandered off from a family hike and gotten lost in an area where Abby and her research assistants had been working for several weeks counting nests.

When an hour of searching failed to turn up any sign of her, the parents called the authorities. By then they were in a state of panic. Abby heard the news on the radio and felt led to join the volunteer effort. Once the authorities learned how familiar she was with the terrain, they used her expertise to set up the grid pattern based on the child's last known location and Abby's knowledge of the area.

It had been Abby herself who'd discovered the child in the predawn hours. Small and frail, the six-year-old had been huddled under a bush half covered by leaves, her soft child's breaths punctuated by whimpers. She was cold, hungry and scared, but she clung to Abby with all the strength left in her little arms, murmuring about how frightened she'd been and how happy she was to see someone who could help her.

Abby had never forgotten the look on the mother's face as she handed the girl over. The whole family was more than relieved—they were wildly jubilant. It reminded Abby of the parable of the sheep and for the first time she fully understood that teaching.

> If a man owns a hundred sheep, and one of them
> wanders away, will he not leave the ninety-nine on

the hills and go to look for the one that wandered off? And if he finds it, I tell you the truth, he is happier about that one sheep than about the ninety-nine that did not wander off. In the same way your Father in heaven is not willing that any of these little ones should be lost (Matthew 18:12–14).

Now, as she threw her gear into the trunk of Henry's cruiser she looked out across the water. Night had fallen and the sea was a vast and empty expanse with only a sliver of moonlight to dispel the darkness. The same places that Abby found wondrous and beautiful in the bright light of day could be cold, rough and terrifying for someone lost and maybe hurt. There was no comfort, no hope glimmering out in the inky night.

Abby said a silent prayer as she jumped into the cruiser, asking God to watch over the people from the plane and to grant the searchers the wisdom and speed to help them in time.

Chapter Three

On the way to pick up the sheriff's department's boat, Henry asked Abby about her experiences with search and rescue in New York. When she'd told him about some of the ones she'd been involved in, he said, "So you're pretty seasoned. Mary tells me you've spent a good deal of time doing field-work back East and I know you work with birds, but I've never had much of a chance to talk to you about it. What exactly is your specialty?"

"The research I've done in the past few years involved studying how environmental changes impact various species' reproduction numbers and nesting habits, things like that. It involves a lot of traipsing around in the woods, looking at a lot of nests and counting chicks."

"I see," Henry said. "I guess I could make a joke about your career being for the birds, but I suppose you've heard that one a few times."

"Once or twice," Abby said, smiling. "Do you have any interest in birds?"

"Well, I like to look at them. Especially the sea birds. The herons, the cormorants, the oystercatchers. And I'm a pretty good hand at identifying which is which, but I can't say I've made a study of them."

"Well, you appreciate them, that's a start," Abby said.

"Yeah, I do," Henry said, turning into the marina. "Except when they're the competition. I like to fish. Freshwater and saltwater. Sometimes we're all after the same catch."

Abby laughed. She liked this man very much. He was at home in his own skin and there wasn't a trace of pretense about him. And more important, Abby was pretty sure he knew his own mind. She hoped Mary would take her time and not do anything rash.

"Give me your opinion on this," he said handing her the map he had folded askew. Abby studied it by the car's interior light as Henry pulled into a parking spot. Based on her own observations, and on what Henry had told her about what the fisherman had seen, she narrowed the likely crash site to about ten mostly uninhabited islands slewed off toward the south of Sparrow Island in the archipelago.

Since the plane was a floatplane, it was possible that it could have gone down over open water. But as Henry had told her, the witness report of the fisherman, as well as those of the pleasure boaters, seemed to rule that out. Other search teams disagreed and, based on other evidence, those teams were headed north to search.

"This guy on Decatur was an old-timey reef netter, so he

was sitting still. He got a pretty good look as the plane passed over. No boaters or pilots have reported seeing any wreckage spread out on the water. Plane goes down on the water, usually it's going to leave some flotsam and jetsam."

The witnesses—or the closest thing they had to witnesses—all heard sounds they interpreted as a crash on land, metal hitting wood. However, none had a view of the plane at the time of impact.

"Sounds carry far over these islands, if you remember," Henry said. "They bounce off the landmasses and drift up the byways. It's like trying to find a cricket in the basement, first it seems to be over here, then over there then coming from behind. So unless you've got a line of sight, you can't trust your ears."

Abby's scientific mind went to the task of prioritizing the search. She marked the approximate position where she'd seen the plane last, then put marks where the other witnesses reported it. She closed her eyes and tried to visualize what she'd seen earlier in the afternoon. Years of research work watching and charting the migration patterns of birds had given her a comfortable orientation in what to others seemed a boundless and incalculable dome of sky. She strained to focus her attention on the glide path and heading of the plane as she'd last seen it.

Back at the conservatory she and Bobby had heard nothing that resonated as a crash. But they were far away and the sounds would have blended with the ferry engines, the drone of other small planes and the purr of outboard motors. And even those would have been overlaid on the sounds of nature all around, to which Abby's ear was much more attuned. And in any case, whatever had happened, it had happened after the plane left Abby's range of sight.

They climbed out of the car and Henry spread the map out on the hood and shined a flashlight on it. "We've set up a grid," he told her. "It's a big area, and like I said, I'm short-handed. San Juan may be the smallest county in the state, but I've got over 175 square miles of land to cover and over 170 named islands and reefs—and that shoots up to over seven hundred at low tide. Here's our plot of it," he told her, tracing a section of the map with a pencil. "Most of the others are concentrating in this grid here," he said, indicating an area farther north.

"Why is that?" Abby asked, frowning. "That's in the opposite direction from where I saw it heading."

Henry shrugged. "Search-and-rescue is relying on the report from the pleasure boaters who last saw the plane heading north. You're pretty sure about what time it was when you saw it?" Henry asked.

"I'm sure," Abby said. "It was sometime around 5:00 PM."

Henry nodded slowly. "That's nearly a half hour after the boaters spotted it. Could be we're talking two different planes, or could be this one doubled back. In any case, I'm more inclined to go with your judgment. If we find anything on the water we can call in the Coast Guard. And I've notified Skagit

County and they're searching south of us in this other sector, but we've got all this to cover," he said, again indicating an area encompassing several islands. "You still think you want to try it? It may be pretty rough."

"Yes, absolutely," Abby said. "I think I can be of some help."

"All right then, let's move out," Henry said.

After they'd hastily transferred their gear into the search boat, Abby settled into her seat and pulled a flashlight and a small notebook from her backpack. They donned their bright orange life jackets, and by the time Henry had unwound the mooring line from the cleat and was reversing out of the slip, Abby was working industriously on compiling a ranked list of islands within the search grid.

Henry was hurrying, but without rushing. Abby could see that he was thinking through each action, going through a mental checklist, accomplishing each task quickly, but with sureness. It inspired confidence.

Since Abby had been back on the island, she'd been around Henry enough to come to see him as a dedicated and skilled law enforcement officer as well as a fine, caring man. But they had never spent much time in conversation without other people around.

Henry supervised the four deputy patrol officers who worked in far-flung District 3 of the San Juan County Sheriff's Office, which included Lopez, Shaw, Sparrow Island and a few other smaller islands. He could have chosen to sit in an office, but he liked to stay in touch with all the islands' residents. It was not uncommon to see him on Sparrow Island on any given day, stopping by the businesses and services in Green Harbor to chat and catch up on the local news. In the big cities they'd call it community policing, but on Sparrow Island they just called it watching out for one another.

It made Abby heartsick to think that Mary might break it off with Henry. It would be different if Mary didn't care for Henry, but Abby knew she did. Mary thought she was doing the right thing, that her motives were pure, laudable even, but in Abby's view they were misguided. Abby thought Henry could speak for himself and should be given the opportunity to do just that.

She wished Mary had never told her. She felt the burden of knowing that Mary was considering breaking up with Henry as she sat here beside him in the boat.

As they started out across the water it was impossible to carry on a normal conversation over the engine and the rhythmic slap of water on the hull. So when Abby had finished her list she tapped Henry on the shoulder and held the notebook up, her flashlight beam trained on the page. "One, two and three," she shouted, indicating the search order of the islands and pointing to their coordinates.

He glanced at it, gave her a thumbs-up and tapped the paper. "We'll come on this first one from the east," he said, turning his head slightly toward her so his words wouldn't be blown away. "It's a teardrop shape and we'll be able to see nearly shore-to-shore except for the northernmost end."

Abby nodded then settled in the seat. She pulled the collar of her coat closer and zipped it up to her neck. The night wind was cold and condensation was settling on her glasses, requiring her to take them off frequently and clean them with the rapidly disintegrating tissue from her coat pocket.

Being on the water at night could be a bit eerie, especially on a night like this. The boat's running lights seemed to slice into the darkness as if it were a solid thing, and Abby was grateful to have a skilled boatsman like Henry at the helm. He'd grown up on nearby Orcas Island and now lived on Lopez, so the buoy markers and waypoints were all practically hardwired into his brain. And he handled the boat like it was an extension of himself.

As they approached the first small island, Henry nudged the throttle back to cut the noise and picked up the handset to the radio. He relayed the search order to his deputy, consulting Abby's list and glancing over occasionally to the map to double-check the coordinates of the small islands.

"Maybe we'll get lucky and find it right off," he told the deputy, talking loud over the static and squawk. "But if we don't it could be a long night. You gonna be okay, Bennett?" he asked.

"I'll be okay, Sarge," Abby could hear the tinny voice through the handset. He didn't sound too convincing, but Abby knew if it was humanly possible, Deputy Mike Bennett would be at his post throughout the night. Henry had the assistance of deputies every bit as dedicated as he was.

As Henry signed off and pushed the throttle forward, aligning the boat with the shoreline, Abby got out her binoculars. She put the eyepieces to her eyes, making a small focusing adjustment. For Abby, looking through the binoculars was second nature. She panned with them as Henry maneuvered the boat around the island, looking for any breaks in the tree line, for any debris or for any unusual shapes in the silhouette of vegetation along the shoreline. The boat's lights barely penetrated the thick undergrowth past the rocks, but Henry had been right about the narrow span of the island. They could just make out an occasional glimpse of the channel on the other side through the trees, the anemic moon catching an occasional odd wavelet with a stingy glint. If there was anything as bulky as a plane out there, they'd be sure to see it.

As they rounded the south end of the island, Henry suddenly veered off at a sharp angle away from land. The boat slewed around, forcing Abby to grab on to the grip rail to keep her balance. She strained to look ahead and saw the telltale ripples in the water and a mass of bull kelp floating above. As Henry turned to her, an explanation at the ready, she shouted, "I know, reef. Looks like a bad one."

Henry pursed his lips and nodded. "Keel killer." He looped a wide arc around then angled back toward shore. He picked up the map and studied it for a moment. Looking up, he was obviously straining to make out the features of the landmass in the enveloping darkness. "We're here," he told Abby, pointing to a spot on the map. "If we hike up to that promontory," he said, gesturing vaguely to his right, "we should have a view of nearly the whole island. Well, when I say view, I mean we'd be able to see any signs of fire, flashlights or maybe even some of this feeble moonlight glinting off wreckage—if there's any to see. During the day, I'm betting you can see all the way into the interior from up there."

Abby agreed that this seemed the quickest and most efficient way to survey the island, then checked the laces on her hiking boots to make sure they were cinched tight. Henry dropped anchor near a narrow strip of sandy beach in a small cove, and they each grabbed their backpacks from the boat and set out.

Abby was glad to be moving again, her blood flowing to limbs stiffened by the cold and damp. She was a healthy woman, accustomed to the outdoors, but still this island was a challenge. The people on that plane might be ill equipped for this, assuming they had survived the initial crash.

She thought of that frail little girl she'd helped rescue. What if there had been a child aboard this plane? Or someone already ill? An involuntary shiver shimmied down her spine, and she pulled her collar closer around her neck and quickened her step. She was both eager to find the plane and dreading what they might see when they did find it. She needed to steel herself. "Hope for the best and prepare for the worst," she said, without realizing she'd spoken aloud.

"What's that?" Henry asked, looking back over his shoulder.

"Oh, nothing, just something Dad used to say," she told him, repeating the adage.

"Always good advice," Henry said.

It was rough going through the huckleberry bushes and nettles. The low-lying manzanita bushes, their rusty leaves and festive berries such a delight in the daylight, proved to be only entanglements for boots in the darkness.

"I'll bet this is beautiful in the daytime," Abby said. "I'll have to come back when all this is over."

"Then I'd have to arrest you," Henry said, his voice light. "This is wilderness area. But I'll bet you could get yourself a permit. They like you scientist types keeping tabs on things so we can learn how to keep it like it is."

"Maybe I'll do that," Abby said, drawing air deeply into her lungs. "I saw a pigeon guillemot rookery back there above where we put in. I'm sure a good count hasn't been done in years. I'll talk to Hugo about it."

As they trekked deeper into the interior of this wild little island, the beams of their flashlights seemed insubstantial—as if timid about ferreting out what lay ahead in this nocturnal world of wildlife tenants. Their progress was hampered by wet slippery leaves concealing stones and opportunistic roots. Every step required a constant state of alertness.

Abby tried to take her cue from Henry, to hurry without rushing. She pushed away the memory of the wonderful dinner her mother had prepared back on Sparrow Island and tried to ignore the hunger that rumbled in her stomach. She knew her mother would save her a plate. Maybe in a couple of hours, she'd be back in the homey kitchen at Stanton Farm having a late supper and everyone would be rescued and safe.

"Right up here there's a little finger of water that comes in from the shore. It'll be a lot faster if we scramble over the rocks rather than go around," Henry said. "Watch yourself."

He played his flashlight over the area just in front of them. In full light Abby knew the moss-covered stones would resemble a faded, well-used patchwork quilt in muted greens, ambers and yellows. But in the beam of the flashlight they looked more ominous than comforting. The mosses and lichens that gave them such soft beauty for the eye also made them slick and treacherous for human feet. There were so many slopes and crevices on which boots could slip and toes could snag.

Head bent, all her focus on safely navigating the rocks, it took a moment for Abby's ears to register the muffled moan that came out of the dark. She jerked her flashlight toward the sound and Henry did the same. Trained in their crossed beams, a head was visible just above the water. Slowly, two liquid eyes appeared, and Henry and Abby stood frozen in their tracks.

The eyes were soon followed by a whiskered muzzle then two more smooth heads popped up, each giving Abby and Henry a scolding look for having been rousted from their resting place by noisy human invaders. Harbor seals.

It was the end of pupping season and Abby and Henry had inadvertently stumbled onto a favored haul out spot; their approach had sent the residents hastily into the water.

Abby and Henry both exhaled huffs of relief. Abby let out a nervous laugh, and Henry shook his head and looked chagrinned. "Seeing a seal is not exactly an uncommon event around these parts. Funny how the dark plays tricks with your mind, huh?" he said.

"For those not accustomed to it, you bet," Abby said as they got moving again.

She looked back over her shoulder and whispered, "Sorry, guys. We'll leave you be now."

"So are you saying you're accustomed to the dark?" Henry asked as they moved across the rocks and toward a marshy area studded with arrowgrass and Hooker's willow.

"Not me. But I had colleagues back at Cornell who were more at home in the dark than in what they always referred to as 'the harsh light of day.' They were doing long-term studies of night birds," Abby said, now needing human conversation to fill the darkness.

"Owls?" Henry said eagerly, seeming to need the same.

"Yes, owls, but also rails, snipes and grouse. Lots of birds are nocturnal. Even song sparrows like to do a late show now and then. They'll break into song in the middle of the night." She looked at the silhouettes of the trees ahead. "Frankly, I'm wishing one would do that right now," she said, following Henry off the rocks and into the salt-stunted weeds as they headed uphill toward the promontory. "Their songs are much more optimistic than the forlorn hoot of the owls."

As if on cue, a muted trill of *hoo-hoo-hoo* drifted down from the trees ahead, answered by a *cr-oo-oo-oo* from somewhere farther inland.

Henry gave a short little laugh. "Guess we don't always get our druthers," he said, half turning and pointing his flashlight toward a hole nearly covered with leaves and twigs. "Watch out for that."

Abby stepped around it. "Those are only western screech owls. They're just sweet-talking one another. At least we're not getting that heavy-duty hoot from the great horned owl. That's such a mournful sound, and it carries for miles."

"Speaking of which," Henry said, "we need to stop now and again for a listen. Not for birds, but for people." He turned toward her, cupping a hand around his ear. "Night as still as this, maybe we'll hear something."

Abby had just been thinking the same thing. She was good at listening for sounds in nature. Her father had taught her early to stand quietly in the forest and identify the sounds all around her. And, of course, as a birder she'd learned all the calls and songs by attentive listening. She stopped and closed her eyes. They stood perfectly still for a long moment, then Henry let out the breath he'd been holding. "Nothing," he mumbled.

"No, not nothing," Abby said. "I heard some small bats

flitting overhead, a dog barking somewhere far off on a neighboring island, something rustling in a bush over there, probably a raccoon. The low thrum of engines from a large vessel—probably a freighter out in the strait—and did you hear that winnowing sound? That's a snipe in flight. They have two stiff tail feathers that make that sound. It sounds like a window fan if you stick a piece of paper in it."

Henry sighed. "Okay, I should have been more specific. I didn't hear anything that would make me think there's *humans* nearby."

"No, me either," Abby said with a sigh.

They trudged on upward to the top of the promontory and Henry took off his hat and wiped his brow with the sleeve of his jacket. "See anything?" he asked as Abby put her binoculars to her eyes.

"No, nothing." She turned to him with a wan smile. "As you say, nothing that would make me think there are humans anywhere around."

They stood in silence as each moved their binoculars back and forth, scanning the breadth and width of the island, searching for anything that might hint at the presence of the downed plane. They saw nothing but the dark shapes of trees and the random glimmer of moonlight on windblown waters.

As they made their way back toward the boat Abby felt her spirits sag. She was tired, hungry and disheartened by having their efforts come to nothing. It was near midnight and despair was on the prowl.

And this was only the first island. She was feeling the weight of responsibility for having set the search order. What if her estimations were wrong and she was causing a delay that would have tragic consequences? Maybe she should have stayed out of this. She closed her eyes and willed the image of the plane back. No, she was certain they were on the right path. There was no doubt.

Just then from the water's edge came a choir of tree frogs. Abby smiled, a bit embarrassed by her little pity-party. Soon the frogs were joined by a song sparrow serenading them. Her nephew Zack would appreciate this fellow, Abby thought. He introduced his song with a rhythmic introduction, followed by equally spaced phrases, then a trilled section. Like Zack's jazz—cool and calming. A passage from one of Abby's favorite Psalms came instantly into her mind: "At night his song is with me—a prayer to the God of my life" (Psalm 42:8).

She and Henry and the other rescuers weren't in this alone, she reminded herself. And being a little tired and hungry was nothing compared to what the people from the plane were probably enduring by now. It could get very cold out here at night at this time of year and some of the larger islands were even more rugged than this one.

Henry had apparently been doing a little musing of his own. "I'm having second thoughts about having brought you out here," he said as they threw their packs into the boat and prepared to move on to the next island.

"Why? Am I slowing you down?" Abby asked. "I can go

faster, Henry. I was taking my cue from you. You set the pace and I'll keep up."

"No, not that at all. You're doing fine—better than fine. But this could go on all night, and I keep thinking about how Mary's getting along while we're out here."

"Mary's fine," Abby said, knowing it was true, but feeling her own little bubble of concern surface. "She's becoming more independent every day."

"Yeah, I know," Henry said. "But still I wish you were with her. She's very special to me you know."

There was nothing Abby could say that didn't feel like a deception, so she simply repeated. "Mary will be fine."

"Well, anyway, it's not just that," Henry said. "I keep wondering what that plane was doing way out here. Something doesn't seem right about it."

"If it was a student pilot like I guessed, it makes sense, doesn't it? He'd want to be out someplace isolated to practice his landings, right?"

"Yeah, I guess so," Henry said nodding. "Yeah," he said, more emphatically. "That would be where they'd want to do it. 'Course, I'd think they'd want to get out away from the salt-water highways if they were that inexperienced, but maybe he was learning to read the water conditions in the channels. That's an art all its own. I guess after so many years in my line of work my mind automatically goes to more nefarious scenarios."

"Occupational hazard," Abby said.

"Yep," Henry agreed. "Occupational hazard. Sort of like

you hearing that snipe doing his window fan imitation. I'd have thought it was just the wind blowing through the trees. You ready to hit the next island?"

"Ready," Abby said.

As Henry turned the boat and headed for the mouth of the little cove where they'd laid anchor, Abby spoke softly into the wind, "Ready and willing. And for the sake of the people aboard that plane, I hope able."

Chapter Four

Mary was feeling very uneasy as she and her parents finally sat down to a late dinner. She glanced at her watch. Past seven. Full dark now. It had seemed perfectly natural for Abby to go and help Henry out with the search, but now Mary was thinking of all the dangers.

She followed suit as her father bowed his head to pray over the abundant meal set before the three remaining diners. He added a fervent entreaty for the well-being of the passengers of the plane and for Abby and Henry's safety, then looked up and smiled, trying to give them reassurance they knew he wasn't entirely feeling.

As they passed bowls and platters, and the clink of silverware on plates began, they tried making small talk about the farm and the flower shop and the news on the island. But with the two empty chairs at the table serving as constant reminders, inevitably their conversations came back around to speculation about what was happening out on the little islands with Abby and Henry.

"They'll make a good team getting help to anybody needing it. And we ought not worry. They both know how to take care of themselves in the outdoors, and they both know the islands," George said firmly.

Mary knew that was certainly true of Abby. She had always been at her father's heels growing up, and she'd inherited his love of the sea and the natural world. Back when he'd still been running his charter boat business, Abby had loved to go out with him. She'd especially loved joining with him when he took people out to see the orcas. Like her father, Abby said she believed if people could see these remarkable whales in their watery world they'd be forever changed by the experience, that it would inspire them to do their part to help protect the orcas and other wild and beautiful creatures as well.

And Abby had delighted in the daily rambles around the farm with her father, spotting and identifying birds on the wing by their markings and songs, and classifying nests by materials and building methods. She'd been the quintessential tomboy.

"That's true," Ellen said, bringing Mary out of her reverie. "We mustn't worry about Abby and Henry. I just hope they can find and help the passengers on that plane. If they're city people they might not be at home outdoors. It will be very dark out there, and it can get pretty cold on these September nights if you don't have the proper clothing."

Mary nodded, lost again in her own thoughts. She was remembering how she'd felt in the minutes following her car crash. It had been terrifying to be out there in the darkness, alone and in pain and not knowing when help would arrive. She squeezed her eyes shut and said her own prayer for the people on the plane, asking God to give them courage and comfort.

"Say," Ellen said, seeming to sense her daughter's distress, "why don't I call Janet and Doug and see if they'd like to come over? They've probably eaten already, but maybe they'll have some of this lemon meringue pie with us."

"That's a good idea," Mary said, smiling reassuringly at her mother. "But, I'll go call. You enjoy the rest of your dinner. You've certainly worked hard enough on it today."

Mary placed the call and found Janet and Doug ready and eager to accept an invitation to share in one of Ellen Stanton's treats. They promised they would, as Janet put it, "scoot right over."

Mary and Ellen had just finished clearing the dinner dishes when they arrived. As usual on Sparrow Island, the news of the plane crash had already spread. As the long-time secretary at Little Flock Church, Janet Heinz was wired into the local news and was always eager to pass it along. She was an inveterate gossip, though there was never anything mean-spirited or judgmental in her chatter. She simply liked people, and she liked talking with them—and about them.

"Any word from Abby?" she asked as she and her husband came in the door at Stanton Farm.

"No, nothing yet," Mary told her, accustomed to Janet's habit of skipping over the preliminaries and getting right to the point. "But they haven't been gone that long. Henry's promised that his deputy will keep us informed about what's going on and will let us know if they're going to stay out longer than planned."

"Well, I think it's great that she's willing to help," Janet said. "Henry's got his hands full right now. There's been practically an epidemic of colds and bronchitis making the rounds and I hear two of his deputies are really sick."

George Stanton poured coffee for everyone while Mary served the pie and Ellen and Janet finished clearing the table. There was lively conversation and Mary was happy for the distraction—for her and her parents. Despite their calm exteriors, she knew they were both worried about Abby going out on the search. But she also knew they were proud of Abby for volunteering to go. Their mother and father had always taught them to be of service to others whenever possible.

As she distributed the slices of pie onto her mother's blue willow plates, Mary thought of Henry. He loved this pie and it thrilled her mother to have him say so, which he did—with great gusto—each time she made it for him.

In the time they'd been seeing one another, Henry had gotten to know the older Stantons well and he had been wonderful to them. Henry was wonderful, period. Mary bit her lip and concentrated on the conversation.

"There's any number of little islands along in that area," Doug Heinz was saying, shaking his head. "Water around 'em is just full up with eddies, reefs and places where there's 'bout nearly a skookumchuck. It's no place to try to land a float-plane. What do you suppose got into that pilot?" he asked, directing his question to George.

"No telling," George answered with a little shrug. "We're getting more and more city people out here these days. They don't always take to the way of doing things in the islands right off."

"You know, I've heard that word all my life, *skookumchuck*," Janet said, "But I never realized what a funny sounding word that is. And I still have no idea what it means. What kind of word is that anyway?" she asked, her insatiable curiosity piqued.

"Comes from the Chinook," George answered. "It means rough water I think. In the literal translation though, most boaters mean it to describe places where there's whirlpools and tricky tides and such."

"So the pilot wasn't likely to have been from around here, or he'd have known the waters a little better," Ellen said.

"Maybe he was trying to fly over that cluster of little islands for a landing on the other side," George said. "Glassy water takes about four times the distance for landing. Sometimes these new guys tend to discount that. You just can't see that surface unless you've got a reference point. That's why they teach pilots to land alongside a shoreline. Parallel to it. Maybe that's what he was trying to do and he just got closer than he meant to."

"Yep, could be," Doug concurred. "But most all those

islands are in the wilderness area. He couldn't have been planning to go ashore, least he better not have been unless he was after a stiff fine. They don't fool around about that. I heard that a fisherman off Decatur saw him porpoising." He made a series of arcs with his hand, indicating how the plane had alternately gained and lost altitude. "Losing his nerve maybe. Or could be engine trouble and he was trying to put down anyplace he could."

"Whatever caused the crash, I just hope everyone is okay," Janet said, shaking her curly, reddish-brown head, and making a *tsking* noise. "They're so far out. There's nothing on those little islands but turkey vultures and river otters."

"Well, I think Abby might beg to differ with you on that score. There's plenty of wildlife out there. But yes, they're a long way out," George said, forking off the tip of his slice of pie. "Which raises the question, if he was trying to land out there beyond the islands, why? Where did he think he was going?"

AFTER AN HOUR of pleasant conversation, and with the last dish washed and put away, Mary and Janet were in the van about to depart for Mary's house.

The two had been friends from childhood and though their personalities were very different, they understood one another in a way only people with a long history can. "I really appreciate this, Janet," Mary said.

"Don't be ridiculous, Mary," Janet answered. "You know

full well I'm right where I want to be, doing just what I want to do. I've been wanting us to have a chance to get together and gab. We haven't had a girls' night in a while."

"We haven't been girls for a long time," Mary replied, smiling. Mary knew Janet was sincere when she said she was glad to be with her and relaxed a bit. One of the most difficult adjustments she'd had to make since the accident was that now she was frequently forced to ask for help. She hated inconveniencing people on her account. She was accustomed to being the one giving the help, not the one receiving it. It was humbling.

As she put the van in gear and backed out of her parents' driveway, she remembered how hard it had been at first, driving the van with the hand controls. She'd gotten the van a few months ago and was still absorbing the surprise of it all. She had practiced with Abby in the school parking lot, a little afraid at first but confident that she'd be able to get the hang of it. She could figure most things out given half a chance. And she did.

The driver's seat Abby used when driving the van could be easily removed from its track. Mary's chair could then glide right into place and be secured by brackets. As she had learned to get herself in and out of it and to operate the vehicle, it gave her the much wanted independence she had craved those days after the accident. It also gave Abby more freedom in her own schedule, and Mary had wanted to be able to give her that. Though Abby always scolded her for using the word, Mary felt as if her sister had already sacrificed a lot to come and take care of her.

"I didn't want to say anything in front of Mom and Dad," Mary said to Janet, now free to express her concerns, "but I'm worried about Abby's being out like this. I mean I know she can take care of herself, but she's lived away from here for a long time and this is a completely different terrain than New York State."

"Abby will be fine, don't you worry about her," Janet said as Mary turned on the windshield wipers to clear the condensation off the windshield. "She's one of the most capable people I know."

"Yes, that she is," Mary agreed with a smile. "That used to be one of the things I envied about her. She and Dad always had a special sort of bond. They both love the outdoors so and Abby loved nothing more than shrugging on a pair of overalls and traipsing off with him to the woods or helping on the boat. I used to get a little jealous."

Janet gave a soft laugh. "Have you told Abby that?"

"Only recently," Mary said, smiling. "Why?"

"Oh, I was just thinking of something Abby told me. It's ironic, that's all."

"You mean her confession that *she* has always been a little jealous of *me*? I know all about that. She's told me a few things recently too. Funny isn't it, how we look at the same set of circumstances so differently?"

"Funny, and silly too. You and Abby each have so many

gifts—it's an embarrassment of riches, really. You're just different people is all."

Mary tilted her head and laughed softly. "We are *definitely* different. I have no *desire* to spend as much time outdoors as Abby does—an afternoon in my garden once in a while is all I need. And she'd be bored to tears staying inside and cooking and crafting, which is what I like to do. But now at least we can appreciate one another's gifts without coveting them. And to think it's taken us till this point in life to recognize that," Mary said, still smiling. "Maybe we never would have if Abby hadn't moved back. I can't tell you how wonderful it's been to have her back here. We've grown closer than we've been in a long, long while. Yet, when I see her ready and able to go out to help Henry like this, I *still* sometimes wish I was more like her. I just hope they both stay safe."

Janet tried engaging Mary in idle chatter to distract her from her worry. "Are you and Henry planning to go to the Autumn Dance at the Community Center next week?" she asked.

Mary turned onto Oceania Boulevard and headed toward her house. "Oh, I don't know. Henry hasn't asked and I don't know if I'll say yes even if he does," Mary said, trying to keep her tone breezy.

"Oh, but you have to come. Henry's always the best dancer there by far. And all of the ladies enjoy a turn around the floor with him." She stopped short and drew in a sharp breath. "Oh Mary, I'm so sorry. Me and my big mouth! I forgot for a moment—"

"Janet, it's okay," Mary said, giving her friend a smile. "Really, it's fine. In a way, it's nice you forget. It makes me feel like nothing has changed between us and that you still think of me the way you always have. As for Henry, there's no reason in the world why he shouldn't continue to do all the things he enjoys. Certainly not on my account."

Janet prattled on, but Mary was only half listening. She looked out the windshield at the pale moon in the sky above. Janet had inadvertently hit on a subject that had been weighing on Mary's mind for such a long while now. She was very fond of Henry, more fond than she liked to admit, even to herself. And she enjoyed her time with him so very much. But Henry was a robust man who liked being active—hiking, fishing and yes, dancing. All things Mary could no longer do. She had begun to feel that she was being unfair to him by continuing to see him.

But she knew Henry, being the compassionate man he was, would never call it off. He would surely feel as if he were abandoning Mary when she was at a low point. This left it up to her to do the very thing she didn't want to do. But it was the right thing, for Henry's sake. *Well, wasn't it?* Mary thought to herself.

The van rocked as Mary steered it off the road and into the garage attached to her house. Janet's own car was parked at the end of the driveway. As promised, Doug had left it there for her and walked the short distance to their house down the road. He'd bid them good-bye at Stanton Farm, saying, "You two gals enjoy your visit. Take your time, Janet."

"It's sweet," Mary said, "that Doug is being so generous about you spending time with me tonight."

"Yes, it's very sweet," Janet agreed. "'Course, he has ulterior motives too. There's a baseball game on television he wants to watch. With me out of the house—and my mother out visiting a friend—there won't be any interruptions. He says I always get the urge to have an extended conversation the minute he turns on a ball game."

Mary had always admired Doug and Janet's easy relationship. Doug was the quiet, even balance to Janet's gregarious personality and they almost always seemed to be having a good time when they were together. It all seemed simple and blessedly uncomplicated.

"Hey, there's a good movie on tonight," Janet said as they went into the house. "It's a two-hankie one. How about I make a big batch of popcorn? We haven't had movie night in a long time."

"Oh, I don't know if I could concentrate, Janet," Mary answered, an edge of anxiety in her voice.

"Mary, you know they'll break into the program if there's any news about the plane crash, and we'll keep the cordless phone right in the living room in case the deputy calls. It'll give you something to occupy your mind—something other than worry."

"You're right," Mary admitted, "I guess I am worrying. Okay, let's watch a movie. Who knows, maybe Abby will even be back before it's over. But, *I'll* make the popcorn. I can manage that quite well since the kitchen's been renovated. You go turn on the television."

"Deal," Janet said and went to the living room. "No butter, I'm trying to diet," she called back over her shoulder.

Mary got the popcorn popper from the lower cabinet and set it up. Soon the exploding kernels were producing a pleasant percussion inside her cheery kitchen. Every sight and smell tonight took her thoughts back to Henry. Their first official date had been to see a movie—some barely memorable romantic comedy. But what Mary *did* remember was Henry excusing himself and returning with an enormous tub of popcorn. The movie, he claimed, was only an excuse to indulge in one of his favorite snacks.

Mary couldn't bring herself to tell Janet all the thoughts going through her mind about Henry. She knew if she told her she was considering telling Henry she couldn't see him anymore, Janet would try to talk her out of it. And Janet was not nearly as tactful as Abby about offering advice. Mary certainly didn't need anyone to remind her of Henry's many sterling qualities. That wasn't the point. The fact was that she wanted to do what was best for *him*. And she knew this decision, as hard as it might be, was one she'd have to make for herself.

Mary emptied the popcorn into a big bowl, put it in her lap and wheeled out to the living room. For Janet's sake, she told herself, she would try to get into the spirit of the evening.

The movie, a young woman's World War II–era coming-of-age story, would ordinarily have kept Mary entertained, but on this night she was distracted. She found her thoughts wandering back to concerns for Abby and Henry and the people from the downed plane. And those thoughts kept leading her to the decision she had before her about Henry. She glanced at the telephone every few minutes, willing it to ring, but the cordless phone on the coffee table remained stubbornly mute.

During the commercial breaks Janet chatted away about all the latest news in the community, about how her elderly mother Emma, who lived with Janet and Doug, was enjoying the handicrafts class at the Senior Center. And about the new altar arrangement she was working on for Little Flock Church. Janet fancied herself the chief flower arranger for the church and she was always eager to have Mary give her arrangements her stamp of approval.

Mary could tell that Janet was trying to keep her mind off her worries, and she appreciated it. She tried to hold up her end of the conversation, but each time the movie came back on, Mary was happy to have the excuse to retreat into silence. She was not a worrier by nature. Generally she had a sunny disposition and an optimistic outlook. But since the accident she tended to be more reflective and thought about things a lot more. Too much sometimes, according to Abby.

Suddenly there was a noise coming from the laundry room as if someone was rattling the knob of the door to the garage. Both women jumped and looked at one another wide-eyed.

"Maybe that's Abby," Janet said.

"But I didn't hear a car drive up, did you?" Mary asked.

"No, I didn't," Janet said, and they both fell quiet. The noise repeated, this time more insistent.

"Abby has a key. Why would she be rattling the door like that?" Mary asked, now a bit alarmed.

They both stared at one another and before either could shake themselves from their frozen state, a voice called out, "Mom? Aunt Abby? Surprise, it's me, Zack. Mom, are you here? I can't get in, my key doesn't work."

"What in the world?" Mary said. "Zack?"

"I'm coming, Zack," Janet called hopping up to go let him in. "Oh, Mary, how exciting. Zack's home!" She walked behind Mary's chair, bending down to squeeze her shoulders as she passed. "Just what you need," she said in an excited voice.

Zack, looking a bit travel-rumpled, came into the living room and bent down to Mary's wheelchair, giving his mother a heartfelt hug. "You look super, Mom," he said, a big grin spread across his face. "Did I surprise you?"

"I'll say you did," Mary answered, her face aglow. "Oh, Zack, it's so good to see you. I'm glad you came early," she said, reaching up and pushing a stray strand of black hair back off his forehead.

"Where's Aunt Abby?" he asked, glancing around the room as if they might be hiding her somewhere.

Mary and Janet told him what had happened with the plane, taking turns filling in what thin details they knew.

"That's awful. Hope everyone's okay," Zack said. "It's great that she could help out like that. She's a smart lady and I tell you what, if I was ever in that situation I'd want Aunt Abby out looking for me." He reached out to pat his mother's hand. "I can tell you're worried, Mom. But you know Aunt Abby can take care of herself. She'd have made a good pioneer woman. And anyway, Henry's not going to let her put herself in danger. You can trust him, you know that."

Mary gave him a smile and tried to take his assurances to heart. Everything he said was true, but that didn't mean *both* of them might not be facing dangers out there. The question her father had raised about why anyone would be attempting to land in that desolate area in the first place had sent her mind to speculating about all manner of dangerous people and situations. She told herself she was being overly dramatic, but a small prickle of apprehension occasionally crept its way into her thoughts.

Zack stood, his usually implacable face spread into a Cheshire cat grin. "I've got another surprise for you, Mom," he said. "It's a super, amazing, incredible, unimaginable surprise gift from Nancy and me to you. Well, not from us exactly, but it was our idea."

Mary laughed. When Zack started stringing together that many adjectives, she knew she'd better hold on to her hat. It was like a jazz riff to him—once he got started he couldn't seem to find a stopping place so he just kept improvising.

He held up a finger. "I'll be right back."

He disappeared through the kitchen and out into the garage

and a few moments later came back in leading a dog, a golden retriever and yellow Labrador mix judging by his size and his wavy golden coat. The dog came in and sat calmly by Zack's side. He cocked his head and looked at Mary expectantly.

"What is this, Zack?" Mary said, looking at him with her smile frozen in place, but a frown stitching its way across her forehead.

"It's a dog, Mom."

"Well, I can clearly see that Zack. What I don't understand is what this has to do with me," she said, apprehension hanging on every word. Did Zack expect her to dog-sit while he was on the road?

"I mean, I'm a little surprised that you got a dog," she said. "Especially with your traveling so much, but—"

"Just hear me out, Mom," Zack said, kneeling down beside the dog and holding up his hand toward his mother like a crossing guard stopping traffic. "This is no ordinary dog. His name is Finnegan and he's a trained mobility assistance dog. When you get to see all he can do, you'll realize he can really be a help to you. He's really amazing."

"Oh, Zack," Mary said, sucking in a breath and choosing her words carefully. "It's so sweet of you to think of this for me, but, honey, you know I'm not really a dog person. And I'm having enough challenges these days just learning to look after myself. I can't look after a dog too. I'm sure he's perfectly nice," she said, glancing at the dog, who still stared at her with rapt attention, "but I just don't think so."

"Mom, you don't understand," Zack said. "You don't have to look after him. Well, not much anyway. He'll be the one looking after you. Wait until you see all he can do."

"But . . . but what about Blossom!" Mary exclaimed. "She's accustomed to being queen of the castle around here. They'd get along like—well, like dogs and cats. No, it just won't work out, Zack."

"Finnegan is a specially trained dog, Mom. He won't bother Blossom. Nancy and I knew you'd be lukewarm about this. All we're asking is that you give the dog a chance before you decide. Tell me you'll at least meet the trainer and let her show you all that Finnegan can do before you say no."

"You brought the trainer with you too?" Janet asked, craning her neck to see if someone else might appear in the kitchen.

"No, not here to the house, but she's on the island. She's staying over at The Bird Nest. She came with me all the way from Illinois. Her name is Lily. It's a long story, Mom, but let me tell you, this is a once-in-a-lifetime chance. And Nancy and I both are really hoping you'll give it a try. That's all we're asking. If you then decide he's not for you, we'll be fine with that."

"He *is* a very nice looking dog," Janet said, and scooted over to pet him and run her hand down his smooth back. The dog allowed it, but held his eyes on Mary.

"Yes, he looks like a very nice dog," Mary said, looking down at Finnegan, who had hardly blinked. "And it seems you and Nancy have both gone to a great deal of trouble about this. So, yes, if it means that much to you, I'll meet the trainer and see what the dog can do. But really, Zack, I hope you mean it when you say you'll accept my decision without any hurt feelings."

"Absolutely," Zack said, nodding firmly. He gave the dog a good scratch around the ruff of his neck. "Just a try, that's all we're asking," he said, grinning from ear to ear. "Finnegan here will convince you of the rest."

Mary smiled, but in her private thoughts she was already rehearsing how to let Zack and Nancy down easy. The last thing she needed in her current circumstances was another being to care for.

The telephone rang and Mary snatched it up while the sound was still reverberating. It was Deputy Mike Bennett from the substation. Abby and Henry had called in, he told her, and asked him to let her know they were fine, but were still searching and would likely be out for a good while longer.

"Ms. Stanton wanted me to be sure to give you the message that you ought to get someone to stay with you tonight," he said. "She was very specific about that."

"Yes, I imagine she was," Mary told the deputy. She thanked him and extracted a promise from him that he'd be sure to let her know the minute he got anymore news.

"I'll stay with you tonight, Mary," Janet volunteered. "I can just run home and get a change of clothes for work tomorrow."

"That's okay, Mrs. Heinz," Zack said. "I'll be back here as soon as I go take Finnegan back over to his trainer. You two go ahead and enjoy the rest of the movie I interrupted," he said, pointing to the muted set. "I'll be back soon, and Mom, we can have a nice talk. I've got a lot to tell you about Finnegan."

"All right then, Zack. That'll be nice. It's wonderful to have you home." She started to turn her attention back to the television, but then turned and called, "Zack, how did you get here anyway? I didn't hear a car."

"Mr. Choi loaned me one of his bicycles," Zack answered, referring to the owner of The Bird Nest. "He said I could keep it as long as I'm here."

"How'd you get the dog here?" she asked.

Zack stuck his head back around the doorjamb. "I told you Mom, he's a mobility assistance dog. He ran right alongside me all the way. If I had needed him to, he would have *pulled* me all the way here. I'm telling you, he's a wonder dog!"

As she heard the garage door shut, Mary looked at Janet and gave a great heaving sigh, part contentment, part lament.

"My life is going to the dogs," Mary quipped.

"Well, you know what they say, 'Don't look a gift dog in the mouth.'" Janet smiled.

"Okay, enough with the clichés. Let's get back to the movie."

Chapter Five

DAWN WAS STILL AN HOUR AWAY. Abby and Henry trudged back to the boat after searching the third island and finding no sign of the plane. Their steps were heavy and the disappointment showed on their faces. They were now almost twenty-four hours without sleep.

This island was slightly larger than the first two, but it had been no more hospitable. It was heavily wooded to the north and thinned out into a comma shape toward the south where a single tombolo—a narrow sand spit—crooking out from the tip as tenuous as a spider's web, connected it to the second island they had searched.

While Henry called in, Abby glanced at her watch. Not yet 6:00 AM. She studied the rapidly moving clouds high in the sky for a moment then turned to look off in the direction of the next island. She wanted to believe the fourth island on her list held the object of their quest.

The island they were about to hit next was much larger than either of the previous three and even more rugged. Abby frowned at the map and sighed. This was taking so long. She worried for the people aboard the plane, and she worried about Mary. She knew there were plenty of people to see after her, but the two of them had established their little routines and she didn't want that to be interrupted for too long.

"Any word on the air search?" she asked Henry when he'd finished his transmission to the station.

He shook his head as he hooked the handset back onto the radio. "Nothing from the other search teams either. The plane will go back out as soon as the sun is up, but they're searching the entire grid—water search too—so they've got a lot to cover. We did get one more witness report in though. Came from another pilot. He saw the plane late yesterday afternoon. He doesn't know anything about the crash site, but he can confirm that there were two people aboard. He noticed the plane for the same reason everyone else did—it's erratic flight path. Said he made it a point to check it out. He's certain there were just the two on board and he's pretty sure it was a man and a woman."

He tugged off his hat and rubbed his hand over his balding pate. He cupped his neck and stretched his muscles from side to side, wincing. "How are you holding up?" he asked Abby.

"I'm tired. I'll readily admit that," she said, letting out a sigh. "But I can keep going for a while yet."

"Me too," Henry said. "But we've got to pace ourselves. We won't be any good to anybody if we let ourselves get to the point of exhaustion. Our judgment will be impaired, and we may need to make some quick decisions when we do find the plane."

Abby nodded. "I understand. The next island is larger, but if I remember, there used to be some rudimentary hiking trails before it became public land. It should be easier going. How about if we search that one, and if we don't find any sign of the plane there, we'll stop and rest?"

"That sounds reasonable," Henry said, looking at the map. He traced along their route with his finger and bit his lip, seeming to make a decision. "You've got to promise me, though, that if at any time you feel like you need to, you'll stay in the boat. Mary will never forgive me if I let you get yourself sick out here."

"I promise I'll do that, Henry," Abby assured him. "But I don't think I could rest a minute knowing those people might be out there in trouble and waiting for us to come and find them."

"You say that now and I know you mean it," Henry told her. "But this could get to be a grueling thing before it's all over. I'm sure you remember that from the other searches you've done. Everyone starts out all gung ho, but if it drags on they start to drop like flies. Sometimes it's a hindrance to the effort because then somebody's got to stop and take care of *them*. We want to work hard, but smart, agreed?"

"Agreed," Abby said.

He reached behind the seat and pulled out a Thermos.

"Let's get a quick cup of joe to warm ourselves up a bit at least," he said, unscrewing the top and pouring coffee into the cup. The steam rose in tendrils in the cool predawn air as he handed it over and Abby shucked off a glove to cradle the warm metal cup in her hand.

"That'll put a little starch in you," he said, inhaling the aroma as he reached for his travel mug nestled between the seats. As he poured, he said, "I tell you, I'm trying real hard not to think about that meal your mother had all prepared last night. I hated to miss it then, and I hate it even more now."

"Me too," Abby said. She dug in her bag for a couple of granola bars to go with the coffee. "It's not what you'd call a hearty breakfast, but it's fuel," she said, handing over a foil packet to Henry.

"Thanks," he said. "I'm sure it'll taste pretty good right now." He stared off at some point on the shoreline up-island, his focus unfixed.

"Henry, are *you* okay?" Abby asked. "You seem preoccupied —with something besides the search, I mean."

"Oh, I'm okay. Like I said, I've just been having some second thoughts about dragging you along out here. There's something that strikes me as just not right about this whole thing. Any pilot worth his salt would know not to try to land a plane anywhere around this area. What was this guy up to?"

"There's that occupational hazard kicking in again. I don't know, Henry. Maybe there was no choice. Engine trouble maybe, or some kind of mechanical malfunction. Maybe it's a honeymooning couple and he was trying to show off for his new wife. Who knows?"

"Well now, there's a poetic take on it," Henry said, sounding none too convinced. "In any case, when we do find something, I want you to stay well back and let me check it out before you go anywhere near. We straight on that?"

"You'll get no argument from me," Abby said, saluting him with her coffee cup. "I'm strictly civilian and happy to stay that way. I'm the Bird Lady, you're the law."

Henry smiled and tipped his head. "Yes, ma'am." His smile faded and he fiddled with the lid on his travel mug. Finally he said, "Truth is, I still can't help but worry about how Mary is getting on without you. I've been feeling guilty about bringing you out here and leaving her all alone." He took a sip of his coffee then turned to her. "Don't get me wrong, I appreciate the help, and you're doing a great job, but Mary's just on my mind is all."

"Mary will be fine, Henry," Abby said, feeling a little lurch in her stomach. "I don't like being away from her either, but one of the wonderful things I'm rediscovering about Sparrow Island is that there are a lot of people willing and eager to help when help is needed. Mary has a whole flock of friends who'll be happy to help her out—as much as she'll let them anyway. As you well know, Mary is intent on being as independent as possible."

Henry gave something between a laugh and a sigh. "Yes, I'm well aware of her determination to be self-reliant. It's one of the things I admire about her. Her pluck, her zest for life. She's really something else, your sister," he said as he tore the foil pouch and extracted the granola bar, examining it as if he was unsure it was edible.

"You've been wonderful for Mary through this whole ordeal, Henry. I hope you know that," Abby said, feeling the need to say something positive to him. She bit into her own bar. It tasted better than a store-bought granola bar that had been rattling around in the bottom of her bag for some weeks had any right to taste.

"If that's true, I'm glad. But, as I'm constantly trying to convince Mary, I'm getting the good end of this deal. I enjoyed spending time with her before the accident and I enjoy spending time with her now. Nothing has changed about that. Who Mary is has got nothing to do with her disability."

"I know. And Mary *will* come around to realizing that sooner or later. But you've got to understand what this has done to Mary's world. She's still adjusting. Maybe you could ask Deputy Bennett to give her a call again as soon as it's a decent hour. She'll be worried about us," Abby said, trying to walk a thin line between encouragement and fair warning. Henry didn't know that now was the time to press his case with Mary.

"Already done," he said, as he crunched through a bite of granola bar and washed it down with a swig of coffee. "And Abby, I know what you say is true. She's got lots of friends to look after her, but none of them are you. You and Mary have a special way with one another."

Abby nodded, realizing it was true. As Henry readied to get underway, Abby thought about that. Over the past few months she and Mary had gotten back to the way they'd communicated when they were little. Despite their different personalities they'd always been tuned in to one another. And now they'd found that long-lost art again. A lot of things went unspoken, but perfectly understood. They could read one another's moods and they found the same things funny.

This was another realization that fit neatly with a quotation by Euripides Abby had run across a few weeks ago in her morning readings. "There is in the worst of fortune the best of chances for a happy change." She'd copied it neatly into her journal and started a list of all the good things that had come about in the last year. She made a mental note to put her renewed closeness with Mary on her list when she got back to Sparrow Island.

Abby watched as a black and orange woolly bear caterpillar made its leisurely way across the grab rail. The old-timers said you could predict how tough a winter it was going to be by how wide the black bands on his back were. If this little fuzzy guy was any kind of predictor, Sparrow Island was in for a mild one. The caterpillar would spin his cocoon and Abby realized—God willing—she would still be here in the spring to see the Isabella tiger moth emerge. Her life was here now.

This had been a year of change. Sometimes it was disorienting for Abby. She was accustomed to order and predictability, and now life held little of either. When she'd first contemplated the idea of returning to Sparrow Island for good, it had been an overwhelming prospect. But she had done what she always did when she was unsettled. She turned to a favorite Psalm (34:4): "I sought the Lord, and he answered me; he delivered me from all my fears." She repeated the verse now under her breath.

They set out for the next island, feeling only slightly rested. The brief respite had been enough to renew hope, but Abby was aware that the longer it took to find the plane, the worse it would be for the couple who'd gone down with it. And even though Henry had remained calm and professional on the outside, his tension was almost palpable. He certainly knew the minutes were ticking by too fast. Abby tried to resist the impulse to look at her watch for the fifth time in the last half hour.

As Henry skimmed the boat across the open channel, Abby noticed that the day that had just begun to dawn was fast becoming overcast. The San Juans, resting as they did in the rain shadow of the Olympic Mountains, had more sunny days than other Pacific Northwest coastal areas—an average of 247 sunshiny days a year, if one could believe the boast of the tourism bureau. Unfortunately, this wasn't shaping up to be one of them.

Henry nudged Abby and pointed off to the port side. "Change of plans," he called. "We're going to have to go back around and loop to the west side of the island. I don't think we've got enough clearance. We're supposed to stay a hundred yards out from the pods in motorized boats."

Abby put the binoculars to her eyes and looked where he was

pointing. Orcas. Under other circumstances this would have filled Abby's heart with pure joy. When she was a girl she'd gotten to know the orca pods well and could even identify individual members. It would be like a visit with old friends. But today it meant taking a detour that was costing them time.

"That's J-pod, I think," she said, straining over the boat noise. She looked at them again, training her binoculars on the ruffled surface of the water. Three or four gray-black bodies appeared along the surface and blew water out of their blowholes, chugging along like living geysers.

"Maybe it's just as well," she shouted to Henry as she slumped back down in the seat. "We can do a visual survey of the coastline and if we see anything, we can put in here." She tapped the map. "There are not that many places to put in on this side of this island anyway."

By the time they reached the southern tip, occasional wisps of fog were curling and lifting off the water. Abby looked up into the dawn sky, now gone gunmetal gray, and wondered what this weather boded for the air search.

Henry picked up the map and handed it to Abby. "We'll hook around the south end and double back," he said, passing an index finger back and forth in an inverse arc over the general area. "You ready to do lookout duty?"

Abby nodded. Henry throttled back and swung the boat around, running parallel with the shoreline. As the noise abated he looked skyward and, as if reading Abby's thoughts, said, "This gets any soupier and the search plane will be grounded for sure."

Abby put the binoculars to her eyes and the two orbs coalesced into one view. Even in the pale light she was struck by the raw beauty of this wild place. A soft gauze of fog enveloped the stately trees and gave it an ethereal look—the forest primeval. But given the task before them, the fog was just another impediment to their efforts, one more thing working against them. It made it nearly impossible to see for any distance.

Abby's eyes felt gritty, and she lowered the binoculars for a moment and gently rubbed her lids. She blinked a few times, and focused again on the shoreline. There was a small gap through a break in the trees and she got a momentary glimpse of amorphous tendrils rising. Thicker, more substantial than vapor she thought. Smoke? Maybe. She blinked and looked again then tapped Henry three short staccato raps on the shoulder. "Back, back. I think I saw smoke."

Henry throttled back and waited for the boat to settle, then reversed. Abby leaned forward, staring intently, waiting for the spot. "There," she cried. "Right through there."

Henry stopped and put his own binoculars to his eyes, surveying the shoreline. "Are you sure it was smoke and not fog?" he asked. "I'm not getting anything."

Abby put the binoculars down and squinted, then looked again. "No, no I can't say I'm sure, Henry." She rubbed her eyes again, thinking of what Henry had said about sleep deprivation impairing judgment. "I don't see it now. Maybe it *was* only fog. Are there inland streams on this island?"

"Several," Henry answered. "Yeah, I see it too now," he said. "But I can't tell if it's smoke. Looks a little too scattered. Tell you what, there's a trail of sorts on the northwest side. If we follow it, I believe it'll come out pretty close to where we're seeing the . . . whatever it is we're seeing. It'll be quicker since we won't have to fight through the brush and there's nowhere to put ashore here anyway."

"Okay, let's go," Abby agreed, willing energy into her legs.

Henry piloted the boat expertly up to an area of broad sloping mudflats on the northwestern side of the island. The land was fringed with plants tolerant of saltwater—pickleweed, sand spurry and arrowgrass. "We'll put in there," he said, indicating a spot where the sea had carved a small curve in the land too shallow to properly be called a cove. "I'll need to move the boat in a little over an hour. Don't want to get caught out at high tide. Some of the currents around here will pull this anchor right up."

As Henry switched off the motor, the only sounds were the faraway puttering of an outboard—probably an early-morning sports fisherman—and the chatter of the birds congregated in the tide pools. The sounds were both peaceful and discouraging. Abby kept half expecting to hear cries for help, or best-case scenario, someone hailing them with relieved shouts. But none came.

By now she and Henry had developed a set routine for securing the boat and getting ready to set out, and they talked as they went through the motions.

"What's Hugo got planned these days for the museum?" Henry asked. "I'm assuming he's working on new exhibits."

"Hugo's always thinking at least three projects ahead," Abby said. "The man just has phenomenal energy. Right now he's working on the Native American exhibition. Dioramas and interactive displays and I'm not sure what all else. It's going to be wonderful."

"The Lummi?" Henry asked.

"Yes, Lummi, but other Salish tribes too."

"Salish tribes?" Henry repeated. "There's more than one?"

"That's what *I* said," Abby answered. "I thought I knew my own local history, having grown up here, but I'm learning lots of new things through Hugo. Salish is a language group, not a tribe in itself. There's a bunch of them."

"Is Hugo going to wonder where you are today?"

"It's my day off. And I'm sure he'll find out through the grapevine where I am."

Abby hoped their search would prove fruitful today and not stretch on any longer. She ran her fingers through her damp hair and took in a deep breath, puffing the air out in one big exhale as she shed her life jacket and stowed it. Surely they must be getting close.

Since this island was so large, they'd need to take whatever they could with them just in case they found the survivors. She retrieved the first aid kit from the back of the boat and added it to her pack, checking first to make sure she was familiar with the contents in case she needed to use it in a hurry. As she watched Henry drop anchor, a passage from Hebrews 6:19 came to mind: "We have this hope as an anchor for the soul, firm and secure." She looked ahead at the grand mass of the mist-shrouded island and held fast to that thought.

Calling their entry point a trail turned out to be a bit optimistic. It was obvious that *something* had trod this way before, but Abby doubted human feet had touched this ground very many times since the last Ice Age when massive, relentless glaciers ground their way through the area, gouging out the channels, sculpting the tops of ancient mountains and cleaving chunks of the mainland into islands.

They went ashore on a small stretch of gravel beach where big tumbleweeds of bull kelp had been blown ashore by storms.

While it was certainly easier going here than on the previous island, the erstwhile trail was overgrown in places and there was still plenty of vegetation and lots of low-hanging limbs to grab at their boots and snag jacket sleeves.

"So," Abby said as they threaded their way through, "have you been out to the museum to see any of the displays?"

"Not yet," Henry admitted. "I've got to tell you the truth. I'm kind of conflicted about the whole idea."

"Oh," Abby said. "How so?"

"Well, I think the idea of having a world-class museum right here to teach our kids—and adults too—about the area is good. Great, in fact. And I'm as proud as any islander of our heritage and culture. And we've sure got lots to celebrate in terms of the natural beauty we get to see every day."

"So, the problem is?" Abby asked.

"I'm not sure I really want to be advertising it. I don't like the idea of too many people finding out about us. Don't get me wrong, the tourism is great and I know a lot of people depend on it for a living. And the tourists we get are a good lot, for the most part. But it seems like more and more of them come and see the islands, then get it in their heads that they want to move here. Then pretty soon they want to change everything so it looks like wherever they came from."

"Yes," Abby said. "There's always that balance, I guess. Of course, I'm a recent resident myself, so I guess I'm guilty of interloping too."

"No, you're not. You're practically a native," Henry said firmly. "You came here when you were, what? Five years old?"

"Yes. My good fortune," Abby said. "Others weren't so lucky."

"I hear what you're saying," Henry said. "And I know you're right. I just hate to see the place change too much."

"Me too," Abby said, pushing aside a clump of oceanspray to get her boot set on solid ground. The clawlike branches attached to her pants legs and she had to shake free. "I think that's actually one of the things that's behind Hugo's passion for the museum and the conservatory. If people see the true nature of the place and learn about its rich heritage and precious resources, they'll come to see that it's their duty to look after it. After all, we're called to be stewards of the earth, right?"

"Right," Henry said. "I wish I had Hugo's faith that's the way it'll go. Seems like lots of people are just out for themselves these days. Guess I'm just being cynical."

"Well, I think you're right to be concerned. But I think Hugo is right too about the way to approach it. Like so many things in life, education is the key. One of the exhibits at the museum is this gorgeous painting and a recording of the words of Chief Seattle of the Suquamish Tribe. He said, 'We did not weave the web of life, we are merely a strand in it. Whatever we do to the web, we do to ourselves.'"

"Never thought of it quite like that," Henry said. "I guess I've been thinking of the museum as just one more tourist attraction. Maybe I need to get over there and visit soon."

"Yes, please do. I'll give you a personal guided tour."

"Thanks, I'd like that." Henry then fell silent. Other than a warning about a trip hazard, and a guess about how long it would take them to get inland, he didn't say anything for the next ten minutes as they hiked through an area of thick growth.

"Henry, is there something else on your mind? You're not still worrying about Mary are you?" Abby asked him finally, as they squeezed between a large rock face and a shaggy-barked cedar.

"I was just thinking about our earlier conversation. About Mary and her . . . I guess you'd call it her pride. That's kind of got me worried in a way. What do you think I could say or do that would convince her that I want to be with her because of who she is and not because I feel some kind of obligation to her?"

"Oh, I don't know Henry," Abby said, trying to keep her voice neutral. She pushed aside a swamp gooseberry bush with her leg, trying not to tromp on it. "Mary makes up her own mind about things. She's easygoing, but once she's decided on something, it's hard to sway her. I don't know how much she's told you about our relationship, but we had a few rocky places along the way when we were growing up. We're so different, it's sometimes hard to believe we came from the same parents."

"You're different, yet you're alike too," he said as they started up an incline. "You both have the same can-do spirit and the same concern for others. I'd say your parents' virtues are much in evidence in the both of you."

"You're kind to say that," Abby said, a bit embarrassed by the compliment. "But in our interests and our tastes, dress and personalities, we're opposites in almost every way. Mary was always the pretty one and I was always the brainy tomboy, trailing along with Dad in the outdoors."

"Yes, but down deep you've both got the same character," Henry said, grabbing hold of a fir sapling to pull himself along as the land bucked sharply upward.

"I can't tell you how grateful I am for this time with Mary," Abby said. "I really feel in my heart that I am being led to stay here and not just to help her out with the physical adjustments. It's been such a blessing to us both."

Henry glanced back over his shoulder, "Maybe you'll be able to help me jump some hurdles with Mary now that you've got experience with it."

Abby laughed softly, conserving her breath as she labored to keep pace with Henry. "Just be patient. That's about the best advice I have to offer," she replied, wishing Mary was the one to hear all this and not her.

Henry gave a mumble of acknowledgment then pointed ahead on the trail where an outcropping of rocks led up to a bald. "Let's see what we can see from up there," he said, moving steadily upward.

Abby picked her way over the smaller rocks, careful to establish firm footing and test for slides until they came to the bald. "How about if I climb up there and take a look around?" she asked, pointing to a large rock sitting at the apex. "You can spot me—I wouldn't be much help in trying to catch you."

Henry chuckled, looking down on her petite five foot three height from his vantage point a good head taller. "No, I don't believe it'd be good for you to break my fall. Okay, but you be careful. The last thing we need out here is for you to break a leg or something."

Nature had kindly provided a series of rocks that Abby was able to use as stairs, leaving her only a few feet to scramble up before she could stand safely and look around.

Unfortunately, the view rendered the effort futile. There was still too much tree cover, and the fog was now as thick as the proverbial pea soup. She put her binoculars to her eyes and scanned anyway. There were several small gaps in the tree line, but she couldn't make out anything in them. They looked like cones filled with cotton candy.

She climbed back down and, by some kind of tacit agreement, she and Henry both began to dig water bottles out of their backpacks. Now that they were standing still, Abby's legs felt like jelly and she noticed a small stitch in her side. Her arms were heavy and it felt as if her eyelids were made of sandpaper. They'd had such a long, long night and the weather was worsening as the morning went on.

Henry was feeling it too, she noted as she watched him place both hands on the small of his back and stretch. "We can't keep this up much longer without a longer break," he said. He squinted in the direction of the crude trail. "I estimate about another quarter mile to the spot where we saw the smoke—or whatever it was."

"Let's push on," Abby said, stashing her water bottle back into her backpack and hoisting it onto her back. "If I stop too long I may not be able to start up again."

Henry grabbed his own pack and slung it over his shoulder. Visibility was growing steadily worse as the fog thickened and the foliage and vegetation grew more dense. Abby was warm from exertion, but where the air touched her skin she felt cold and clammy.

Still, any inclination she had to complain was halted by thoughts of how the survivors of the plane crash might be faring by now. The clouds were gathering in great gray columns and the threat of rain brought a new urgency to the rescue effort. They had to keep going as long as they could. But she had to admit that Henry was right—she couldn't go on much longer without rest and still have her wits about her when they finally found what they were searching for.

An involuntary shiver crawled up her spine as they walked on. The fog obscured the trail ahead so completely that it seemed as if they might walk off the face of the earth if they took another few steps. Abby's feet felt leaden and it took all her concentration to keep moving at a good pace, while also watching out for roots and rocks that might send her sprawling. She was so intent that at one point she let go of a branch she had pushed aside without realizing Henry was close behind her and thwacked him a good one across the chest. She started a round of apologies, but Henry simply waved them away, urging her onward.

The fatigue pushed them both into silence as they conserved their flagging energies. With the fog cocooning them and the only sound that of their labored breathing, they trudged along. Abby felt herself being lulled into a stupor. *One foot in front of the other*, she told herself. *There may be people out there in deep trouble, and they're depending on us.*

Suddenly there was a commotion in the underbrush just a few feet away. The weeds shook and the air was filled with caterwauling and trilling. Abby scrambled backwards, almost knocking Henry down. They both looked up wild-eyed as two indistinct mounds erupted with fury from the undergrowth.

Abby suppressed a scream as she looked back at Henry, who had his hand on his sidearm, ready to draw.

Chapter Six

MARY AWOKE LONG BEFORE her alarm sounded. In the pearly gray dawn she could just make out the shapes of the furniture in her bedroom, her low dressers along one wall and the beautiful vanity along the other. After an uneasy night, it was comforting to wake up and see everything in its place.

She had slept fitfully, half expecting Abby to return and let herself in through the garage during the wee hours of the morning. But still, she *had* slept. She had been warm and snug in her own bed, while Henry and Abby, if they'd slept at all, had probably only caught a catnap in the boat or on the cold hard ground. They had been out all night.

Mary closed her eyes and tried to get back to sleep, but it was no use. Worry over Henry and Abby had teamed up with her excitement at having Zack home and she knew she wouldn't sleep another wink.

Deputy Bennett had told Mary that Henry and Abby were headed out toward the uninhabited islands to the south and southwest of Sparrow Island. She hoped they'd be able to do much of the search from the boat. Hiking those islands would be pretty rough going, even for them. On the other hand, she supposed that made it even more important that they get to the victims of the crash as soon as possible.

Mary had to acknowledge the tiny twinge of jealousy that was still plaguing her. If Abby had been helping anyone else in this way it probably wouldn't have affected her quite like this. But Abby was helping Henry, helping him out in a way Mary never could. Abby was able-bodied—an equal to Henry.

She rolled her head to the side and saw Blossom curled up in her favorite chair in the corner. "I ought to be ashamed of myself," she told the cat. "I, of all people, should know how important it is for the victims of the crash to be found and tended to as soon as possible, and here I am letting the green-eyed monster get the best of me."

The cat stared at her as if to say, *What do you expect, you're only human.*

"I know, I know," Mary told her. "I wouldn't be out there hiking in the wilderness, accident or no. So I've got no business feeling sorry for myself. I've never been outdoorsy like Abby. I'm more the type who serves by staying inside and cooking up a pot of hot soup to have waiting when they return."

She fingered the edge of the blanket and fluffed her pillow. She stared at the ceiling for what must have been a full minute, then let out a sigh.

She looked back to the corner. "Don't be so smug,

Blossom, you hear?" she told the cat, who had taken to grooming her whiskers. "Wait until you see what Zack has brought home. You may be a little jealous yourself."

Mary's words echoed softly in the room. They sounded louder than she intended in the predawn still. She cast a sheepish glance toward the door. If Zack heard her carrying on an extended conversation with the cat, he might really start to worry... and not just about her physical well-being.

"Yes, indeed," she said more softly. "He's brought home a dog. And no ordinary dog," she whispered. "He's a *wonder* dog."

Blossom seemed singularly unimpressed. Mary continued her ceiling-staring vigil for another moment. The dog was another thing to ponder. Mary loved her children more than anything in the world, and the thought of disappointing them was almost more than she could bear. But she just didn't see how she could take on the responsibility of a dog right now, even a dog as sweet as Finnegan. And she couldn't imagine what the dog could do for her that she wasn't already learning to do for herself.

She hoped Zack had meant what he said, that he and Nancy would be satisfied if she'd just give the dog a tryout. And that they would accept her decision with no hurt feelings. She resolved to be as cheerful and upbeat as she could through the whole thing. But if the dog was as smart as Zack said, maybe his canine senses would tell him she wasn't too keen on him and he'd not perform at his best. That could be her out.

Mary had a sudden flash of memory and realized that she

had dreamt about the dog last night. In her dream Nancy had been visiting from Tampa, along with her husband Ben and the children. Emily had been out in the yard with Finnegan, running with the wild abandon of a seven-year-old, arms all akimbo. Nicholas, who at three thought everything was a hoot, was throwing his little head back and laughing until he was out of breath. He'd clap his chubby hands and say the dog's name over and over, in a syncopated rhythm. *Finn-e-gan, Finn-e-gan.*

In her dream, the dog could talk, and he was telling her grandchildren that he was here to give their grandmother a tryout, but wasn't sure he was going to stay. Mary smiled to herself and turned back to the cat. "Maybe I'd better not get too smug either, Blossom," she said.

It was full light now, and Mary was growing increasingly restless. The idle comment her father had made about the pilot's possible motives for trying to land a plane in that inhospitable area kept niggling at the edges of her thoughts. Mary wasn't naïve. She could think of lots of reasons someone would chose a remote location like that to land, and most of them were not something she'd care to have Abby getting caught up in. Henry either, for that matter, even if it was his job.

ABBY GASPED AS THE ROUND CRITTERS let out an ear-piercing shriek and came closer. But then she saw feathers fluttering as if the animals were trying to get airborne. Abby knew then that their rotund bodies were too susceptible to gravity to allow them much success.

"Wild turkeys," Abby said, her voice sounding high and reedy in her ears. She sucked in a deep breath, trying to will her heart back into a regular rhythm.

"Okay, that does it," Henry said, shaking his head. "We've definitely passed the point of effectiveness. We need to get an hour's sleep and begin again."

"I agree. But we're so close. Should we at least go ahead and check the area where we thought we saw smoke before we stop?"

Henry pointed down the trail. "I think we just did." About twenty feet away was a clearing where someone, probably hikers, had set up a rough campsite. A stream spilled from a hill on the northern side and heavy vapor swirled up and disappeared into the fog. This was undoubtedly what they'd seen from the boat. No wreckage, no sign of recent human activity. Just a little waterfall.

Abby's shoulders sagged and she had to work hard to keep from whining. "After all this, nothing," she said. "Worse than nothing," she added glancing around at the human detritus that had been left carelessly around. Food wrappers and bottles, plastic tabs and bits of paper.

"Do you know who David Douglas is, Henry?" she asked, her voice sounding faraway and indistinct to her own ears.

"Yeah, Scottish guy, right? Explorer who listed all the plants and animals and stuff through this part of the country. The one the big fir is named after?"

"You get an A," Abby said, her voice still soft. "When he came back here about ten years after his first trip and saw what had happened when the settlers started moving in, he looked around and said 'too much civilization.' I think he was right." She turned back toward Henry. "Maybe, if they'd visited our museum first, they'd have had more respect for the land."

She put both hands to her forehead and skimmed her hair back off her face. "You're right, Henry. If I can be frightened out of my wits by a wild turkey, which I've heard dozens of times in my life, and if I can mistake vapor for smoke, I'm not going to be much good. I'm ready to go back to the boat and rest a little while."

After a long, silent trek back to where they had put in, Henry swung the boat around into a finger inlet that made a natural slip more protected from the tidal pull. A flock of western grebes, instantly recognizable by their swanlike necks and black heads, were startled by the boat's approach. Ungainly flyers, the grebes opted to turn bottoms up and dive to get away from the perceived danger. Abby winced. She hated disturbing the birds.

Henry insisted Abby take the covered cabin while he took one of the boat's sleeping bags out onto the deck. Abby heard him snoring before she'd even gotten her sleeping bag opened up to drape over her.

Tired as she was, she couldn't seem to sleep. She imagined the victims of the crash, wounded, cold, hungry, scared. She wondered if they had any survival skills at all. Even for her, at home in nature as she was, the conditions out here were inhospitable and getting more so by the minute. The fog, the cool temperatures and the overcast sky had made for a dark and dismal day. And it looked as if the rain wouldn't hold off much longer. It was hard to keep hope alive on such a day. She prayed for the survivors and for strength of body and spirit for all those trying to rescue them.

It seemed to her that she had barely closed her eyes when her watch started beeping insistently. Abby blinked several times to clear her eyes and squinted the dial into view. Almost nine o'clock. The whistle-hoot of a quail somewhere off in the brush seconded the notion. It was time to get moving again.

MARY LOOKED UP at the overhead transfer bar, a triangle of metal suspended above her bed. It swayed slightly as the ceiling fan moved the air about and the silver bar caught the early morning light. She tilted her head to one side and studied it. Time to get up.

She remembered her first days using the bar. She'd successfully transferred herself on her own to her chair only after much practice. In those early days she always had Abby or the occupational therapist there to spot her, but she had been absolutely disciplined about her upper body exercises and she had gotten continually stronger. She remembered the first time she did it solo. The therapist had told her she herself would know when she was ready. She had strained and grunted, but she got herself from the chair to the bed. Abby was so proud of her, she actually clapped.

Even though she had done it many times since then, she

still approached the task cautiously. She turned to see that her chair was in the right position and checked that the brake was on, then grabbed the bar and made a few tentative pulls to test her strength. She then pulled herself up, swung herself off the bed and into the chair.

Mary took a few moments to smooth out the blanket on her bed and to rearrange her twisted nightclothes. She always felt triumphant after these small victories, so happy she didn't have to be a burden and ask for help. Once Mary felt presentable, she turned and wheeled from her bedroom toward the kitchen.

Blossom sprang from her perch and followed along, meowing a cantata. Mary chose to believe it was in praise of her accomplishment—though she knew in truth it was simply feline excitement about the possibility of a can of Tuna Delight in the offing.

Mary looked out the window and noticed the amber glow of the early morning was now being subdued by a rapid-moving cloud formation. She frowned. This certainly wouldn't help the search effort.

As she was spooning the coffee into the filter, the telephone rang. Deputy Bennett, sounding horribly congested and absolutely miserable, spoke on the other end of the line. "I hope I didn't wake you, Mrs. Reynolds, but Sarge asked me to pass a message on and I knew you'd be anxious to hear."

"You didn't wake me, Deputy. And yes, I am very eager to hear whatever news you have."

"Well, I'm afraid it's not much ma'am. They still haven't found anything and, as you can imagine, I think they're pretty tired. He called nearly an hour ago, but wanted me to wait until a decent hour to call you. They were planning to rest a bit, and by now they're probably headed out to the next island on the list. Miss Stanton wanted to make sure you've got somebody there with you."

"Indeed. Please, the next time you talk with them, let them know my son is here with me. I'm well taken care of. It's them I'm worried about. And you too, Deputy. You don't sound well at all."

"I'm hanging in, Mrs. Reynolds. Deputy Washburn is going to come in and relieve me for a couple of hours. He's been out sick too, but between the two of us we'll cover the station until Sergeant Cobb gets back in—somehow or other."

Mary wished him a quick recovery and rang off, with the deputy's assurances that Henry and Abby would be fine still echoing in her ears.

It struck Mary that everyone seemed to keep repeating that statement, as if saying it out loud would make it so. She rolled over to the window and looked out over the water. "Abby and Henry will be fine," she said firmly, even as she watched the fog starting to collect in the low-lying areas along the shoreline.

She flipped on the coffeemaker and, as the aroma began to fill the kitchen, she moved to the table to do her morning devotions. She opened her well-worn leather Bible and turned

FLIGHT OF THE RAVEN

to the reading indicated by the devotional guide her pastor had given her. As happened so many times, today's verse was surpassingly attuned to her worries and concerns. She read the passage from Proverbs 3:5–6:

> Trust in the Lord with all your heart
> and lean not on your own understanding;
> in all your ways acknowledge him,
> and he will make your paths straight.

Mary smiled as she read, thinking back to a conversation she'd had with her pastor, James Hale, back when Abby had first broached the subject of staying permanently on Sparrow Island. Inside, Mary had been thrilled with the idea. She and Abby had gotten so close, and Mary had been afraid they would lose that closeness again across a new gulf of time and distance if Abby went back to New York. She longed for Abby's continued company and friendship, and for them to continue healing old wounds and misunderstandings.

But she hadn't wanted to express any of that to Abby. She confided in her minister that she didn't want to influence Abby's decision, and she didn't want Abby staying out of some misguided sense of obligation to her. She didn't want to impose her needs on Abby's decision.

Rev. James had listened in his patient way, his countenance open and warm, and then said to Mary, "If you're asking me for guidance, Mary, I'd say tell Abby how you honestly feel, then trust that God will lead her to the right decision. And urge Abby to do the same." He smiled and added, "The first thing we always have to do is get ourselves out of the way." The little twinkle in his eye let her know he appreciated how hard that sometimes was for her.

As Mary reflected on today's reading, she knew she had to apply that same guidance to the things troubling her now.

First off, there was Abby and Henry's safety. She had to stop letting her imagination run away with her. "Trust," she whispered softly, reaching over to run her finger around the rim of the coffee cup Abby kept on the lazy Susan on the table. It featured a brightly colored kingfisher painted on the side. Mary smiled. The kingfisher was said in legend to be a harbinger of peace and prosperity and to ward off bad weather. Abby and Henry could probably use a flock of them about now.

Next she turned her thoughts to the problem of how to let the kids down gently about the dog. She'd go through the motions, but . . . Mary suddenly realized she was doing the very thing today's reading cautioned against. She was relying on her own understanding. "Trust," she repeated again. She would learn about the dog and she would try her best to keep an open mind.

And finally, there was Henry. She enjoyed her time with Henry so much, and what *she* wanted was for things to continue just as they were. But was that right? Was she being selfish?

At first seeing Henry had been confusing for her. She'd felt disloyal to Jacob, despite the fact that he had been gone for ten years now, *and* despite the fact that she knew Jacob, of all people, would want her to be happy and enjoy life.

And soon she was enjoying it, very much. Henry made her laugh, and he was a thoughtful and attentive man. They could talk easily and they were comfortable with one another.

Then the accident had happened. Henry had been the first responder. He had been calm and kind and comforting during those dark moments, and she would be forever grateful for that. Now maybe it was time to repay his kindness by setting him free from any duty he felt toward her. It would be one of the hardest things she'd ever had to do, but she thought it best.

Before Mary had a chance to realize she'd backslid into relying on her own understanding again, a sharp rap at the front door startled her from her reverie. Mary wheeled to the foyer where she saw Margaret Blackstone's face framed in the glass panel in the front door.

Mary rolled over to let her in and Margaret entered in a flurry of brightly colored polyester. "Morning Mary, how ya holding up?" she said, her Brooklyn accent still as thick as the day she'd arrived on Sparrow Island twelve years ago.

"I'm fine, Margaret," Mary told her. "A little worried about Henry and Abby, and of course—"

"I've heard all about it from Janet," Margaret plunged ahead. "That's why I'm here. One, I wanted to check up on you. I know Zack's here, but I also know he's a jazz musician and they sleep their hours upside down so I knew he wouldn't be up for a while yet. I wanted to make sure to look in on you before I went into the school this morning."

Mary opened her mouth to reply but didn't get an opportunity to say anything.

"And second," Margaret rushed on. "I know this is not my business, but that's never stopped me before. I cannot for the life of me figure out why you don't want to keep him around. What's the matter with you Mary? He can make you very happy if you'll just let him."

Mary's hand went to her mouth. Had she really been that transparent? Janet knew her so well. Had she figured out that's what was troubling her last night? Her confused feelings about Henry? What had she said or done to give it away? What had Janet told Margaret?

"It's not every day you find that kind of fidelity. You'd have a true companion, Mary, who'll be with you for a long time."

Now it was Mary's turn to interrupt. "Oh, Margaret, hold the phone. We've never discussed anything that serious."

"You have to discuss it with him?" Margaret said, looking at Mary with a quizzical look on her face. "He must be smarter than I thought. But what do I know about these things? What's the matter, don't you like him?"

"Well, yes, I like him. I like him very much. He's wonderful, but—"

"Well, then *keep* him," Margaret said. "He'd be awfully good to have around. And I think you'd be very happy with him. Word is, he's a handsome guy too."

Mary frowned. "Well, yes, I think so, but I guess that's in the eye of the beholder. What do you think?"

Margaret put a hand on her hip. "Well, I haven't seen him yet. I thought Janet said he was still over at The Bird Nest with the trainer."

Mary sucked in a breath and bit her lip to keep from laughing. "Finnegan! You think I should keep Finnegan."

"The dog. The whatchamacallit dog. The helper dog. Finnegan, is that his name?" Margaret stopped and frowned at Mary. "What did you *think* I meant?"

"Nothing, nothing at all," Mary said, still trying to suppress a giggle.

"Well, that's my two cents," Margaret said, still looking at Mary with an appraising squint. "I know you didn't ask for it, but you got it just the same. I'd better get going now. You know school principals are smart people, but none I've worked for could find a thing in that office without my help. Is there anything I can do for you before I go?"

"Not a thing. I'm fine. You have a good day, Margaret. Thanks for coming by," Mary said as she rolled toward the door to see her friend out.

"You too, hon. And don't you worry about Abby and Henry. They'll be fine. I just hope the people on that plane are too."

Margaret scurried out to her car while glancing down at her watch. "You remember what I said. You think twice before you give up a good thing, you hear?" she called. "You know I love you, hon, but sometimes you let your pride get in the way. You've got to give these things a chance. Don't be hasty."

"Good advice," Mary called, waving a good-bye as Margaret got into her ten-year-old Honda and drove away.

Good advice as it applied to Finnegan anyway, Mary thought as she wheeled back to the kitchen and poured herself a cup of coffee. She looked out the window at the mist-veiled island off in the distance. But the longer she delayed with Henry, the harder it would be.

She breathed in the aroma of the fresh-brewed coffee and reached out again to touch her fingertip to the kingfisher on Abby's cup.

Chapter Seven

A FEW STRAY GROUNDS FELL into Henry's mug as he emptied the thermos of stale coffee. Abby sniffed at her own cup. It was definitely the dregs, but it was amazing how wonderful a cup of bad coffee could be under the right circumstances. She pulled two more granola bars from her bag and noted that there was one more left, the wrapper in a sad state and the bar broken into many pieces from the feel of it. She also found a small bag of vintage trail mix and two more small bottles of water.

Henry produced a little jar of pimento cheese spread and a sleeve of saltines from his own pack. "I think they're from the last time I was out fishing, so the crackers are probably pretty soggy, but the jar hasn't been opened, so the cheese is still good." He popped the top off. "Oops, I take that back. Unless it's supposed to be green on top, I think it's gone bad."

It was past nine, but Abby's body wasn't registering morning. It craved more sleep. She stood and shook out her arms and legs and twisted her neck back and forth a few times to work out the kinks.

She headed to the back of the boat to check the emergency supplies while Henry radioed in again. Since this boat was primarily used as simple transport between islands and not as a rescue vehicle, there wasn't much on board. She found two cans of soup, a small camp coffeepot with two foil pouches of coffee and several MREs, the meals ready to eat that the military had developed and that most rescue squads now carried for emergencies. She stuffed two of the MREs into her bag. If the survivors of the crash had been without food for this whole time, these self-heating meals would be welcome fare. She was about to slam the lid on the locker shut, but then she noticed a small handheld water filtration pump. She hefted it and found it fairly light. She stuffed that into her bag too, and then after a moment of indecision, grabbed the little coffeepot and the foil pouches as well.

She ran her tongue over her fuzzy teeth and longed for a toothbrush—a toothbrush and a hot shower. Oh, and a decent meal and a full night's sleep. She could picture her mother's table back at Stanton Farm, set with the blue willow china and laden with roast beef, twice-baked potatoes, fresh green salad and that luscious lemon meringue pie. Her mouth began to water.

Stop! she told herself, ashamed of her weakness. Here she was pining away for creature comforts, when the couple from the plane might be out there fighting for their very lives. She thought of Mary and what she had shared with her about the moments after her crash. She'd been alone, frightened and in pain. Her words echoed in Abby's ears. "I tried to be brave and prayed for strength to keep me from falling into despair. But,

Abby, I was so scared, and with every passing minute I was losing hope that I would be found in time. It felt like falling down a well."

Abby peered into the recesses of the next storage locker and brought out a couple of flares and crammed them into her pack, then let the lid fall and twisted the latch. "Ready to head out?" she called to Henry as he signed off the radio and turned to see what she was doing.

"Yeah, just about," he replied, fresh resolve evident in his voice. "The search plane is grounded now, but early this morning they thought they *might*—and that's a big might—have seen something on this next island we're about to hit. Fog was too thick for them to get a good visual."

"Maybe we're getting close," Abby said. "That's encouraging."

"Yeah, except this island's bigger than the others and more rugged too," he said as he moved to the back of the boat to stow the loose gear they'd moved on deck. "Do you know the story of Justice Island up in Echo Bay?"

"I know it's part of the Sucia Island Marine State Park, and I know it's a nesting area for bald eagles and a pupping ground for seals, but that's about all. It's a fairly recent addition to the park, isn't it?" Abby asked as she checked her pack and rearranged things for better balance.

"It came in while you lived away. Did you ever hear how it got its name?"

"No, I don't believe I ever did," Abby said. "Tell me."

"Well, you know this area has a long history with smuggling.

Back in the mid-eighties a fella came in here during the winter months and looked around for a base of operation for his drug-smuggling enterprise. He scouted around and finally bought a piece of property on a deserted island that seemed like it would be perfect. No one around to bother him or snoop into his business. Quiet, tranquil. But then, of course, spring came and the tourists and boaters started to arrive and he realized he'd situated himself right in the middle of a busy marine park."

"I take it he wasn't among our more successful smugglers," Abby said.

"The land was confiscated by the U.S. Marshals when he was convicted in 1986. It was turned over to the state."

"His loss, definitely our gain," Abby said.

"Yeah, well, this island we're about to search, it was a favorite of the smugglers in the old days. They were a smarter bunch. They picked it for good reason. It's isolated and it's harsh. I renew my offer here. If you want to wait in the boat, nobody's going to think less of you, Abby."

"I know that Henry," Abby answered.

"Our cell phones are useless out here. No signal. I wish we had some two-way radios. That way I could leave you with the boat and if I find something I could radio you and you could relay it to the Sparrow Island station. But the long-range ones are expensive and the department only has three sets and the deputies on patrol need those. I should have brought my own little dinky ones I use when I'm out fishing with buddies. They're short-range, but that would be *something* anyway."

Abby tensed. "I think I've got a set. How could I have forgotten that? They should be in my bag." She grabbed up her pack and started to rummage through it. "I don't want to stay with the boat, not yet anyway, but still it would be good to take these along. We could spread out a little more and still stay in contact. It would make things go faster." She hunted around a little longer but finally came up with only one walkie-talkie. "I forgot," she said, deflated. "Hugo and I were using them the other day when we were working out on the conservatory grounds. He still has the other one. I forgot to get it back."

Henry smiled. "Well, if Hugo comes within two miles of us out here, we'll be able to say howdy to him. Otherwise I guess we'll have to stick together."

"I'll go as long as I can hold out, but I promise, I'll tell you when I've had it," Abby said. "I don't want to become a liability to you. Deputy Bennett checked in with Mary this morning, correct?"

"Oh yeah," Henry said, a broad smile spreading across his face. "I'm to tell you not to worry. Zack is home. Mary says he's taking good care of her."

"Zack's home?" Abby said, clapping her hands together. "Oh, Mary must be over the moon."

"I'm sure she is," Henry said. "About *that* anyway," he added, a frown darkening his genial face.

"Well," Abby said, casting a sidelong look at Henry, unwilling to pursue that line of conversation, "that's one less worry for us. We know Mary's being well taken care of."

"Absolutely," Henry said, his affable manner back. "And here we go," he said as he started the engine. "Both my deputies and the Coast Guard are waiting to hear from us. If we find anything, we're to radio in and they'll send out help," he said, as he turned out into the channel.

"How's Deputy Bennett holding up?" Abby asked.

"Mike sounds pretty bad," Henry answered, shaking his head. "My other deputy, Artie Washburn—do you know Artie?" he asked, keeping his eyes straight ahead as he maneuvered out into the open water.

"I think I met him once," Abby answered, conjuring up the image of a young man of Native American ancestry who was in some way related to Wilma Washburn, who served as the conservatory's receptionist, secretary, bookkeeper and general go-to gal. "Seems like a nice young man."

"Oh yeah. He's tops," Henry said, raising his voice to talk above the wind. "He's getting up out of his sick bed to come in and join Bennett. They'll spell one another as best they can and keep the station covered. They're good men, both of them."

Abby took inspiration from the deputies' examples. If they could work ill, surely she could go on simply tired and hungry. She turned to Henry and gave him a thumbs-up and the most optimistic smile she could muster. The brief nap had done little to restore her eyes and weary legs, but the news from the search plane certainly renewed her determination.

Henry had to moderate the speed of the boat in the thickening fog. Even though they were of similar depth and configuration, these channels got nowhere near the traffic of Wasp Passage or Harney Channel, which were Washington State Ferry routes around Shaw and Orcas Islands. But there *were* hardcore fishermen and boaters who'd be out on the water regardless of the conditions. Plus they were getting close to the Strait of Juan de Fuca, which got all manner of water traffic, all the way up to cargo ships, oil tankers and even aircraft carriers and their tenders. Sometimes boats from the strait detoured up the channels.

Abby pulled the drawstring tightening the hood of her coat around her face and closed her eyes to rest them. Her body's fatigue warred with the bad coffee and the adrenaline caused by the prospect of finding the plane. She felt both tired and edgy—longing for rest, but at the same time eager to get going.

Henry had decided the best tack was to follow along the eastern side of the island, where a large sandy spit prevented them from getting snug into shore. Abby spotted a multitude of shore birds and land birds feeding together. Her mind automatically started to register species: a black oystercatcher, a Bonaparte's hull, a common murre, a Virginia rail and several types of plovers. She made a mental note to come back out to this island with her camera for more pleasant pursuits when this was all over.

Looking through her binoculars she followed along the spit until it was swallowed up by dense forest. It was a struggle to keep the binoculars steady. The boat's motion and the fatigue in her arms conspired to pull them away from her face. And now the fog had promoted itself to a light drizzle and occasional drops fell from her hood and seeped down onto her glasses.

As they rounded the south end of the island, Abby looked up, awed by the sight of a sheer rock cliff rising out over the sea like a medieval fortress. Waves, bigger and more violent than the gentle waves that lapped at the shores of Sparrow Island, crashed against the scree at the bottom. Nature's battering ram. These formidable rocks had resisted the onslaught of the sea for long years. Abby took a deep breath.

"We'll put in just around to the west," Henry called over the engine. "We'll have to put in on the rock beach. It's the best we can do. With over 370 miles of saltwater shoreline in our fair county, you'd think we'd be able to find better places to put in, wouldn't you?"

Abby nodded and put the binoculars back to her eyes. "The tops of the fir trees up there nearly disappear in the fog," she called. "I don't think I'll be able to see anything from here."

No sooner had the words left her mouth than a couple of broken treetops came sharply into view. "Wait!" she shouted. "Wait, I got something. Up there, at the top of that cliff, over to the right. Here, look," she said, handing Henry the binoculars as he throttled back and let the boat settle.

Henry trained the binoculars on the spot Abby indicated. "Yeah, I see it. Looks like fresh breakage. I don't see any debris though. Did you?"

"No, just the splintered trees. But like you say, it looks fresh."

"Yeah. Could be just a lightning strike, or could be it looks fresh because it's wet. But it's definitely worth checking out."

Henry slid back down in his seat and looped a turn back to the base of the cliff, getting in as close as the rocks would allow. "These were formed when the tectonic plates played bumper cars," Henry said, glancing up and down the side of the cliff face, which was scored with large cavities. They both trained their binoculars on the top of the cliff and scanned down to the water immediately below.

"What's that?" Henry asked, pulling his binoculars away and pointing Abby to a spot of water that lined up just to the right of the splintered trees.

There was something in the water, submerged except for a piece of white material with what looked like it could be metal running along the edge. It was just barely above the surface. A massive rock formation jutting up out of the water stood sentinel, preventing them from moving closer.

"It could be from the plane," Abby offered. "A piece of the pontoon maybe?"

"Could be." Henry stood up. "I can't tell anything about it from here. It could be just a piece of splintered timber, although that sure looks like metal, doesn't it?"

Abby looked again. "Yeah, but it's hard to say for sure. It could be just curled bark turned inside out. I sure wish we had some sunlight."

"I don't dare try to get in any closer," Henry said, balancing on the balls of his feet and trying for a different angle. "Not if we want to keep our hull intact." After a moment he growled in frustration. "We're gonna have to do this the hard way. Let's get on around and put in and go see for ourselves."

Abby felt the adrenaline starting to course through her veins again. "We're getting close. I just feel it."

Henry nodded and put on all prudent speed to get back to the access point. "In law enforcement, we usually like to go on hard evidence," he said, but then turned to her with a tired smile. "But just between you and me, I feel it too."

BACK ON SPARROW ISLAND, Zack came into the kitchen, his dark hair sleep-mussed and his voice still froggy. "Mom! How long have you been up? *How* did you get up? Who came by? Why didn't you call me?"

"I got up all by myself, Zack," Mary said. "As I told you on the phone, I do it all the time by myself."

"I know, Mom, but you still should have called me," Zack scolded. "You could have hurt yourself. Aunt Abby's gonna think she left you with a slacker."

"Your Aunt Abby," Mary began, leveling Zack with a look, "is very proud of me and my progress. And you should be too, Zack. Now let's back up and try this again. How about a 'way to go, Mom'?"

Zack smiled and came over to plant a kiss on his mother's forehead. "Absolutely. Way to go, Mom. Later you'll have to show me how you do it. Guess this means you've been doing your exercises."

"Every day. Rain or shine. I'm getting positively—how do you kids say it? Buff? I'm getting really quite buff." She raised one arm and flexed a muscle.

Zack laughed. "I'm sure you are, Mom. It's a little hard to tell with that frilly pink bed jacket you have on though."

"Don't be deceived by outward appearances, Zack," Mary said, happy to be the object of Zack's playful teasing.

"I try never to be. You and Dad taught me that," he said, his smile growing softer. "Well," he said, slapping his hands together, "you've gotta keep your strength up. How about I make us some breakfast?"

"It's already under way. There's batter in the fridge for those cornmeal waffles you like so much. And the waffle iron is there on the counter. I wasn't sure what time you'd get up and I wanted them to be fresh and warm."

"You're just showing off today, aren't you?" Zack asked, his voice again light. He plugged in the waffle iron and the two of them chatted about island news and Zack's travels while they waited for it to heat.

"Did I tell you I'll probably get to see Nancy next month?" Zack asked as he poured a portion of batter into the iron and closed the lid.

"No, you didn't," Mary said. "How is it that you'll get to do that?"

"We're doing a gig in Clearwater. Three nights. It's pretty close. I'll be able to go over to Tampa at least one afternoon and have dinner with them. Who knows, maybe I can talk her into cooking for me and the guys. She makes a righteous chicken piccata."

"I know she does. It's my recipe," Mary said. "Oh, I'm envious, Zack. It seems like it's been a long time since I've gotten to see them all."

"Well, Mom," Zack said, getting a plate from the cupboard then fetching orange juice and butter from the refrigerator, "I feel sure Nancy will want to plan a trip up to see how you're making out with Finnegan—*if* you decide to keep him, that is."

"Zack," Mary began, a warning note in her voice, "what happened to 'no pressure'?"

"I'm kidding, Mom," Zack said, pouring orange juice into Mary's glass, then into his own. He sat and folded his hands and blessed the food then turned to his mother, his tone serious. "Really, Mom, we hope this is something that will really be a help to you. But if you decide it's not your thing, we'll respect that. All we're asking is that you make an informed decision, and that you keep an open mind until you see all that Finnegan can do. Forty-eight hours. That's all we're asking. Deal?"

"Deal," Mary answered firmly. That was something she could promise without reservation. Mary never did anything halfway. If Zack and Nancy wanted her to learn about what service dogs do, she'd put her whole heart into it. But that didn't mean she had to use one herself. She was getting by fine. She had Abby. And hadn't she gotten herself into her chair without help this morning, thank you very much!

When Zack had polished off all the waffles save the one Mary had eaten, the two of them tidied up the kitchen and got ready to go pick up the dog and his trainer. It took Mary a while to get herself dressed, as it usually did these days. She chose a colorful skirt in a geometric block pattern that brought to mind a Mondrian painting. It took a bit of doing, but she was finally able to get it straightened under her and then put on her favorite pair of loafers.

It gave her pause when she went to put on her shoes. Abby usually did this for her, and it had been a while since she'd held the shoes in her hands. She looked at the scuffed soles and the left heel a bit worn on the outside. She bit her lip and fought the sense of sadness and loss that threatened to over-take her.

She rolled quickly to her dresser, choosing a dazzling pea-cock blue sweater to complement her outfit. She had no trou-ble at all getting it on and the beautiful color cheered her. She went over to her vanity to put on a good face—in more ways than one. One thing Mary was determined not to do was give in to self-pity. She was lucky to be alive and she had so much to be thankful for. She strove always to keep her eyes on the positive.

Minutes later she was in the living room, checking the bag on the side of her wheelchair to make sure she had everything she needed.

"Let me check in with Henry's deputy and make sure he has my cell phone number," she called as Zack clamored down the stairs dressed in fresh jeans and a thermal shirt. "I want him to be able to reach me if he hears from them."

There was no more news, the deputy informed her, but he would keep her number close at hand and let her know the minute he heard from them. "Sarge has given me strict instructions about that," he told her.

In the garage, Zack had to check out Mary's new van from stem to stern before they could get going.

"This is so cool," he told her when they were finally in it and on their way to The Bird Nest. "You drive it with this joystick? How cool is that? Can I try driving it that way?"

"Sure, Zack, but not for the first time on the public roads. I remember when I was learning to drive it. Abby and I went over to the school parking lot and I practiced, practiced, practiced."

"That's where you and Dad took me to learn to drive. We can go there and I can try driving with the hand controls."

"You bet," Mary answered.

"This sure looks like a good van. 'Course, what do I know? I know music, cars are a mystery. Has Al seen it yet?" Zack asked, referring to Sparrow Island's auto mechanic and owner of Al's Garage.

"Oh yes," Mary said, laughing. "Never ask Al Minsky's advice about an automobile unless you've got a while to listen. He has checked it out thoroughly and pronounced it excellent in every respect. I think he's already familiar with every part, including all the retrofits for the hand controls."

"Well, he's the one who'll be working on it," Zack said. "The man takes pride in his work. You know, you're lucky to have Al. Everybody on the island is. We've had our band's van break down a couple of times out on the road. It's not everywhere you find an honest, reliable mechanic."

Mary was a bit taken aback by the comment. Zack didn't give out such words of admiration lightly.

"Yes, we're all lucky to have him here, and not just because he's a good mechanic. He's a good man as well, and he makes a contribution to his community and cares about his neighbors."

"Got it, Mom. I meant it both ways."

There had been a time when Zack couldn't find much good to say about Sparrow Island. About anything in fact. She and Jacob had worried about the small, intense boy as he struggled to find his place in life. It was hard because the boy saw everything in absolutes. There was no middle ground. But the answer turned out to be black and white—literally. Eighty-eight keys in ebony and ivory. Zack was a new person from the moment he sat down to play "A Day at the Circus" in his first piano primer.

The house seemed very quiet these days. She looked forward to having it filled with music again while he was home. He always brought his keyboard and the new music he had composed. And Abby would be just tickled pink. She loved to hear Zack play, especially one piece he had written in his aunt's honor. He called it "Birdsong," and Abby swore she could identify different bird calls in the notes and in his phrasing and tempo.

At the bed-and-breakfast, Mary and Zack entered the

lobby to find the proprietors, Martin and Terza Choi, with Finnegan and a slender young woman. She had honey blonde hair pulled back into a ponytail at the nape of her neck and a pleasant, freshly scrubbed face.

"Oh, Mary," Terza Choi said in her slightly accented English, "he's a beautiful dog, this one. So smart. And he is so well behaved." She bent to stroke the dog's head.

"Yes, yes," Martin added, "a very good dog. You're going to like him, I'm sure of it. You can bring him to The Bird Nest anytime. He's a good guest."

Zack introduced his mother to Lily Hanlon, the dog's owner and trainer. Mary was immediately taken with the young woman. She was dressed simply in casual slacks, a turtleneck and a down vest and greeted Mary with no trace of self-consciousness.

But there was something beyond appearances that struck Mary. A genuineness, a warmth. If asked, she wouldn't have been able to describe the quality, but she was definitely drawn to it. And as she watched Zack's face while he was talking to the young woman, she realized she wasn't the only one.

Martin and Terza excused themselves to take care of their other guests, a group of women who were regular visitors. Lily gave Finnegan a command and he went into a prone position, but seemed alert. Lily settled on the sofa near Mary's wheelchair, while Zack shifted around on the piano bench. Mary knew his hands were itching to play.

"Maybe we should start with a general explanation of what a

service dog is, Mrs. Reynolds," Lily said. "Zack tells me you're eager to learn about them."

Mary smiled. "Well, I'm always eager to learn new things," she said vaguely. "And please call me Mary."

Lily returned her smile. "Mary," she said slowly. "Most people are familiar with guide dogs, some call them Seeing Eye dogs. But there are other types of assistance dogs: therapy dogs for the mentally ill, seizure alert dogs, autism assistance dogs, hearing ear dogs and, of course, search and rescue and other kinds of working dogs. Finnegan was trained as a mobility assistance dog, but since the lady he's been with gradually lost her hearing, he was trained for that as well."

Mary nodded politely. She had to admit, this was interesting. At the very least she'd be learning something through this exercise.

"Let me give you a little background on Finnegan," Lily went on, reaching down to scratch the dog around the neck, but keeping her eyes on Mary. "I got him as a puppy. He was a shelter dog. We look for dogs that are alert and make eye contact. That have good energy, but aren't hyperactive. I knew right away that Finnegan would make a good service dog."

Mary looked down at the dog, who kept looking up at Lily as if waiting for a command.

"He's a great dog, and I've got to admit that when they said they were going to retire him early, I was pretty happy about it. I wanted him back. I've missed him." Her smile faded a bit. "But he isn't happy. He needs to work." She tilted her head, and

Mary saw understanding in her eyes. "Like people, he doesn't like to be counted out too soon when he still has a contribution to make."

Mary looked away and cleared her throat. "Well, he looks like a perfectly nice dog. I'm sure you've done a wonderful job with him."

"Zack has explained the nature of your disability, and I think you'd be good partners," Lily continued. "But there's always an ill-defined, immeasurable something—call it chemistry—that only comes through when you spend time together. So I guess what I'm saying is, if you choose Finnegan, he has to choose you too. It's a two-way street."

Mary tried to keep her face composed and not reveal her relief. Surely the dog would sense her reticence. She wouldn't have to disappoint Nancy and Zack. She'd simply allow the dog to reject her. The tension she didn't even realize she'd been holding in her shoulders released. One less worry. Now if Henry and Abby would return to the island with news that everyone aboard the plane was safe and sound, Mary could truly relax and enjoy her time with Zack.

"How about we go for a walk and you can take us through a bit of your daily routine," Lily said. "We can see where Finnegan might be of help to you, and you two can get to know one another."

"That sounds like fun," Mary said, and meant it. She could enjoy this now that the responsibility for the outcome had been shifted onto the dog.

As Lily proceeded to put on Finnegan's bright blue cape with the patch sewn on the side that identified him as a service dog, Mary pulled her phone from the bag on the side of her wheelchair and gazed at the screen. No calls. She thought maybe she'd failed to hear the electronic chime.

"Putting the cape on Finnegan signals that he's about to go back to work," Lily was saying. "The same for his harness. You can use them both, or one or the other. Some people don't like to use the harness. They use a long leash and wrap it around their waists. Finnegan is trained for both."

"And what purpose does the harness serve?" Mary asked, now genuinely interested—but only in an academic sense. "I've seen them on guide dogs, but it's not as if Finnegan can guide my steps."

Mary wished she could call back those last words. They made it sound like she was feeling sorry for herself, and she didn't want to leave that impression. But Lily simply smiled and continued, "No, he can't do that for you. And I understand you've made remarkable progress with your mobility in the chair. Zack says you're a speed demon."

Mary's eyes widened as she looked over at Zack. He shrugged. "That's what Grandpa told me. And I see what he means. Sometimes I have to practically trot to keep up with you."

Mary laughed. "Maybe that's true," she said slowly. "So how does that affect the dog?"

"It doesn't," Lily said. "I'm just saying I know you're getting along fine with the chair, but there may be certain instances where Finnegan can give you a little help, like if you're going a longer distance and you want to rest your arms a bit, he can take over for a little while. Or with ramps or slopes, he can give you a little extra boost. You ready to give it a try?" she asked, as she snapped the fastener on the harness.

Zack stood and rubbed his hands together. "How about if we start off just walking down Shoreline Drive a bit, then back to your shop," he said, gesturing in the direction of Island Blooms. "My mom's florist shop," he said, turning to Lily. "It's just next door."

"That would be fine," Mary said. "I need to check in with Candace anyway."

Outside a light mist was falling, not enough to properly be called rain, but enough to make Mary worry about Henry and Abby's keeping dry. The day that had started out okay had now turned dreary and was headed fast toward dismal. The temperature was still pleasant, but Mary knew that if this kept up all day, that would soon change as well. She normally enjoyed the crisp fall bite in the air, but she surely wished the bad weather would hold off awhile longer until Abby and Henry were back.

She caught herself, stuck again in a loop of worry, and thought back to this morning's devotional reading.

"Trust," she said, under her breath.

Chapter Eight

HENRY PUT IN AS CLOSE as possible to the rocky beach and dropped anchor. The water here was a bit rough and, as an extra precaution, he threw a mooring line up onto shore and wrapped it around a cypress trunk to try to keep the boat's swing to a minimum.

As Abby checked her pack once more, Henry radioed in to give their location. The voice that came back was garbled and peppered with static.

Henry looked up. "The cliff's blocking the signal," he said. He looked around and frowned, then put the mike back to his mouth. "Listen, Bennett, Washburn, whichever one of you this is. We're getting nothing but babble on this end. If you're receiving this, we have a possible—I repeat *possible*—out here." He gave the coordinates and told them where they'd put in. He explained that he'd have to relocate to get a clear signal and that he'd call in again as soon as they had something to report.

Henry hooked the handset back onto the radio and turned to Abby. "I don't want them diverting anyone out here until we know for sure what we've got, despite our feelings on the subject. We can go inland and check it out in no time. Then we'll come back here and move the boat around and call in."

"It shouldn't be far if what we saw at the top of that cliff really was from the crash." Abby glanced at her watch. "It's almost ten. We can be there and back by noon. If someone is hurt, maybe I can help while you come back to call in. Or maybe they both walked away from it and just need a lift back to the mainland. We could all be back in time for lunch."

"Maybe," Henry said, his tone noncommital. He lifted the lid on a storage box on the side of the boat and brought out a couple of plastic-wrapped foil blankets used to preserve body heat in people suffering from hypothermia. He tossed them into his bag. Then he took out two folded rain ponchos and tossed one to Abby. "We may need these if this ever decides to turn into real rain," he said. "Stash it in your pack."

"I've got one already, but I'll take this one in case someone else needs it," she said, zipping it into her pack.

"I may regret this," Henry said, pulling a rolled wool blanket from the box and lashing it to his pack by the straps. "The thing smells like a wet goat, but it could come in handy."

As they scrambled ashore Abby realized one provision she didn't have was dry socks. She usually kept an extra pair in her pack, but had been forced to use them a few days prior when she'd attempted to, as Hugo put it, "jump the creek in two bounds," out on a conservatory trail. She hadn't gotten around to putting a fresh pair in to replace them.

Henry took the lead as they fought through heavy vegetation just beyond the rocks. As they continued underneath the canopy of the trees, the droplets falling on them began to multiply as every branch, twig and leaf seemed to drop the moisture they'd been hoarding. They stopped to shrug on their ponchos before continuing on their way. With Henry in his brown hooded poncho, and Abby in her own bright red version, anyone who had been there to see them might have thought they'd come across Little Red Riding Hood in the company of a Franciscan monk traipsing through the forest, Abby thought.

Henry searched for the path of least resistance, which sometimes made for a serpentine route up an ambitious incline. The majestic spires of the Douglas firs they'd seen from the boat were now hidden from view by the spreading western hemlocks and red cedars, which thrived under the closed canopy. As the forest closed in, Abby began to *feel* like Little Red Riding Hood, except her big bad wolf was the temptation to give up and go back to the boat. If she could sleep for just another hour and rest her legs . . . "Ah, Sandman, what big eyes you have," she muttered under her breath as she marched along.

They had to fight their way through the low vegetation, salal and soopalallie. Every step was a struggle. But as they topped the hill Abby could see they'd be able to make better time, at least on this little plateau. The forest floor up ahead became virtually bare except for mushrooms and coralroot.

They continued their practice of stopping every ten minutes or so to call and listen, hoping for a response. Though none came, Abby's confidence that they were on the right track had returned. She was tense with anticipation and called on her reserves to push her tired legs and aching back.

Abby saw movement out of the corner of her eye and turned to look. It was only a brown creeper spiraling his way up a big fir, busily using his curved beak to probe into every small crevice for insect prey. But as Henry cupped his hands and shouted, she noticed something beyond where the bird was busily working. Across the forest floor ahead, a splash of orange caught her attention. She adjusted the focus on her binoculars, but it was too far away and obscured by vines and thimbleberry. She couldn't make out what it was.

She got Henry's attention and pointed. "Over there. It may be just a bracken fern, or maybe a chanterelle, but I don't think so. It's too brightly colored. It doesn't look organic."

They made for the object, their pace quicker. Abby found herself slightly winded when they reached the spot, but this time they were rewarded for their efforts by a small piece of what looked like a tail rudder.

"This is it," Henry said, his voice firm. "We're close. Let me remind you again. When we find it, let me check things out before you rush into anything. Stay well back and if anything looks fishy, you head for the boat."

Abby assured him she would restrain herself, which in her current state of exhaustion would not be difficult. She took a moment to orient herself and trace the trajectory from where they had seen the breakage in the treetops to where they stood. She squinted ahead and saw another splash of something too bright to be part of the fall palette.

So now we're in another fairy tale, Abby thought. They followed the debris trail like Hansel and Gretel being guided by bread crumbs. The more they found, the more difficult the choice of going forward or going back to the boat seemed to become. They were both calling out frequently. But aside from the distant blare of a boat's horn, and the intermittent croaky calls from some toads in the underbrush, there was an expectant hush over the island.

"Oh no," Henry said, as he hauled up short and looked ahead. The land rose so sharply they were going to have to scramble up a near vertical embankment to continue in the direction they needed to go.

He turned to say something to Abby, but she spoke first. "I can make that Henry. No problem."

"I'm glad you're confident," he said. "Wish I could say the same thing for myself. Let's give it a go."

The wet leaves on the thick layer of duff made finding a good foothold a gamble at best. Even when it seemed firm in the testing, it would give way midstep. At one point Abby slipped and slid down a few feet before she caught herself on a sapling. She was unharmed, but her jeans legs were now wet and covered in muck. Wet socks were now the least of her problems.

When they reached the top of the hill, they struggled to a standing position and looked down into the small clearing below. At the far edge, half in the bordering thicket of trees, they saw it. Like a big clumsy bird in a too-small nest, the plane sat tilted at an angle in a scruff of shrubs and small trees. One pontoon had its bottom sheered off and the other was twisted up away from the plane. The wings were comprised of a continuous strut across the top of the plane. On the side tilting down, the wing had been clipped off near the fuselage and the jagged end was buried in the undergrowth almost as if it were growing up right out of the earth.

They both stared for a moment, taking in the sight. Then Henry held his arm out as if putting up a gate. "Let me go down first," he said, authority in his voice. "You wait here. If I need you, I'll call you down."

"Right," Abby said, continuing to stare at the wreckage. It had been a beautiful plane, but someone had obliterated the tail numbers with a sloppy, amateurish paint job. It almost looked as if they'd simply taken a can of spray paint to it. And there was similar defacement on the door, where a rough oval obscured whatever had been there originally. The immediate area was strewn with bits of paper and other debris, but there was no sign of the couple. Not from this distance anyway.

As Henry walked off down the hill toward the wreckage Abby noticed a single raven circling overhead. He let out a plaintive shriek as if trying to warn them off. A shiver ran up Abby's spine.

THE GREEN AWNING that sheltered the front of Island Blooms was welcome indeed, as a few plump drops of rain were beginning to fall by the time Mary and her escorts had made their way back down the street.

Finnegan walked beside Mary's chair whether she held the harness or not. He kept looking over to her, and Mary couldn't decide if he was just doing his job or if he was appraising her, trying to decide if she was good owner material.

They stopped on the sidewalk in front of the shop and Lily was temporarily sidetracked, admiring the arrangements in the two large multipaned windows on either side of the door. Along with the usual florist selections, there were dried arrangements designed with materials indigenous to the islands.

"These are beautiful," she said. "I've never seen some of these things. Did you do these?"

"Not all of them. Candace did some, but the dried arrangements are all mine," Mary answered. "They're made with things that have been gathered from the islands and preserved: hairy cat's ear, pearly everlasting, fireweed, Japanese beach peas, salsify. And that one there," she said, pointing to a smaller basket in the front, "is called old-man-in-the-spring. Its flowers are just tiny little buds, no petals."

"Even the names are so unusual," Lily said. "And you obviously have an artist's touch. These are just stunning."

"Where others see weeds, Mom sees beauty," Zack said. "That hairy cat's ear is like a glorified dandelion. Most people spend their time trying to get it out of their lawns, but Mom gathers them in like strays and gives them a place of honor in her window."

Lily laughed. "You know what they say, to each his peach. I like your view of life much better, Mary." She looked at Mary. "Did you notice that even though I stepped away, Finnegan stayed with you? He knows he's working now. That's a very good sign."

Mary looked down at the dog who stood placidly by her chair. "I'm afraid I'm going to run over his paws or something," she said, looking over the side of the chair. "He stays so close."

"You don't need to worry about that," Lily said. "By instinct and by training, he's good at spatial relationships. He knows where the chair is, and he's very tuned in to your movements. He'll stay out of the way." She looked toward the door of the shop. "Is this door pretty easy for you to maneuver?"

"Most of the time," Mary said, wondering if this was a test for her or for the dog. "I sometimes have to fiddle about a little to get the door open, especially if I'm carrying anything in my lap, but I get it eventually."

"Let's try this," Lily said, and reached into the canvas bag she carried and came out with a device she proceeded to attach to the doorknob. It had a short leather strap hanging down from it. "It doesn't interfere with the way anyone else uses the entry," she told Mary as she stood up. "Now, it's important to give short commands and to be consistent. Finnegan already knows this one, so it should be easy. I want you to say his name then say . . ." She stopped and glanced down at the dog then looked at Mary and winked. "Say D-O-O-R," she said, spelling in a stage whisper.

Mary looked up at Zack, who seemed to be enjoying himself immensely. "Okay, here we go," she said quietly. Then she turned her head to the dog and said, "Finnegan, door."

The dog walked over immediately, grabbed the leather strap in his teeth and started pulling downward, which turned the knob. Then he used his head to nudge the door open and went inside a few paces before turning back toward Mary.

"What do I do now?" Mary asked, looking inside to see the surprised face of her manager, Candace Grover. And who could blame her? It wasn't every day they had canine customers strolling in to order flowers.

"Just go right on in," Lily said, with a sweep of her hand.

"What is all this?" Candace said, moving her petite body out from behind the counter as Mary rolled in behind the dog. "Hey Mary. Zack? When did you get here? Whose dog is this? What a pretty boy! What's his name?"

She halted her barrage of questions as she looked in Lily's direction, her eyebrows arching.

Mary made the introductions and explained what they were doing and Candace immediately jumped on the Finnegan bandwagon. "What a grand idea! Oh it would be so much fun to have a dog around the shop," she said. "We could put him in a little bed over there—"

"Yes, well, as I said, we're just learning about all this right now. Just in general, you know," Mary interrupted. She looked over at Finnegan, who let out a small chuff.

"Candace, Henry's deputy hasn't called here has he? With news from Henry and Abby?" Mary asked.

"No," Candace answered, a look of concern replacing her smile. She pushed a lock of her strawberry-blond hair from her face. "When was the last time you heard from them?"

"It wasn't that long ago," Zack volunteered. "But she's worried, you know." He glanced out the window at the darkening clouds and a small frown pleated his forehead. "I keep telling her they'll be fine, but you know . . ." He shrugged then turned as the door opened and a woman entered, shaking water from the plastic bags she carried in each hand. Her long black hair was braided down her back. Her flowing peasant skirt was accessorized by a bright yellow rain slicker and galoshes.

"Hey Mary, Candace," she said, her English carrying the cadence of the Spanish that was her native tongue. "I've brought you some things," she said slowly, taking in the others present, her eyes coming to rest on the dog.

"Hi, Ana," Mary said. "How are things at In Stitches?"

"Oh, you know," Ana said. "A little slow this time of year for the store, but the quilters have all got hot needles. They're just working away over there, and I'm getting more orders than I can handle for the wall hangings." Ana turned and registered surprise. "Zack? Is that you? I hardly recognized you. Oh, it's so good to see you, young man."

"Mrs. Dominguez," Zack said. "It's good to see you too. My mother tells me you've got a thriving business going with your wall hangings. Good deal."

He turned to Lily. "Wait until you see her art," he told her. "She makes these extraordinary wall hangings with all kinds of natural materials from the island: driftwood, feathers, madrone bark, cedar, even stones."

"I'd love to see them," Lily said, extending her hand and introducing herself.

In answer to Ana's questioning glance toward the dog Mary explained what they were doing then rushed on before Ana too joined the Finnegan fan club. "So what have you brought us, Ana?"

"Oh, a little bit of this and a little bit of that," Ana replied. "Ida and I were out in the canoe yesterday doing some gathering," she said, referring to the young waitress at the Springhouse Café. "We got a little carried away so I brought some things over to share. We were out for hours. It was such a beautiful day." She looked out the window and made a sour face. "Not like today."

"Thanks, Ana," Candace said, taking the bags to the counter. "I've got some things in the back for you too. Let me just get them."

Mary explained to Lily about how she and Ana both used natural materials in their work and how they often shared the bounty of their gatherings. "Of course, now mostly it's Abby, or sometimes Candace, who gathers things for us. Sometimes even Henry brings things in from his fishing trips," she added, and the dark cloud of worry formed on her face again.

"What's wrong, Mary?" Ana asked. "You don't seem yourself."

Mary was glad when Zack answered for her. He told Ana his mother was worried about Henry and Abby out on the search.

Of course, there was more, thought Mary. But it was an error of omission only, she justified to herself. She was, indeed, still very worried about them. But her decision about Henry was occupying her mind as well. The thought of her life without his company made her heartsick. But how could she in good conscience go on with things the way they were? She'd be glad when he came back so she could get this over with and get on with the business of adjusting to life without him.

"Oh, Mary, try not to worry," Ana said, patting her arm vigorously. "Or you either, Zack," she said, turning her face to him. "*Arriba los corazones*. Take heart, it will be all right. Abby, she knows what she is doing."

Mary smiled, but cast a wary eye toward the window and the rain falling outside. "I'm sure you're right, Ana. I just wish I'd hear something more from them." She instinctively reached down to stroke Finnegan's back. His fur was soft and she felt somehow comforted by his calm presence.

Looking up, she caught Zack smiling down at her, and she quickly pulled her hand away. No sense in building up false hope.

Candace came out of the back with a bag of pods, dried

flowers and bits of ribbon for Ana, who said her good-byes, opened the door and made a dash through the rain, heading for her stitchery shop.

"You two must be getting hungry by now," Mary said to Zack and Lily. "It's almost noon. Just let me help Candace put the foil and the ribbons around these arrangements for the Ladies' Auxiliary Luncheon, and we'll go on down to the Springhouse Café for lunch. How does that sound?"

"Sounds great," Zack said, walking over to the window and peering up at the sky. "Long as you don't take too long. Looks like the rain may be getting worse."

For Mary the movements involved in arranging flowers came naturally, but today she found herself all thumbs, her hands mirroring the agitation in her mind. As she went to cut the last ribbon, her scissors escaped her grasp and clattered to the floor. Without hesitation, Finnegan went over, and picked them up and put them gently in her lap.

"Why, thank you," Mary said, surprised at both the dog's skill and his intuitiveness. She hadn't even given him a command. She made a little face as she wiped a trace of doggie drool from the handle. But as he looked up at her, seeming somehow to need her approval, she couldn't help but reach out to pat him. "He really is a smart fella, isn't he?" she asked Lily, and then realized she was preaching to the choir as Lily simply nodded and smiled.

Mary quickly finished her task, then pulled her cell phone from her bag, looking hopefully at the screen again. Seeing no messages there, she said, "Okay, Candace, we're going to lunch. If the deputy calls here could you please have him call me on my cell phone? They've been out there such a long time now."

"Of course I will Mary," Candace said. "Now, try not to worry."

"That seems to be the byword of the day," Mary said, smiling ruefully. "But when I look out there, it's hard not to." She glanced toward the windows at the darkening clouds scudding by.

Chapter Nine

As Abby watched Henry walk off toward the wreckage she had to resist the urge to call out after him. She glanced at her watch. Eleven o'clock.

Not knowing what was down there was making her afraid. She felt herself trembling, though whether it was from fear or exhaustion she couldn't say. What she did know was that she felt a new admiration for Henry. A big part of his job involved entering into situations without knowing what awaited him, yet he did it. With care, but with no hesitation.

He cupped his hands and called out a few times, his voice carrying both reassurance and authority as he made his way to the fractured fuselage of the plane. It was tilted at such an oblique angle and its front end was covered in shrubs and torn-away tree branches, that he couldn't see into the cockpit. He climbed around the debris littering the area near the docked tailpiece. He made his way along the side of the plane then disappeared from sight around the nose. Abby spent a couple of very long minutes waiting for him to come into view again.

"Come on down," he called finally, beckoning to her. "I think this is going to take both of us."

Abby started down the hill, trying to read the situation from the tone in Henry's voice. There didn't seem to be any added urgency, but there was still plenty of tension.

When she reached him, he motioned to the left side of the plane, which was tilted over at such a sharp angle the window was almost buried in the ground. "Here's the situation," he said. "There's not a sound coming from in there. We need to get a look in a window to see if the pilot and the passenger are still in the plane, but I can't see in there from either side. One's too high and the other's flush against the ground. The inside's partially collapsed, and I couldn't fit through there, even if the thing was stable, which I'm not at all sure it is."

"Just tell me what you need me to do, Henry," Abby said.

"I need you to climb up on my back and have a look through the window into the cockpit. I hate to ask you to do that, Abby, because I don't know what you'll find. It could be bad. But obviously I can't be the one to look. You can't boost me up—I'm not what you'd call petite," he said smiling without mirth. "If there was any other way, I wouldn't ask you to do this, but time is definitely an issue here."

"Say no more, Henry," Abby said, putting down her pack. "How far around can we get?" She started to move around to the front of the plane, bracing herself on the trunk of a lodge-pole pine that had been scarred by the crash.

"Careful," Henry cautioned. "Like I said, I'm not sure how

stable this wreckage is. Don't lean against it. There's a washout just on the other side, and it may slide."

The ground was marshy and Abby studied the lay of the land. Up on an embankment on the other side of the plane she saw water from an underground stream trickling over the rocks, moving down toward a larger stream. Where a small meadow ended, there was a copse of woods running along a ridge to the north. To the east, the earth dropped away in a steep slope all the way to the shore.

They had to fight their way through hardhack, swamp gooseberry and lashes of trailing blackberry, but they finally reached a point where they could have a look. Henry leaned against a tree and bent over until his back was almost level with the ground, bracing his hands on his knees. "Grab hold of that branch for balance and use my knee as a step," he told her. "Just take a quick look and tell me what you see. Don't . . ." he began, but his voice trailed off. "Just take a quick look is all."

Abby wiped a few droplets from her glasses then followed his directions. The window was fogged, but when she stretched her neck and pulled herself a little taller by holding onto the tree branch, she had an unobstructed view through a small section of clear glass. She sucked in breath.

"There's no one there," she told Henry.

"That's good," Henry said, his voice muffled. "They made it out okay then."

"Looks like they made it out," Abby said slowly, staring

transfixed at the sight before her. "I'm not so sure about the okay part. Henry, there's a lot of blood on one of the seats in there. Someone is definitely injured. We've got to find them—soon!"

She lowered herself carefully back to the ground and they started to pick their way around the wreckage. "There's no chance they were thrown clear," Henry said, shining his flashlight over and under the wreckage. "So where did they get out?"

"There's a breech over here," Abby called, as she made her away around the front of the plane, "just back of the cockpit. The wash and what was left of the wing kept the plane from collapsing against the ground."

"Wait up," Henry said, picking his way gingerly around in front of her. He reached out for the propeller and motioned for Abby to move back. He gave it a couple of tugs and the plane creaked and groaned, but kept its position. "You stay back. I'm just going to check the perimeter and then have a look."

He hunched over and pushed his way through the branches of a low-limbed cedar that scrubbed against the side of the plane.

After what seemed like a very long time, but was in reality probably less than a minute, Abby heard him say. "Yeah, this is how they got out. There are footprints." He was silent again, and Abby grew impatient. She moved out away from the plane and, holding on tight to one of the cedar limbs to brace herself, worked her way around until she had Henry in sight. He was crouched down, shining his flashlight in through the opening in the fuselage.

Abby looked around and started picking up bits of paper from the ground. The crash had made confetti of someone's personal life, little bits of receipts and letters, newspaper and pages from books. She stuffed them into her pockets, thinking she'd look at them closer later and see if there was anything useful on them. She squatted down and twisted her head to peer at Henry. "What else can you see?" she asked him. He looked up sharply, but relaxed when he saw she was well away from the wreckage.

"There's blood smears in the cabin too. You're right—one or both is definitely injured. There's a briefcase in here that's had its hinges sprung. It's jammed under the seat. Looks like that's where all this paper came from," he said, nodding toward the litter on the ground. He directed the flashlight back toward the area just in front of the opening and moved it back and forth. "Only one set of footprints," he said. "And a wide drag mark." He put his head back in the opening and examined the rough edges. "Looks like they've made some kind of travois with tree limbs and a green blanket maybe. There's another blanket in here, same color as the fibers caught here in the jagged edges." He thumbed the side of the breech. "And they've chopped off those limbs over there." He pointed toward a couple of stubs where pine limbs used to be. "Those are definitely tool marks, not splintering."

"Surely they haven't gone far," Abby said, staring at the drag mark. "Especially not with one pulling the other." She looked up at the ever-darkening sky. "It looks like we're in for bad weather for sure. We need to find them quick, Henry."

"Yeah, sure does," Henry said, glancing upward. He shined the flashlight back into the opening and, half-kneeling and half-standing, stuck his upper body back inside. Suddenly there was a loud snap, and Henry let out a strangled wheeze and then dove for the ground. Instinctively Abby did likewise, flattening herself against the marshy earth. Before she could get her wits about her to call out to Henry, a raven flew out from the damaged fuselage and swooped skyward. He gave his wings a couple of noisy flaps, then let out an urgent, ear-piercing *caw* and dove, passing just over Abby's head and out across the clearing.

Neither of them moved for a minute, then Abby broke the silence. "What in the *world* was he doing in there? That's strange behavior."

"I don't know," Henry said, standing and dusting off his pants. "But he 'bout took the top of my head off."

Abby picked a couple of pieces of rotted leaf from her face and gave the front of her poncho a couple of ineffectual swipes. "That's twice in twenty-four hours I've been frightened by a bird, for heaven's sake," Abby said. "What kind of ornithologist am I?"

"Unusual circumstances," Henry said. "I hate crows anyway, no offense to your birds. San Juan chickens they've taken to calling them. You eat outside, the sneaking little bandits will steal the food right off your plate if you don't watch out."

"That wasn't a crow, it was a raven," she told him. "Ravens are bigger. They have a more hooked beak and a shaggy throat, like that one did. And there," she said, pointing skyward, "see how his tail is almost a diamond shape?"

"Like out of Poe?" Henry said, staring up at the bird now riding a current of air high aloft. "Well, that's a cheery touch."

"I still can't figure out what he was doing in there," Abby said. "Did you know ravens—all the corvids, for that matter—are supposedly the most intelligent birds? They'll actually work at solving a problem. There's a famous experiment where a vat of water was placed in front of the bird, but his beak couldn't reach it. He added stones to the vat until the water level rose and he could drink from it. They've been seen to use tools, too, like a drinking straw, to get at insects. And they post sentries when the flock is foraging and will mob any perceived enemy. Seems odd that lone one was *inside* the wreckage."

"Who knows?" Henry said, scowling at the bird, still perturbed. "Maybe he was looking for something to pilfer." He looked around, then pointed toward the ground. "Tell you what, let's follow this trail and see if there's a chance we can locate and evacuate these folks ourselves. If they made it out of here, chances are they're in good enough shape to make it to the boat. It would take me nearly an hour to get back and move the boat to call in. Let's see if we can find them first. How good a tracker are you?"

She knelt, unconcerned about soiling her clothes. They couldn't get much worse. She looked closely at the drag marks. "Well, not bragging, but I'm a pretty good sign cutter. Dad learned from an old Lummi friend of his, and he taught me. For Native Americans, it's part of their heritage. They can follow the most delicate signs—bent branches, overturned rocks, smells and slight variances in footprints. They can learn a lot about what or who they're tracking along the way. I'm not that good, but then there's nothing subtle about this," she said, pointing to the drag marks. "They've left us an obvious trail. Looks like it goes off there back out toward shore. Maybe they gave up on being rescued and went looking for help."

"Unless they're familiar with the area, they'd have no way of knowing the island's uninhabited, I suppose," Henry said. "But they'd have been better off to stay with the plane. At least they'd have some shelter here."

Abby stood up. "Let me get my pack," she said, "and we'll follow the trail. Maybe they found shelter under a bluff or in a cave somewhere. It got pretty cold last night. I hope they at least have on a few layers of clothes and know how to make a fire."

"No sign of smoke, but as we've already found out, that doesn't mean anything. Could be masked by the fog," Henry said. "Thing I don't understand is this leads off through the roughest woods and on out toward that sheer cliff. Why wouldn't they go up through the meadow there where it's easier going? Or better still, go down that way, toward the channel."

Abby frowned as she came back around the plane, shouldering her pack. "I don't know," she said, looking up at the hilly patch of horsetail and velvet grass. "Maybe they thought they'd be more visible to a search plane on the cliff. But, then again, how would they know the cliff was there? Unless they flew over it before they crashed."

"Maybe," Henry said. "But even the most clueless city dwellers would know not to go off to high ground, it'd seem."

"Maybe they were disoriented," Abby said. "Or maybe they had in mind to set a signal fire."

"There's a thought," Henry said, nodding. "That would make sense." He frowned. "Of course, they could have done that right here. Something just doesn't add up."

They set out, each on the lookout for fresh marks to indicate the trail. Henry pointed toward two partial shoeprints from a pair of athletic shoes in a muddy dip. Both were pointed in the wrong direction. "That's odd," said Henry. He looked more closely. "One of them is having to make a pretty good effort to bear the load, walking backward and pulling the other person up the hill. Look how these are dug in. Big shoes, probably male."

"Now see, you're not such a shabby sign cutter yourself," Abby said.

The rain was now falling in big round droplets and Abby feared the trail would be washed away before they were able to follow it to the end. Henry must have felt that way too because by unspoken agreement they both started to walk faster.

As they moved under the canopy of forest again, darkness

seemed to be making a premature approach. What light there was illuminated everything in a pale, gray-green cast. Even the bright red berries of the mountain ash and holly were muted, like the colors in an old masters' painting.

The rain ricocheted down off leaves and branches, a drum corps of percussion in the otherwise quiet forest. The incessant drumming drove the sense of urgency, and Abby had to remind herself to pay careful attention to her steps. Fatigue was already doing strange things to her perceptions, causing her to misjudge distances. That, and the fact that her rubbery legs were not responding as they should, could easily cause her to stumble and fall.

She tried to imagine the couple—but then asked herself why she thought of them as a couple. All she and Henry really knew was that it was a man and woman in the plane. They could be father and daughter, mother and son, even brother and sister. She hoped they were warm, and that they hadn't given in to despair, that great black chasm that had threatened to swallow Mary in the minutes after her accident.

Abby said the simple prayer uttered by almost everyone at some point in life when one is too tired, too distracted and too harried to pray. "Help," she said softly as she put one heavy foot in front of the other.

AS THEY LEFT ISLAND BLOOMS, Mary turned to Lily and said, "Maybe we should leave Finnegan here with Candace while we go to lunch? I'm sure she'd love to dog-sit."

"Oh no," Lily answered. "For the next forty-eight hours Finnegan goes everywhere with you. That's the way it works normally. Under these special circumstances, I'll take care of feeding and grooming him for you though. That is, until your sister gets back, so we can go over all that together."

"But what will we do with him when we go in to eat," Mary asked.

"He'll go right in with us," Zack said. "Haven't you ever seen guide dogs in restaurants before?"

"Well, yes, guide dogs," Mary said. "But this is different."

"Service dogs are welcome almost everywhere," Lily said. "Once in a while you'll run across someone uninformed who'll give you a hard time, but it really doesn't happen often. We have cards that you can give out that explain the legalities of it in those rare cases. For the most part, people respond very positively to service dogs. Too much so sometimes. But we'll talk about that later."

Candace had given her two big umbrellas, and they used them as they walked the short distance to the Springhouse Café along Shoreline Drive. With the patter of the rain on the umbrellas as a backdrop to their conversation, Mary learned that Lily was from Evanston, Illinois, and that she worked part-time as a veterinary assistant and part-time for an organization called Pet Partners.

"Obviously you love animals," Mary said. "But what made you choose this particular field to get involved in, if you don't mind my asking?"

"No, I don't mind at all. I get asked often. I have a personal reason. My younger brother has a disability, quite similar to yours, actually. He had a diving accident when he was ten years old. I was fifteen then and I saw how frustrated he was with some of his daily activities," she said. Her tone was matter-of-fact and Mary found she appreciated that. Since she'd been in the chair Mary had seen how uncomfortable some people were when they talked to her and how they picked their way around a minefield of words. They didn't seem to know whether to bend or stay upright when they talked with her. They were just awkward around her. Lily's plain nononsense approach felt like a breath of fresh air to Mary.

"And your brother got a dog?" Mary asked.

"Yes. His name was Bono—his trainer was a big U2 fan," she said, more to Zack than to Mary. "He became part of our family."

"How old is your brother now?" Mary asked.

"Jeff's twenty-one, he's a student at Northwestern, premed. He's on an intramural crew team—he's using all those upperbody exercises he's done all his life to good advantage. He has a wonderful girlfriend, loves his classes and is living a very full life. His new dog, Miles, goes everywhere with him."

"Miles?" Mary asked.

"He's a jazz buff," Zack cut in. "Jeff, not the dog. Although, come to think of it, I think the dog kind of likes it too. Anyway, Jeff got to name him, so he's named after Miles Davis. That's how Lily and I met. Jeff came into the club to hear us play and

I went over to talk to him during the break. I asked about the dog and he told me if I wanted to learn about service dogs I should call Lily. So I did."

"What about Bono?" Mary asked.

"Bono's living out his retirement with our parents, which has turned out to be a very good thing. My dad has arthritis and Bono's a great help to him. It's been a bonus blessing."

As they reached the Springhouse Café, Mary looked down at Finnegan, who had walked just beside her chair, adjusting his gait to her speed. When Zack swung the door open, Mary hesitated. The front entry of the Springhouse Café featured a gift shop with all manner of breakable items lined upon the shelves. One swish of Finnegan's tail could send things flying.

"It's okay," Lily said, sensing her hesitation.

Finnegan moved with measured steps through the shop, keeping his body in tight to Mary's chair. When they were inside the café and seated at the table, he moved around beside Mary's chair. Lily instructed Mary to give him one quick command, "Finnegan, rest," and he settled down on the floor.

"Doesn't the smell of food excite him?" Mary asked, amazed that the dog wasn't agitated by the aroma of grilling hamburgers and French fries.

"Oh, I'm sure he's making like Pavlov's dog." Lily laughed. "But he's been trained to ignore distractions and he has a strict feeding schedule. It's important for you, though, as his partner, to try to minimize the distractions whenever you can. Sights, sounds, smells . . . it can be a lot for him to sort out."

Ida Tolliver, a waitress at the café, came to take their order. But as was the practice on island time, she visited for a few minutes standing near Zack's chair. Ida was very pretty, with blonde hair and eyes Mary had always thought of as the violet color of the Eaton's asters that grew along the roadsides in the San Juans.

After Ida had been introduced to Lily, she asked Zack about his music and his travels. She listened with a longing look as Zack told her what he'd been up to for the past couple of months. Ida wanted nothing more than to escape the island and move to a big city and have an exciting life. But her parents had passed away when she was still in high school and she had to support herself. She hadn't been able to go to college, not that she had any idea what she'd want to study if she did. At twenty-four, Ida was, as Abby put it, in her "seeking" phase.

She asked for news of Henry and Abby and the plane, and Mary told her what little she had to report.

"Gosh, I hope they're okay," Ida said, then caught herself. "I mean, I'm sure Abby and Henry are," she said quickly. "But I hope the people from the plane are too."

Ida had been in the restaurant's kitchen when they had come in. So as she moved around the table to start taking orders, she was startled by Finnegan, who was having himself a wee nap on his time off.

"There's a dog in here!" she exclaimed.

Lily quickly explained about the dog and Ida's face lit up. "How cool is that?" she asked, turning back to Mary.

Before she had a chance to get any more wound up about it, Mary cut in, "You know, Ida, we're just starving. What's good today?"

Several other islanders came into the café while they were lunching, each coming over to ask Mary if she had any news from Abby and Henry. And each got the full explanation of what the dog was all about. Mary noticed that they all broke into smiles when they were told about the dog and what he could do. It seemed almost contagious.

Mary looked up to see her pastor, Rev. James Hale, come into the café. His eyes passed over all the tables as if looking for someone. Ida called out to him, "Reverend, Rick DeBow called and asked me to tell you he won't be able to meet you for lunch. He's hung up on a job over at The Bird Nest."

"Fine. Thank you, Ida," he called back. He walked to the center of the room and raised his voice. "Hi folks, can I interrupt you all for a moment? I just wanted to let you know that we're having a prayer vigil tonight for the people on that downed plane. Join us if you can and tell all your family and friends about it. Six o'clock at Little Flock. Of course, you don't need to wait until then to say a prayer for them and for those out searching for them. God is open twenty-four-seven, you know."

People nodded and the hush that had fallen over the café was soon again replaced by murmured conversation, the clink of dishes and the hiss of the griddle.

Rev. James spotted Mary and came over to the table. He greeted Zack with a couple of slaps on the back.

"Good to see you, Rev. James," Zack said, introducing Lily and asking after the family.

It had taken Mary a little while to get used to Rev. James Hale's more casual style of ministry. The previous pastor at Little Flock Church had been a good man and a good pastor, but he'd always maintained a certain formality with his congregants. Rev. James had a more personal style of ministering.

Unlike the others, after Rev. James was given the explanation for Finnegan's presence, he stood a moment looking pensively at the dog before a satisfied smile spread over his face. Mary knew Rev. James well enough by now to know that look. He was one to think things through. He wasn't taken in by the charm of the dog. He was thinking about *Mary* and what it might mean down the line for her if she kept the dog.

"We're just giving this a tryout for a couple of days," Mary said, needing somehow to lower expectations, especially for this man who knew her foibles so well. "I may not be a good candidate for a dog like this. Who's to say?"

Rev. James pushed his sandy-blond hair back from his forehead and adjusted his wire-rimmed glasses. He turned calmly to Mary, smiling all the while. "As long as you have an open mind and an open heart, I'm sure things will work out just as they're meant to. He certainly is a good-looking dog."

He turned to Lily. "I'm not supposed to pet him or anything if he's working, right?"

"He knows he's off duty right now, so it's okay. But it was really good of you to ask," Lily replied.

She turned to Mary as Rev. James stooped to pet the dog. "That's one of the things I was telling you about earlier. Some people are so drawn to the dog they'll want to pet him and play with him. You need to try to gently discourage that if he's working. That's sometimes hard, especially with children. The best thing to do in that situation is to stop if you can and have Finnegan sit. He knows he's on a little break when you do that and he can interact with them a little without it throwing off his concentration."

"Well, I must say," Mary said, "so far, people have certainly reacted positively to him. I can't believe how they just take to him right away."

"He's a great icebreaker—a good ambassador. My brother says he's had conversations with any number of people who probably would never have approached him if his dog hadn't been with him. Including, I might add, that girlfriend of his I mentioned," Lily said, laughing.

"Yeah," Zack said, as if the thought had suddenly occurred to him. "You know, I might not have gone over to talk to him that night if he hadn't had the dog along. I never thought about that before, but it made him seem just more, I don't know, friendly I guess. Approachable. Or maybe it just gave me some way to ease into the conversation."

"Well, I know one little person who would be thrilled to see the dog," Rev. James said as he stood, still looking down at Finnegan. "Maybe if the rain lets up, you could bring him by the house and let Toby see him—he's my two-year-old son," he explained to Lily. "He's crazy about dogs, any breed, any size, any color. All his favorite books have dogs in them. But I haven't been able to talk my wife Patricia into getting one. She thinks it'll be too much work."

"That's what I've been telling Zack," Mary said. "I'm not sure I'm up to seeing after a dog right now either. No offense, Finnegan," she said, looking down at the dog.

"Ah, but some things are worth the effort, aren't they?" Rev. James said, smiling his warm smile. "It's good to have a dog around. One of my old seminary professors had a homely looking little beagle that went everywhere with him. Came with him to the office, slept at the foot of his bed at night. Someone asked him once why he was so attached to the dog. He said the dog inspired him, that he got up every morning determined to be as good a man as the dog already thought he was."

Lily laughed. "That one I've got to remember," she said.

Rev. James reached down to scratch behind Finnegan's ears. "Toby and I are working on his mom. Maybe Finnegan here can give us a little help."

Mary's phone let out a trill and she dug in her bag for it. Deputy Washburn, sounding every bit as ill as Deputy Bennett had been, told her Abby and Henry had called in, but were having transmission difficulties. "There's all kinds of glacial deposits and sandstone cliffs and whatnot out there that mucks up our communications sometimes. But we expect to hear from them again soon," he said. "They may have found something, but we're not sure just what, our conversation was pretty patchy. But we know they're okay anyway. Thought you'd be anxious to hear that."

Mary thanked him and shared the small bit of news.

"God be with them all," Rev. James said softly. "Sounds like they're getting close."

Chapter Ten

As Abby and Henry moved along, careful not to disturb evidence of the trail, Abby started to sniffle. That was all she needed, a head cold starting in. She reached into her pocket for a tissue and brought out a piece of paper she'd picked up from around the plane. She glanced idly at it as she separated it from the tissue. It was an envelope fragment with a partial name, Atkinso-, and a postmark she couldn't make out.

As she attended to her sniffles and moved along, part of her brain was engaged with following the trail, but the other part was busily pondering the name. She needed Mary here. Crossword puzzles were her forte. "Okay, Mary," she said under her breath, "help me figure this one out."

"You say something?" Henry asked.

"Uh, sorry," Abby said, still sniffling. "I was just having an imaginary conversation with Mary."

Henry laughed. "I've been having quite a few of those myself lately. I feel a lot better now that I know Zack's there with her, but I still want to get you back to her as soon as I can. For your sake as well as hers. No offense, but you don't look so good."

Abby looked down at her mud-caked clothing and felt her wet hair stringing down on her checks. She sniffled again. "I feel a cold coming on, I think, but I can make it."

"Not to mention we're both getting near that exhaustion point I warned you about. But it should all be over soon—one way or the other," he added ominously.

As they walked on, each pausing occasionally to point out some new sign on the trail, she told him about the last name she'd found on the paper. "It's probably Atkinson. I keep thinking I've heard that name recently, but I can't remember where."

"Well, it's not that uncommon a name. Isn't that one of those newfangled diets?"

Abby gave a wheeze that passed for a laugh. "No, that's Atkins."

"Knew it was something like that," he said, his words coming slowly. "Visibility is still pretty bad," he said, his voice broken by little puffs of exertion as they started up yet another knoll. "But at least the rain's almost stopped."

Abby looked up, but could see little of the sky through the trees. "At least for now. But those clouds don't look like they're finished with us. It's going to be dark and gloomy in the woods, even at this time in the afternoon. Hope our flashlight batteries hold out."

"I've got extra and, if worse comes to worst, there's a lantern in the boat. Let's just hope we find them before we need either."

"Your lips to God's ear," Abby said, shooing away the crane flies flitting around her head. Abby knew they didn't bite, but these insects, which looked like jumbo mosquitoes and seemed suddenly to be everywhere, could certainly pester.

Following the trail was easier in some ways than the search thus far had been. But it was slower, since they had to make sure they weren't veering off the trail the man and woman had left. There was something pitiful about the two ruts the travois had made. It must have been desperation that had made one of them decide to try to drag the other one to get help.

Why, Abby wondered, hadn't the one who was still capable of pulling simply gone for help alone? Wouldn't that have been faster and more efficient?

But then she thought again of what Mary had told her about how she'd felt on the night of her accident. It would be hard to leave someone in that condition alone, especially in an area as rough as this. Whoever these two were, they were in it together. The thought made Abby quicken her steps, despite the protests of her tired legs and cold feet.

Henry had been right about the dangers of fatigue. Abby found herself unable to sustain a clear line of thought. Her mind kept bouncing around from one thing to another. The hunger in her belly didn't help, nor did the throbbing in her head that had syncopated itself to her every footstep.

At one point they came to a cedar nurse log at least a hundred feet in length with three good-sized saplings already rising up out of it to take its place in the nutrient rich soil that had nourished it for so many years. Abby looked up and down the log studded here and there with fan-shaped angel's wings fungi, wondering how the couple had managed to get over it. Then she saw the disturbance in the spongy wood where the travois had been dragged across it, gouging out two deep troughs and scattering the rotted wood across the forest floor.

Just beyond the log the trail took a sudden turn and Abby and Henry both stood studying it, trying to divine what could have made the couple turn away from an area of low undergrowth to a route thick with brambles and bushes. Then Abby looked up. "You may want to get out from under that tree," she said, moving away a few feet. She pointed out a large area spattered with guano. "Nesting site," she said, pointing up to a rocky outcropping pegged with trees. "Looks like three or four different species."

"Well," Henry said, "doesn't take a sign cutter to figure these are probably city people if that would be enough to make them go from clean forest floor to that to avoid a few bird droppings." He pointed toward the thick underbrush.

"It might not have been just that," Abby said. "Maybe it was the sounds. A bunch of birds together can make a lot of racket. And like we said earlier, if the owls get into the mix, it's pretty eerie. Maybe the noise scared them off in a different direction." Abby walked over a few paces into the detour. "I'll bet they wish they'd braved the birds right about now though," she said, pointing down toward the brush.

"*Hmm,*" Henry said, "stinging nettle. Hope they're covered up good." He stood up straight and shed his pack. "Let's have a water break. We don't want to get dehydrated. I think we're getting close to the shoreline. Listen to the waves."

Abby blinked and closed her eyes. A dangerous practice, she decided. She believed she could fall asleep right there, standing on her feet. Her clothes were so muddy and stiff they could probably hold her up.

She heard the waves, regular and insistent, beating against the rocks. She tried to orient herself and realized they must be getting very close to the sheer cliff where they'd seen the first sign of the wreckage. They had hiked over half the length of the island. No wonder she was tired. She heard the crackle of the paper as Henry unfolded the map and studied it.

She wasn't sure if she decided to sit down, or if her legs simply mutinied, but she found herself sprawled against a rock near a prickly pear cactus. People were always surprised to find cacti in this watery land. They associated it with dry, parched places. Abby couldn't identify with the dry part right now, but she certainly felt parched. She dug a water bottle out of her pack and took a few long, quenching sips. She opened the plastic bag of trail mix and grabbed out a small handful, then offered it to Henry, who took it distractedly as he continued to study the map. The mix was stale and soggy, but the nuts and fruits had one property Abby could fully appreciate—they were edible. She needed something to keep her from bottoming out. She was getting concerned that she wasn't going to be able to go on and that she would become the liability she'd promised Henry she wouldn't be.

Suddenly there was an electric blue flash through the trees. A Stellar's jay swooped overhead letting out a grating squawk, rousing Abby out of her stupor.

"They've got to be around here someplace," Henry said, glaring at the bird. "Look where they've come from," he said, pointing back over the trail. "Even without a knowledge of the island, common sense should have told them to go the opposite way."

"All the more reason to find them soon," Abby said. "They obviously aren't thinking clearly. And I'm not sure we will be either if we go on much longer."

She struggled to her feet. "Like you say, we've got to be close," she said, giving Henry a hopeful look.

He nodded and put both hands around his mouth, forming a make-do megaphone. He gave several shouts, but the only answer was the flutter and snap of flapping wings as the nesting birds took flight. Abby cringed. She didn't like disturbing their habitat, but she knew the more pressing concern of finding the couple had to take precedence.

As they shouldered their backpacks and started to move on, Henry stopped abruptly and pointed ahead, "Is he *following* us?"

Abby looked where he was pointing and saw a raven sitting on the limb of a cedar. He made no attempt to fly but stared straight ahead at them almost as if he had been watching for them, though Abby knew that was giving the bird awareness and intentions he didn't possess.

"I doubt it's the same bird, Henry," Abby said. "And anyway, we're the ones invading his space."

She tilted her head slightly and stared back at the bird. "You know, it's amazing how much these birds show up in myths, from all over the world. Sometimes he's good and sometimes he's bad. He's a messenger in one, a creator in another. He's a thief, a trickster or a spy. In Norse mythology, Odin had two ravens—Thought and Memory—who flew around the world every day and brought news of everything that was happening back to him."

"Well, maybe that one will tell us where the people from the plane went," Henry said. "What's he got in his beak?" he asked, pulling back as the bird dropped something on the forest floor and noisily flapped his wings and took flight.

Abby walked over and picked up a bright silver book of matches. She held them toward Henry. "They love anything shiny," she said. "Maybe he's a helper. These may come in handy."

"Yeah, well, still seems like something out of Poe to me," Henry harrumphed.

"Well," Abby said slowly, knowing the fatigue was making her babble as she marched along, "they really are cunning birds. They can mimic the calls of other birds perfectly. And they've been known to bait hawks to get them fixated on prey, then when the hawk has done all the work, the raven will come in and chase the hawk away and take the meal for himself."

"And you still like this bird?" Henry asked.

Abby shrugged. "We've all got good and bad aspects to our nature. The raven can also sing a beautiful full-throated song when he wants to. He's the biggest songbird there is." Abby looked to where the bird had been perched. "Or maybe he's a messenger, after all. Look there."

Henry looked to where she was pointing. Light slanted in under the canopy of trees. It was flat and gray, but it was daylight.

"We're at the cliff," Abby pronounced, throwing down her pack, which had gotten so heavy it seemed to her someone must have been slipping rocks into it from time to time.

"I can't imagine they tried to make it through here at night. It would have been just too hard a trek," Henry said. "And if they waited for daylight, we ought to be right behind them, so where are they?"

"That's what I was thinking," Abby said. "Maybe we'll be able to see them once we get to that edge. Maybe they've found a way down onto the beachhead."

"If we're where I think we are," Henry said, "the only way to the water is straight . . ." His voice trailed off as they came to the last tree before the ground gave way to solid rock.

The trail the travois had left was still as distinct as ever, but it ended, literally, in thin air. The marks had dug two notches in the sandstone at the edge of a sheer drop. Henry knelt and peered over the edge. Abby, not trusting her rubbery legs, sat down on the ground and leaned on one elbow to peer over.

On a rock ledge, about twenty-five feet down, a green blanket was caught on a gnarled shrub of juniper, two pine branches dangling crisscrossed below.

Abby gasped. "Oh Henry, do you think they went over the edge in the darkness?"

"Maybe they *did* try it at night," Henry said. He squinted down at the rock scree at the bottom of the cliff. "It's near high tide," he said solemnly.

From somewhere on the island came the clear, wild laughter of a loon.

ZACK SUGGESTED THAT SINCE the rain had let up and they needed to get in some more walking practice anyway, they should take a stroll over to let Toby see the dog. When Mary saw Rev. James's big grin, she didn't have the heart to refuse. And in any case, she always enjoyed seeing Patricia and little Toby.

"Hold on just a minute," Rev. James said and went to the counter and asked Ida for some fresh, hot French fries to go.

"My vice," he said, as he looked back at them sheepishly.

"Don't worry, I won't tell, Reverend," Ida said as she served them up. She handed him the bag and drew her pinched fingers across her lips.

Little Flock Church was just back beyond Mary's shop, and the Hales lived in a little cottage-style house just behind the church on Harbor Seal Road, so the walk wasn't very long.

On the way over Lily suggested that Mary experiment with varying her speed to see how Finnegan would react. When she went faster, so did he. When she slowed, he matched her without ever glancing in her direction.

As they walked along, Rev. James munched on his fries. As with everyone he met, he was interested in Lily, and by the time they were halfway to his house he'd extracted practically her whole life story.

"What about you," she asked, "how long have you lived here?"

"Oh, I'm a newbie to the island. To this island anyway. I've been here five wonderful years," he said, smiling broadly. "I grew up on Santa Catalina and, after years on the mainland, I was ready for island life again. We love it here."

"Yes, I can see how you would," Lily said. "It's beautiful. And the people are all so nice. Zack told me he grew up on an island, but I never pictured it like this. It's got its own pace and rhythm."

"You know, it's a strange thing," Zack said. "I confess, I haven't always appreciated what a great place this was to grow up in. I guess it's true that some people have to go away before they can really appreciate their home."

"I know I did," Rev. James said.

"Not me," Mary said. "I couldn't wait to get back to Sparrow Island after college. I've always loved it here."

A chorus of honks sounded overhead and they all looked up to see the familiar V-formation of geese flying South.

Lily looked down at Finnegan to judge his reaction. He watched and shifted on his feet a bit, but then put his attention back on Mary.

"Well, that's one test," she said. "That wasn't a familiar experience for him."

"This is migration season," Mary said. "We'll have geese, and I don't know what all else through here in the next couple of months. Abby could tell you if she was here."

By the time they made the turn at the church, the rain had stopped. The sidewalk ended and they walked out across paved road. From there on, they were on a slight incline and Lily said, "Ah, this is a perfect training ground. Mary, if your arms get a little tired—or even if they don't—this would be a good place to practice having Finnegan pull you for a short time."

Mary certainly didn't wish to admit it, but her arms *were* tired. With the fitful night's sleep she got, she was just plain worn out.

"What do I do?" she asked Lily. "Do I need to give him a command?"

"Just reach down and take the harness. Notice that it pivots so you can hold it at whatever angle is comfortable for you. His command is 'pull,' but I doubt you'll even need it. When you pick up the harness he'll do the rest."

Mary reached over and picked it up. Finnegan turned his head slightly toward her then put his body into motion. The wheelchair glided along. Mary smiled. "Well, thank you, kind sir," she said to Finnegan. "You are ever the gentleman."

Mary found she was really enjoying learning about the dog. Even if having a dog wasn't for her, she'd be able to share what she learned with others she'd met during her rehabilitation.

"When you want to take over again, you just let go of the harness, and he'll adjust his pace to yours," Lily said. "He's getting quite attuned to you already."

They were coming to the driveway of the house and Patricia Hale's greeting saved Mary from having to reply. Patricia was in the garage, sliding candles through the slits in small tagboard circles. "These are for the prayer vigil this evening," she explained. "Have you had any word?"

"Nothing definite," Mary said. "But Henry called in to his deputies and they think maybe they're getting close. I'm hoping we'll hear something soon."

"Wouldn't it be nice if this turns into a thanksgiving service tonight?" she said to her husband. "What a blessing that would be."

"That it would," he replied.

Toby, who had been playing with his toy cars a few feet behind Patricia, came running forward. Rev. James reached down to pick him up and swing him in a big arc before bringing him to rest in his arms. "Hi ya, buddy," he said. "Look who's come for a visit. Can you say hello to Mrs. Reynolds and her dog friend, Finnegan?"

When Toby saw the dog, his eyes lit up, and he tried to scramble down.

"Could we let Finnegan out of his harness for a few minutes?" Mary asked Lily. "Is that too confusing for him?"

"Not at all," Lily said. "That's one thing about dogs. They like simple. They don't tend to complicate their lives with too much shaded thinking. Why don't you try taking it off him and see how the fasteners all work."

As Mary was working on that, Zack explained to Patricia Hale what the dog was all about. Patricia, even in worn jeans and a faded turtleneck sweater, and with her beautiful mane of red hair pulled back in a casual ponytail, still looked every inch the Hollywood actress she had been at one time. And Mary had learned that she was as beautiful a person on the inside as she was on the outside.

"Oh, Mary, that's marvelous," she said as she watched Toby wiggle from his father's arms. "I never knew there was such a thing."

When Mary had the harness and cape off, Lily produced a tennis ball from her bag. "Playtime is a reward for him," she told Mary. "He's not so much different from us humans in that respect. He needs time each day when he can do things for the pure joy of it," she said. "Sometimes we underestimate how much we need joy in our lives." Again Mary saw that knowing look in her eyes and was struck at how wise beyond her years this young woman was.

As Mary watched Toby run and play with Finnegan in the front yard, she couldn't help but think of Nicholas. He was a year older than Toby, but he was just as full of energy. Mary thought back to her dream last night and smiled to herself. *Maybe Finnegan was still trying to make up his mind about her,* she thought. He was a good dog and remarkably well behaved. He would make someone a very good helper. But she still just didn't see how he would fit into her life.

As the others talked she slid her hand into her bag and looked at the display on her cell phone for what seemed like the tenth time in the last half hour. No more calls.

She excused herself and wheeled a ways down the driveway and put in a call to her parents. Although she had talked to them earlier in the day, telling them about Zack's surprise visit and the dog, and had given them a quick update each time the deputy called, this time she just needed to hear their voices.

"Why don't you and Zack come over for dinner?" Ellen Stanton asked. "And his friend and the dog, too, of course."

Mary told her about the prayer service. "I think we'll take a rain check, Mom, if you don't mind. I need to go home and change before the prayer service, and we'll see you there. Maybe Abby will even be back before then," she said, wishing she could will it to be true.

Rev. James wandered over after she rang off and stood casually beside her chair watching his son and the dog. "So, how are you feeling about the dog, Mary? I understand this kind of caught you by surprise."

"He's a nice dog," Mary said, hedging. "And I'm so grateful that the kids are thinking of me." She turned toward him and sighed. "I just don't see how I can take care of a dog though. Even a dog like Finnegan. I don't want to disappoint the kids . . . and I'm just so taken with Lily. And I like the dog,

I really do. More than I expected I would. But I just can't see how I can take on another pet."

Rev. James smiled his warm, patient smile. "Well, Finnegan wouldn't exactly be a pet. There's a reason they refer to them as working dogs you know." He squatted down beside her chair. "You need to do what's right for you, Mary. Zack and Nancy will understand, whatever decision you make," he told her, looking her in the eye. "And I certainly wouldn't presume to tell you what to do. But I will say this. Don't close your heart to new possibilities, Mary. Not in regard to the dog, nor to anything—or *anyone*—else you might invite to share your life. You know Mary we're all called to be *fully* human and *fully* alive." He tilted his head and looked at her over his wire-rimmed glasses and touched her arm lightly. "You're allowed more than one intention at the prayer service tonight, you know. Bring all your concerns."

Chapter Eleven

THIS DOESN'T MAKE ANY SENSE," Abby said. "They got this far and then just stumbled off the edge of the cliff? How could that have happened?"

Henry continued to stare down at the rocks below. "No sense at all," he said slowly. "Even at night. Not unless you're walking backwards." Henry looked at Abby, his face now in a tight frown. "Like you're turned around pulling something."

Abby felt all the blood drain from her face. Could it be that they were so disoriented that they'd simply walked off the face of the earth? She squinted at the vegetation that grew up along the face of the bluff—stonecrop and chickweed. She pulled out her binoculars for a closer look. She couldn't see a single bent or broken twig. She got up and walked over to look more closely at the trail markings. "Henry, look at this," she said, turning slowly. "Have you ever seen a killdeer's broken wing display?"

"Sure, lots of times. They'll feign a broken wing and lead intruders away from the nest until they have them well clear, then they'll miraculously recover and fly away. They do a pretty convincing acting job too."

"Well, we may be dealing with a couple of killdeer. Look closely here."

Henry bent down to look at the signs Abby pointed out. "The trail leads up here," she said. "Then there are the gouges in the soil up near the edge of the cliff there as if they went over. But look at this. It looks more as if something was pushed into the dirt from this side, like this," she said, picking up a stick and moving down the bank. She jabbed at the dirt and sandstone along the edge of the cliff as if thrusting with a sword. "And," she said, holding the stick sideways and laying it out a few feet back on the trail, "these marks don't match those marks." She aligned the end of the stick along the track marks and put her hands on the stick as an indicator of how far apart the two marks were. "They're not the same width," she said, moving the stick forward and laying it alongside the two gouges on the edge of the precipice. "Those weren't made by the travois. The width is a good six or seven inches off."

"You're right. And look at this." He pointed to where the grass was growing up between the rocks on the trail. It was bent back toward the woods. "These should be bent in the other direction if they went off the edge."

"And here," Abby said, following along. "This shoe impression. The weight is on the ball of the foot, not the heel." They continued along the path, backtracking. "It looks like they tried to walk inside their old footprints, but they weren't careful enough." She looked up at Henry. "They've gone back the way they came."

"That's it," Henry said. "We're going back to the boat and calling for backup. And *you're* going back to Sparrow Island. When people are stranded in the wilderness and are trying to *keep* from being found, it's usually because they're up to something immoral, unethical or illegal. Most times all three."

"You won't get any argument from me," Abby said. "This is your area of expertise. If they're in good enough shape to stage this ruse, they can't be that badly injured. It's all yours."

"Let's get back to the boat pronto," Henry said, starting back down the trail. "If we angle off back over this way, we can cut off about twenty minutes of hiking, I think. It's a little rougher, but at least most of it is downhill."

"Lead on," Abby said, relieved to be turning this responsibility over to Henry, but at the same time feeling a little guilty about cutting out. Whatever this couple had going, and however it was to resolve itself, it was growing increasingly unlikely that they were helpless victims. Too much about their behavior didn't add up. But having come this far, Abby didn't like the idea of leaving Henry in it alone. She hoped he planned to wait for his men before he went out again.

Who were these people and what was this all about? The name she'd seen on that scrap of envelope was still bouncing around in her brain. Atkinson. She could almost capture where she'd heard it before, but then it would slip away again. It was frustrating.

When they came to the place underneath the nesting site they'd spotted earlier, Abby paused and looked closely at the trail. "Look, here's where they took off from. We didn't notice it before because we were so intent on trying to figure out why they took the hard way." She pointed to some faint impressions on the hard-packed earth, leading away from the trail and back out toward where Henry had moored the boat. "There's a method in their madness."

"Like they say, if you're gonna bluff, bluff big. Worked too, at least for a little while. These two seem to have a game plan, though I can't imagine what it could be."

"Is this where we need to angle down?" Abby asked, trying to get her bearings.

"Yeah, off through here," Henry said. "Like I said, shorter, but rougher. I want to get you off this island and get backup units out here as soon as possible. Until I have reason to think different, I'm no longer calling this a rescue. Now it's a pursuit. These two are now persons of interest, wanted for questioning."

As Abby ducked under a low-hanging branch she heard water droplets falling. At first she thought she'd simply disturbed the dew clinging to the tree, but in a few moments a gentle but constant patter started up.

"Great," Henry said. "That's just what we need." He took a compass out of his pocket and studied it for a moment. "Least the rain stopped long enough so we could follow that trail before it washed it away."

Abby's sniffles had turned into sneezes and she reached into her pocket to try to find another tissue. Again she brought out the small pile of paper fragments she'd picked up around the outside of the downed plane. She was relieved to find a tissue— her last. As she followed in Henry's wake, she examined each of the small pieces of paper. Lots of receipts. Another partial envelope, and this time she could make out the entire last name before the torn edge truncated it. "Look at this, Henry. The name is definitely Atkinson. That jog anything for you?"

"No, can't say it does. I know there's no wanteds or BOLAs on anyone by that name. Those I keep up on."

"BOLA? Oh yes, a be on the lookout advisory. Well, I guess we've just issued our own. At least to each other," Abby said, looking around, now listening for every little sound.

"Yes indeed," Henry said. "You see anything that strikes you as odd, you let me know, and then you get down low to the ground and stay there."

"Henry, do you think they were leading us away from the plane?" Abby asked as she mused about the possibilities. "You think there's something in or about that plane they didn't want us to find? That was awfully peculiar, the way the tail numbers and the panels had been painted over like that. Maybe we should go back to the plane and go through some of the stuff and see what we can find out about these two. It wouldn't take long and it might tell you what you're dealing with."

"Abby, I thought you said you'd leave the police work to me," he said. "And, in answer to your question, yes, I think they were trying to get us away from that plane. And it worked!

The question is why? I've been running it through my mind. We've traipsed all around that airplane, so if it turns out to be a crime scene, we've contaminated it. 'Course, we thought it was a search and rescue then, so that'll be overlooked. But from here on in, it's by the book. I call in my investigators. You go back to Sparrow Island and take care of Mary."

"Sure," Abby said, a little stung by his abruptness.

"Look, Abby," Henry said, his voice softening as he stopped on the trail and looked at her. "I appreciate everything you've done. You've been a tremendous help. But I want you out of harm's way. I'd never forgive myself if anything happened to you. And Mary would never forgive me either."

"I know," Abby said, pulling up the hood on her poncho. "And I'm ready to get back to civilization, believe me. I can't wait to take a hot shower and put on some clean, dry clothes," she said, looking down at the sad state of her clothes. "My curiosity just gets the best of me sometimes."

"Don't worry, I'll let you know how it all turns out. I promise. Every detail. But in the meantime, let's get on back to the boat before we have to break out the flashlights again. There's not much light with this cloud cover and it's only going to get darker. I don't want whoever is out there to be able to spot us in the dark and not the other way around. Makes us too vulnerable. This is one time I'm with your night-birding friends. I think I'll be more comfortable in the dark."

MARY, WITH FINNEGAN AT HER SIDE and Lily and Zack following along, arrived at the prayer service a half hour early. Night was falling and the air felt heavy. A bank of rain clouds smothered the last light from the sky.

Inside the church, Mary struck a match and touched the flame to the wick of a candle. Contrary to her hopes, Abby had not returned to the island in time to turn the prayer service into an offering of thanksgiving. And worse, they hadn't called in to the substation again either. Deputy Bennett had tried to pass it off as business as usual when Mary finally gave in to her anxieties and called just before they came over to the church, but Mary could hear the unease in his voice.

Little Flock Church was warm and lit only by candlelight on this cool rainy evening. As people came in they greeted one another in hushed murmurs, each taking a candle at the door where Patricia Hale was handing them out.

Mary's parents came to sit with her, Zack, Lily and Finnegan as the minister began. Rev. James led a short service and then invited the congregation to sing. As the strains of "Abide with Me" filled the church, Mary found her eyes welling up. She thought of how Henry and Abby and the other searchers were putting themselves on the line for the benefit of total strangers. Sacrificing their time and energies and taking risks for their fellow man. It was such admirable selflessness.

This sent her mind back to the need to release Henry from any sense of obligation he might feel toward her—to set him free. She asked God to give her the strength to do it. This could be her act of selflessness. It would bring her great sadness, but when you really cared for someone else, Mary believed you had to be willing to sacrifice your own wants and needs.

As usual, Rev. James spoke words that were just the right mixture of comfort and challenge. He then invited everyone present to take home a small votive candle and keep it lit as a reminder to continue to pray until the passengers of the plane were found and the searchers all came back safely.

"Put it in your front window if that's a safe place for it," he told them. "That's what they used to do in the old days when sailors were out to sea. They kept a candle burning in the window to help them find their way back to home and hearth. It's a sign of loyalty and love for those who are away from home, as some of our loved ones are tonight."

As people began to file out, almost all of them came over to speak to Mary and the elder Stantons, giving them assurances that they would say a special prayer for Abby and Henry. And, of course, they all asked about the dog. Blessedly, Lily was there to patiently answer all their questions.

"That must get very tiresome," Mary whispered to her as they left the church.

"I suppose it could be," Lily said, tilting her head. "If you and Finnegan do partner, that's one thing you'll have to get used to. People usually ask questions, or if they don't, you can tell they want to," she said. "But I look on it as a chance to spread the word about these animals and how much they can add to people's lives. It really is a mission for me. A chance to educate people about a very positive thing."

"That's a wonderful way to look at it Lily," Mary said, a little ashamed of her own impatience.

Lily gave a little shrug. "Don't misinterpret me, Mary. I'm not trying to convince you to keep Finnegan. You can't do this for someone else. It has to be your choice and it has to be right for you. It's very important that you *both* want this partnership if you decide to keep him. If you're not committed to it, it won't bring what it's intended to bring to your life. And Finnegan will pick up on it. He senses things."

Mary nodded. Finnegan wasn't the only one who could sense things. Lily was a very intuitive young woman.

George and Ellen were thrilled to see Zack, but Mary could see that they were worried. The strain showed on their faces. But Finnegan made them smile. They were both very keen on the dog and were as taken with Lily as Mary was.

Ellen turned to Mary and Zack. "I hope you'll all come to the farm for a big Sunday dinner. I'm preparing a special meal in honor of Abby and Henry. I'm sure they'll be back any time now," Ellen said, with only the slightest tremor in her voice.

"You know you can count me in, Grandma," said Zack. He turned to Lily. "Wait until you taste her cooking."

"I'll look forward to it," Lily said. "But it would have to be early, I'm afraid," she said, looking at Zack. "Our flight leaves that evening, and I'm not sure how long it takes us to get back to the airport from here. And if Finnegan goes with us, we have to allow some extra time for boarding."

Mary saw a fleeting frown on Zack's face, but he adopted a breezy tone. "It's okay. Grandma always has Sunday dinner right after services. We'll have plenty of time, even if we end up taking Finnegan back with us."

Mary looked over at the dog sitting patiently by her chair. It made her a little sad to think of him going away. She realized she'd gotten a bit attached already. But leave he must, she told herself firmly. That was the trouble with getting attached to animals—or people. When the time came to part, it was often painful.

Earlier that afternoon, Lily had taken Finnegan back to The Bird Nest with her to groom him for his first visit to Little Flock Church, while Mary and Zack had gone home to change. Now Finnegan would have the chance to meet Blossom for the first time, and Mary would have a deal-breaking reason to send him away. She felt a little conflicted about that as she drove toward the house.

Blossom, despite her humble beginnings, had become a haughty feline. She had joined the Reynolds household one morning a couple of years back when Mary had come across the kitten, bedraggled and ill-fed, outside the back door of Island Blooms. Mary had taken her inside and cleaned her up. Underneath all the grit and grime was a beautiful white Persian with electric blue eyes.

Mary placed an advertisement in *The Birdcall*, Sparrow

Island's weekly newspaper, hoping no one would answer it. When no one did, Blossom became part of her family and quickly became accustomed to the pampered life Mary offered her.

Zack and Nancy both knew how Mary loved the cat. If Blossom and Finnegan didn't mix, they would surely understand Mary's decision.

When they arrived at Mary's house, Lily instructed Mary on how to let the dog help her get inside the house. With short commands, she had Finnegan opening the door from the garage for her and holding it open. "This is a real help when you're coming home with bags of groceries," Lily said. "It's not that you can't do it yourself, it's just that this makes it quicker and easier. These all seem like small things, but when you add them up, they really make a difference in your daily life."

Inside, Zack lit the three candles they had brought home and set them in the foyer window. "For Aunt Abby," he said, lighting the first. "For Henry, and for the passengers on the plane," he said, lighting the other two in turn.

"Would you like me to go through some of the other tasks Finnegan is trained for?" Lily asked. "Or have you about had enough for the day?"

"How about if we eat first?" Mary asked. "It seems like it's been a long time since lunch." Mary didn't like to admit that she was tired, but this had been a long day and the stress of worry had taken its toll. She needed the quiet mealtime to renew her energies. But she wanted Zack to see that she was giving this trial period her all.

Lily took Finnegan's harness and cape off. He looked from her to Mary. Lily laughed. "He wants you to give him a command. This one's a little unconventional. I started it by accident and his previous partner kept it up. Say 'off the clock.'"

Mary did as instructed and Finnegan sneezed, then turned and went into the living room. The others watched from the foyer as he sniffed his way around the furniture as if getting to know the room. Finally he settled down on the rug in front of the fireplace for a nap.

Mary told Lily to make herself at home. Zack served up soup that Mary had put into the slow cooker earlier in the afternoon, while Lily made a salad. Mary was just cutting some big slices of rye bread when she heard the patter of tiny feet coming from the stairs. Blossom had been in her favorite spot in the window in Mary's old room upstairs, now Abby's bedroom. She still liked to sun herself there during the day and often went back to that familiar spot when everyone was away.

"*Uh oh*, here comes trouble," said Mary, wheeling into the dining room.

Zack and Lily followed and they all watched as Blossom pranced into the room. She spotted her mistress and came over for a moment to rub against Mary's leg. Then she saw something more interesting in the living room. She approached the big beast slowly, stopping every few steps to lift one delicate paw in a pointer's stance.

Finnegan raised his head and looked at the cat warily, but

did not move from his spot. Blossom moved in, step by halting step, until the two were nose to nose. They stayed that way for a moment and then Blossom sniffed and started to circle Finnegan, inspecting him from head to tail. Finnegan stayed still, occasionally cutting his eyes in the direction of the cat as if expecting her to pounce at any moment.

But Blossom seemed satisfied that she was superior to the dog and jumped up into the chair by the fireplace and began grooming.

"Oh yeah," Zack said, smiling broadly. "Big trouble. We should all have troubles like that."

After dinner Lily asked Mary questions about her household routines. Mary was surprised to realize how many times her response was that Abby took care of that. Too many times. Starting with the laundry. "I can do it, it's just awkward, so it takes me longer," Mary said. "But how could Finnegan help with laundry?"

Lily showed her how the dog could, piece by piece, get laundry from the basket into the washer, and out of the dryer. "In your case, he doesn't need to do it all. If he helps you, it just makes it go faster and reduces some little aggravations—like getting something out that's stuck way back in the dryer and is hard to reach. Like I said, it's a little thing, but those little things add up over the course of the day."

Next Lily had Mary practice getting Finnegan to retrieve objects she dropped and showed her how he could help her with things like getting her jacket on, opening cupboard doors and fetching her grabbing stick for her when she needed to get something from up high.

Again Mary marveled at the discipline and intelligence of the dog, but more than that, at his seeming delight in helping. And unlike her experience with humans, Mary wanted him to help her because it seemed to please him to be able to do it. They were both getting something out of it. She looked over at the dog with his big warm eyes and tried to steel herself. She couldn't allow herself to want him to stay. She couldn't stand another loss.

Chapter Twelve

As the sky darkened and the rain picked up, Abby strained to separate out every other sound from the cadence of the pelting rain. A twig snapping underfoot made her jump. A rustle in the bushes made the hair stand up on the back of her neck. And if she listened hard enough she could swear she heard human voices drifting down from somewhere north on the island.

But she also realized her exhausted state, not to mention the head cold she was developing, was probably fueling her imagination. Her feet seemed twice as heavy as they should be and, even though they were hiking at a good pace for such rugged terrain, she felt as if she were moving in slow motion.

Henry had fallen silent as they made their way back to the boat, pausing often to listen. He went ahead of Abby and wordlessly indicated trip and slip hazards as they cautiously descended the steep hill heading toward the boat.

The trees had thinned out along a rocky outcrop, and they were afforded a clear view of a patchwork of sky and what was left of the dying light. But the clearing also exposed them to the rain that was now beginning to hammer down in great, heavy drops.

Suddenly there was movement behind them and they both turned toward the sound. A gray-brown rabbit, startled by their approach, took off in bounding leaps, its tail flashing white in its quick departure. Henry was midstride when he looked up at the rabbit. When he put his foot down, he stepped on a pile of rocks covered by half-rotted leaves. The disturbed rocks began to tumble and Henry reached out to grab hold of a branch on a young red alder tree to catch himself.

The rocks slid out from under his feet and continued to slide until nearly all of his weight was swinging from the thin tree branch that, with a sudden loud *crack*, broke and sent him tumbling head over heels down the side of the hill.

Abby stood frozen, watching Henry's body in the brown rain poncho rotate with sickening thuds and scraping noises for what seemed like a very long time. Then it all stopped.

"Henry!" Abby, finally able to get a message from her brain to her feet, started to move down after him. "Henry, are you okay?"

There was no answer. She called again and hurried down the hill with as much speed as she dared, holding on to trees and zigzagging down the hill like a slalom skier. The rain was smacking on the hood of her poncho and pouring down in front of her face, obscuring her vision.

"Henry," she called again. "Henry, answer me."

"Abby," called a feeble voice. "I'm okay, Abby," she heard faintly. "Well, I'm not okay, but I'm alive and conscious anyway," he said, his voice tight and halting.

Finally she reached him. A large boulder had stopped his progress and he slumped against it, holding his leg with both hands and grimacing. He had cuts and scrapes on his face and head. A trickle of blood ran down his forehead and a bright red stripe cut across his bottom lip. A bruise was forming on his cheek.

"I think I broke my leg," he said to Abby as she knelt beside him. "I can't put any weight on it."

"Here Henry, let me have a look," she said, moving around in front of him. She pulled the extra rain poncho out of her bag and put it over Henry's head and shoulders and had him hold it out over his leg making a sort of tent. His arms were trembling, but he managed to hold it in place as she got the first aid kit out of her pack and used the scissors to split Henry's pant leg up to the knee. She looked carefully at his shin. There was no break in the skin, but Henry couldn't tolerate any manipulation of his foot. Abby had seen plenty of broken bird's legs, but she was clearly out of her depth here.

She knew it was important to immobilize the leg, but her main concern was getting Henry out of the rain and then getting to the boat to call in for medical help.

Henry seemed to be reading her thoughts. "You're going to have to go on to the boat and call in. You'll have to move the boat out to where you can get a clear signal," he said, stopping every couple of words to suck in air. "Can you do that?"

"Yes, of course, Henry. Don't forget Dad ran a charter business for years. I grew up around boats. I can do it, don't worry."

"That's right," Henry said, grimacing as he tried to get in a more upright position. "Good thing."

"First I've got to get you out of this rain."

"I'll be okay."

"Henry, you can't move. I'm not leaving you here. The hillside is not stable. If it keeps raining, we might get a slide. Not to mention we don't know what other dangers there are about. Don't forget the couple from the plane. We still don't know what they're up to."

"I haven't forgotten them for a second, believe me," Henry said through clenched teeth.

Abby looked around and found two fairly straight sticks and fashioned a makeshift splint with the tape from the first aid kit. Henry was in obvious pain, and she hated to bring him more, but it had to be done. She had to move him. She couldn't leave him out here exposed, but she didn't dare try to move him without giving the leg some support.

She looked around until she found a forked branch on a bigleaf maple hanging low enough for her to reach. She brought out a small folding camp saw from her bag and sawed off the limb to make a crutch. It took several minutes, and she had to keep stopping to wipe away the rain that was dripping down into her face, but it finally gave way with a satisfying snap. She trimmed the leaves and turned to Henry, visually measuring him to determine where to cut the limb to fit his frame.

"You're a regular Girl Scout, aren't you?" Henry said.

"'Tomboy' is the way Mary always put it," Abby said.

"Mary," Henry said, sounding far away. "I hope Mary's okay."

Abby didn't like the sound of his voice. She was afraid he might lose consciousness. "Right now, we need to make sure you're okay, Henry," she said, moving a little farther down the hillside. "I'll be right back."

She turned and surveyed the hillside and was relieved when she spotted an overhanging bluff not too far from where Henry was. If she could get him into that, he'd be out of the downpour and he'd have his back protected from—well, Abby thought, from whatever it needed protection from. She could only deal with one worry at a time.

She went back and told Henry the plan. "It's going to hurt, probably quite a lot," she told him. "But by the time I get back from the boat it's going to be completely dark, so we need to do it now. Do you think you're up to it?"

"I can make it," Henry said. "You need to get to the boat. My deputies know to come looking for us if we don't call in, and they should be here soon. But they don't know what they're coming into. And they need to know about this development," he said, gritting his teeth as he tried to get into a standing position. "Remember, tell them this is no longer a rescue but a pursuit, and to approach with caution."

"Got it," Abby said, helping him to stand up.

Using the boulder that had done the damage, he managed to get himself upright. Abby picked up his hat from the ground a few feet up the hill and tried to straighten out the bent brim. She put it on his head to keep the rain off his face and handed him the maple limb crutch.

"Good fit," he mumbled. His speech was still a beat too slow and Abby wondered whether he might also have a concussion. It made her second-guess herself. Maybe she should try to get him to the boat and get him back to Sparrow Island for treatment. But if he had a head injury, perhaps moving him wasn't a good idea. She couldn't decide which course of action was better. Abby hated dithering. She usually trusted her own judgment, but right now she was so fatigued she couldn't seem to get a grasp on things.

As it turned out, it wasn't her decision to make anyway. Henry was still very much in charge. It was all he could do to make it to the bluff. But he was clearheaded about Abby's next move. She had to leave him and get to the radio in the boat, without further delay.

The overhang of the bluff was high enough for Abby to stand underneath, though Henry had to duck as he hobbled under. It was dry and he was able to get himself situated in a sitting position against the back wall. From there he'd be able to see anyone trying to come up on him.

"I'll be back as soon as I've called in," she assured him. "Is there anything you'd like me to bring back from the boat?"

"No," Henry said, resting his head back against the earthen wall and holding up a hand. "But here's what I want you to do. I want you to get in the boat and move it out where you can get a clear signal and *stay there* until my deputies or the Coast Guard get here. Do *not* come back here. Tell them what we've found and where I am, but *do not come back onto the island.* Are we clear?"

"Henry, I can't just *leave* you here," Abby protested.

"You're not leaving me here," he said, rocking his head slowly from side to side. "You're giving me one less thing to worry about. I'll be fine here. Remember your promise that you'd let me do my job."

"Okay, if that's what you want me to do, that's what I'll do," Abby said, but she didn't like it one bit.

"Have you ever fired a gun, Abby? Do you want to take my service revolver? Like you said, we don't know what this couple is up to. If you run across them on your way to the boat, you may need protection. They could be dangerous."

"The only thing I've ever shot is a tranquilizer gun, Henry. And, no, I don't want to take yours. It wouldn't do me any good, regardless of their intentions. I'd never be able to shoot anyone. Besides, from what we've seen, they're trying to get away from people, not come looking for them," she said firmly, hoping it was so.

Abby took one of the foil blankets from Henry's pack and tore it from the package. "Shock is still a possibility. Let's at least get this around you." She found a hand warmer packet in her own bag and cracked it and put it under the blanket. "This will radiate a little heat," she said. She examined the contents of her backpack and left Henry the rest of the trail mix, the last granola bar and an extra bottle of water. She took a spare set of batteries for her flashlight from his pack and then draped the wool blanket over him. The wet air had done nothing to improve the smell.

"Ah, I knew I'd regret bringing that thing along," Henry said. "Now it smells like a whole herd of wet goats."

Abby tried to muster a smile while she tucked the blanket around his legs as best she could to keep in his body heat. When night fell, so would the temperature, and it would be colder still here underneath the bluff where sunrays never probed. Abby didn't like leaving Henry alone, but the simple fact was that she had to go for help. Staying with Henry was not an option.

"I'll stay away from the island like you say," Abby told him, "*until* the others come, but then I'll lead them back here. They'll have trouble finding this place, especially in the dark."

"Only if my deputies think it's safe," Henry said. He was having difficulty talking. His tongue seemed too thick and his voice sounded an octave too low. Abby hoped it was only from the split and swollen lip he'd gotten on his tumble down.

"Try to sip this water every once in a while," she told him. "And it's probably not a good idea to go to sleep if you can help it," she said, grabbing up her flashlight and shining it directly into his eyes.

He squinted and looked away, but not before she'd seen that his pupils seemed to be reacting okay.

"I usually try not to sleep on the job," Henry said, wincing as he tried for a weak smile. "And with these two unknowns loose on this island—assuming of course that they *are* still on this island—I'm still very much on the job."

Abby turned to go, torn over whether this was the right course of action. If Henry took a turn for the worse or anything bad happened to him, she'd never forgive herself.

But Henry was still in charge and the decision was his. At least she'd be able to get word to Mary and let her know they were still alive—if not entirely well. How much should she tell Mary at this stage? she wondered. Probably the less the better, at least until Henry was examined and they found out how serious his injuries were. No sense worrying her needlessly. And if it was bad news, she'd know soon enough.

She said a quick prayer for Henry, that God would watch over him and keep him safe, then started down the hill.

MARY CRANED HER NECK TO LOOK at the clock tipped sideways on the bedroom floor. Ten o'clock. She took a moment to assess the situation. It could be much worse. She wasn't hurt, not physically anyway, she told herself. But the floor was cold and it was nearly dark in the room. *Pride goeth before a fall*, she chided herself. *Literally, in this case.*

Finnegan stood alongside her, anxiously transferring his weight from one paw to another, whining softly. He turned and went out to the hall and let out a couple of loud barks. "That won't work, Finnegan," Mary called to him. "There's nobody here. It's okay, boy. I'm fine."

Mary struggled into a sitting position and scooted herself back against her bedside table. "This is what happens when you get overconfident, Finnegan," she told him as he padded back into the room. "But I'm okay," she added again, her voice soothing. "Come over here, boy."

Finnegan did as instructed and Mary ran her hand over his head. He sat beside her and looked at her as if awaiting instructions. "Well, this is a nice mess I've gotten myself into, Finnegan," she said to him.

This is what she got for meddling in Zack's business, she told herself sternly. Though it really wasn't meddling, was it? She'd simply wanted to encourage an attraction that was clearly already budding.

After dinner and her work with Finnegan, Mary had spent as enjoyable an evening as was possible, considering her worries. The more time she spent with Lily and Zack, the more she liked the young woman, and the more she liked how Zack was when he was with her.

When she hadn't heard anything by nine that night, Mary decided to call the substation again. Deputy Washburn had told her that if Abby and Henry hadn't reported in by midnight, the sheriff's office would be sending someone out to, as he put it, "give them a hand and get everybody squared away." His words had been casual, but Mary had sensed a little wariness.

Zack had been getting ready to take Lily back to The Bird Nest. "I'll be back soon, Mom," he had said, "and we can watch TV or something. Maybe play a hand or two of rummy. You gonna be okay here by yourself for a few minutes?"

"Oh, Zack, not that that doesn't sound wonderful," she had told him. "But you know, I'm really quite tired. It's been a long day and I think I'll just turn in. That way I'll be rested and we can visit tomorrow when Abby's home."

Her words had been true—to a point. She had been tired after this busy and stressful day. But she had also seen the look on Zack's face when he looked at Lily. The boy was smitten.

"Why don't you take Lily on a drive around the island before you take her back to The Bird Nest? She might not have another opportunity to see it. Take her up to see the lighthouse. It really is beautiful." *Especially in the moonlight*, she had thought, but didn't say aloud.

"Lily?" Zack had turned to her. "It's rainy, but this will probably be the only chance to see the lighthouse while we're here. You game?"

"That sounds nice," Lily said. "Are you and Finnegan all set? Any last-minute questions?" she had asked Mary.

"I think we are simpatico," Mary had assured her, looking over at the dog. "I'll call your cell phone if I have any trouble," she had told Zack. "Take your time and enjoy yourself."

"Okay," Zack had said, unable to suppress a pleased smile. "But remember, the cell doesn't work half the time. If you really need anything and you can't reach me, you'll call Grandma and Grandpa or one of your friends, right?"

"Of course, Zack. But I'll probably fall right to sleep. If the deputy calls with news, I'll have the phone right by the bed. You don't need to hover. I've made a lot of progress."

"That you have, Mom," Zack had said, the wrinkle in his forehead disappearing.

Zack had gotten her settled into bed and then turned to go. He had looked back when he got to the door and had given her a grin. Finnegan was resting on the floor beside her bed and Blossom was snuggled into her chair in the corner. "Now that's a nice picture," he had said.

"Zack," Mary had said slowly.

"I'm just saying . . ." He shrugged then, letting the words trail off. He blew her a kiss goodnight, promising to look in on her when he returned.

Mary had assured him that she would probably be asleep by the time he got out of the driveway, but it hadn't turned out that way. Try as she might, she couldn't disengage from the worries of the day. She had picked up her book from the nightstand and tried to get interested in it. She had been enjoying the novel just two nights ago, but now she was too distracted to get into it. She had put it down and picked up her knitting and did half a row on a new brightly colored afghan she was making for Little Flock's Holiday Bazaar. But when she lost her concentration and dropped a stitch, she had sighed and put that aside as well.

She then said her nightly prayers and reached over to turn off the lamp, wanting nothing more than to escape into the peace of sleep. Maybe when she woke up, she had thought, Abby and Henry would be back safe and sound, having found the occupants of the plane and delivered them safely back to civilization.

Of course that positive thought had only led her to more distress when she thought of Henry and the prospect of breaking off their relationship. Round and round her worries had gone. Then an anxious thought suddenly occurred to her. What if Zack hadn't taken the key? The new door to the garage locked automatically unless a little lever was flipped near the knob. He wouldn't be able to get back into the house.

Time was when people didn't lock their doors on Sparrow Island, but after a few unfortunate incidents during tourist season when so many strangers were around, most islanders were a little more cautious these days.

She had decided that the only thing to do was to go and unlock the door. And anyway, a cup of chamomile tea would be just what she needed to help her get to sleep. She had turned on the lamp and had looked up at the transfer bar and then at her chair. Everything was in the proper place. Or so she had thought.

Finnegan had lifted his head, watching her every move. She had grabbed hold of the transfer bar in order to repeat the now familiar procedure. But she had failed to realize that the brake on her wheelchair was not set. In the excitement of

Zack's visit and the break in routine, she must have forgotten to set it. Just as she had swung over her chair, her legs hit it. The chair had slid backward, knocking against the nightstand and sending the telephone and the lamp to the floor.

It was too late, for Mary had already let go of the bar. She didn't so much fall as simply slide down to the floor.

When everything came to rest, Mary had made a quick assessment. Nothing was hurt, not physically anyway. But there she was with only the light from her nightlight in the bathroom casting a dim glow out into the room. The telephone handset was across the room and her cell phone was in the pocket of the chair, which had been pushed backward a few feet. Mary did not have the upper body strength necessary to climb up from the floor to the chair.

That was how she ended up in her current situation, her back against the nightstand, pondering her options. And as she looked at Finnegan sitting there in front of her, his amber eyes not leaving her face, she realized that she *did have* options. As Lily said, it was a small thing, but a very important one.

"Finnegan, phone," she told him, pointing to the darkened corner where the handset had come to rest.

The dog gave a little whimper, then went straight for the phone and brought it back to Mary. She checked and was relieved to get a dial tone.

"Okay, Finnegan," she told the dog, "here's how I see it. I can call Zack and disrupt his evening with Lily, or I can call Mom and Dad and have them drive over here at this hour on a rainy night to get me back into bed. Or I could call Margaret or Janet. *Or*, there's another option," she said, putting the phone down beside her. "If you can get me that comforter off the bed, I can make myself a pallet right here on the floor and have a little nap until Zack comes home. After all, I'm not hurt. There's no *need* to call anyone. And now I remember that Zack did take the key before he left. He'll be able to let himself in."

Finnegan looked at her and tilted his head.

"Oh dear," she said. "I suppose there's no command for comforter. Well, maybe I can get it." She reached and could just snag the corner of the comforter with her fingers. She began to pull on it. Finnegan watched for a moment, then walked over and grabbed hold of it with his teeth. With a couple of quick tugs he had it off the bed.

"There," Mary said. "Well okay. You think you're a pretty smart guy, eh? Well, you might as well get me the pillow too," she mumbled, "and the blanket to put over me. And you could go make me that cup of tea while you're at it, Wonder Dog."

Finnegan looked at her and let out a soft bark as if asking her to speak up. "Pillow!" she said, a hint of frustration coming into her voice. She pointed toward the bed.

Finnegan put his front paws up on the edge of the bed and grabbed the pillow delicately by its corner and dragged it off and into Mary's lap.

She sat looking at it for a moment, then laughed softly. "Okay, I'm sorry," she said. "I underestimated you. You really are good at your job." She pointed to the bed. "Blanket," she said.

197

Finnegan looked at her and whined, but she repeated the command and he put his front paws up again and began to sniff around. When he had nose contact with the blanket Mary said, "Yes, blanket," and he grabbed it and pulled it until she could get hold of it. Together they managed to get it off the bed.

After a little arranging, Mary had herself a snug little bed. She put the phone beside the pillow and draped the blanket over her. Soon she felt comfortably warm. Finnegan settled down right beside her, watching her closely. After a few moments, Blossom came over and insinuated herself between Mary and the dog, making sure Finnegan knew the pecking order in the household.

"It's good to have you here, Finnegan," Mary said, stroking the dog's back. "And I'll give you a pass about not bringing me that cup of tea." He turned and gave her a long, unblinking look and she felt a peace settle over her. "We don't have to decide anything tonight, do we boy?" she asked, her voice soft in the dimly lit room. "Not about anything. Rev. James is right. I need to get out of my own way."

Chapter Thirteen

THE PATH DOWN THE HILL was steep, but the rain had stopped. The tree cover had thinned out and now Abby found she could wade through the more boot-friendly hair grass with little resistance. It only grew about six inches high and was easy to bend. She put her boots down heavily and tromped with each step. Her usual habit was to try to disturb nature as little as possible when she hiked, but in this particular instance, she wanted to make sure she was leaving an obvious trail to follow on the way back to get Henry out.

She glanced up the hillside and made a mental map of where the bluff was. On a sunny May afternoon this hillside would be a sight that might inspire a modern-day Monet to haul out his paints. Goldback fern would be splashed about, its black stems rising like a profusion of metallic wires from the rock crevices, its leaflets, dark green on top and yellowish below tufting out in triangles from the stems. And there would be the wildflowers: airy cream-colored sprays of alumroot, brilliant yellow wooly sunflowers, vivid orange poppies and Indian paintbrush.

But on this darkening September evening the hillside was all grays and blacks except for the red barked madrones leaning out of the cliff, their red-orange berries hanging in gaudy clusters.

Abby knew that back on Sparrow Island lots of prayers were being said. She felt them and took strength from them. She began to hum softly as she picked her way carefully down, stopping intermittently to look back and check her relative position. She also kept looking at her watch. Each minute that passed was time away from Henry—away from him when he needed her help. When she saw that a half hour had already passed since leaving him, she quickened her pace.

Now that the rain had stopped, she heard every noise. The twilight world was alive with creatures and insects that normally would only have aroused her intellectual curiosity. But on this evening every buzz and rustle made her heart beat faster, every thud and pop made her breath come quicker.

When, at long last, Abby could make out the boat in the distance she had to resist the impulse to run toward it. The rocky beach was treacherous and she was by now acutely aware that she was impaired by fatigue. She was going to have to turn on the flashlight, she decided. She switched it on, but covered the lens with her hand, only allowing a small bit of light to shine through right in front of her feet. She studied each rock carefully before stepping on to it, giving her tired brain time to catch up and process what she saw.

When she was near the boat she heaved a great sigh of relief.

But as she stepped closer, her sigh turned to a gasp. She passed the flashlight beam over the length of the boat, so shocked she was no longer thinking of the danger in giving away her position. All of the storage lockers on the boat had been ransacked and things were strewn all about. She played the flashlight all around frantically, then thought better of it and snapped it off.

She stood there, listening. But there was only the sound of the wavelets slapping against the rocks. She quickly scrambled into the boat and worked her way to the front.

There, things were worse—much worse. The radio handset was on the seat, splintered into pieces, its cut wires splayed out like the strings of kelp that floated around the reefs. The radio itself had been hammered into bits for good measure.

Abby looked around wildly, turning on the flashlight only briefly to get a better look. She then cut off the flashlight again and slumped down, squinting at the shoreline. She stayed there, very still again, listening. She heard nothing that didn't belong to the island night.

She took a deep breath and tried to steady herself. A decision had to be made and she needed a cool head. She couldn't leave Henry up there alone, at least not for long. It was clear now that the couple posed a real danger. It seemed a fair assumption they'd been the ones to do this.

There would be plenty of water traffic out in the channel, she thought. She could take the boat out and give the Mayday signal. Maybe she could hail another vessel and get access to a working radio and call in.

The plan started to solidify in her mind and she moved into the driver's seat. "Yes," she whispered emphatically, giving herself a little pep talk. "Yes, that's what I'll do."

This boat was similar in many ways to the fishing boat her father kept at the marina. Her confidence rose. She had observed Henry's approach to the island very carefully. She'd be able to navigate out.

She turned the key. The engine chugged but wouldn't turn over. Abby's heart sank. Someone had fouled it, probably by shoving in a handful of sand. Apparently the radio wasn't the only thing they'd sabotaged.

Now what? Abby asked herself. Her thoughts were swarming and she felt off-kilter. The panicky part of her was screaming, *Do something!* But Abby knew not to listen to that part. She drew a deep breath and paused a moment to center herself and ask God for strength and guidance. "Show me the right path," she said softly.

She looked around anxiously and then went to the back of the boat and began hastily gathering things. The sleeping bags were gone, as was the small stash of food, but the lantern was still there. She picked it up, hoping the mantle was still intact. She grabbed Henry's thermos and cup and looked around for anything else that might be of use. She took a length of line and a piece of fishing net that had been used to batten down some loose gear on deck. She picked up the long metal lid that had been pried off when the vandals broke into the storage lockers. She knew a use for that. She put it all into the net and hastily wove the line around the outside and gathered it up like a sack. She hefted it over the side of the boat then followed it over.

Getting back to Henry was a challenge. Abby's legs didn't have much left to give. She had to stop and rest at intervals before she could go on. When she was finally within distance of where she thought Henry might be able to hear her movements, she began to stop every few feet and call out in a hoarse whisper, "Henry, it's me. Henry, you okay?"

The first couple of times she got no response, but the third time his voice came back in the darkness, low and urgent. "Abby? Abby, I thought I told you not to come back here. Are my deputies with you?"

"No, no deputies. Just me," she said as she ducked under the bluff and put down her awkward sack.

"I thought I told you not to come back here," Henry repeated, an edge of irritation in his voice.

"Yeah, well, I didn't have much choice," she said, ignoring his tone. She told him about the boat. "They've made sure we can't get off the island. And that we can't call for help. Maybe they're more dangerous than we thought. Or else they're planning their own getaway and want to make sure we can't follow."

Henry sighed and ran his hand over his dirt-streaked face, wincing as he touched the cut. "Bennett will send someone out," he said. "He'll get concerned when he doesn't hear from us. Problem is, it could be a while before they get here. And even then, they won't know what they're coming into."

"What should we do?" Abby asked.

Henry shook his head slowly. "Me being out of commission sure limits our options," he said. "I'd say we set a signal fire down near the boat, but I think it's early yet for that. We don't want to alert anyone else to our position, but we need to be close enough to warn my men. That could be tricky."

Abby nodded. "So we stay put for now?"

"I think that's just what we have to do," Henry said. "This is all guesswork, but I suspect that they'll give us until around midnight to call in, then Bennett or Washburn will send out the cavalry."

"Okay," Abby said, getting into a standing position. "So if we're going to hunker down, we need to make good use of the time." She stood and started to walk out from under the bluff.

"Where are you going?" Henry asked.

"To get us some camouflage," she said, careful to keep her voice low as she walked down the hill.

She stopped and looked around for downed limbs. She found a couple of nice-sized maple and a bonus red cedar and dragged them to the front of the bluff. She got out her saw and hacked away at some salal bushes and other shrubs, then piled them and a couple of armfuls of leaves up in front of the branches to build up the density. When she was satisfied, she pushed the ends of the branches aside and climbed back under the bluff.

"Good thinking," Henry said. "Lets us see out, but they can't see in unless they get right up close."

Abby was too tired to even reply. She set the flashlight on end, casting bizarre shadows on their faces and on the underside of the bluff. She sat for a moment, resting her head back against the cold rock. She pulled the matches from her pocket and tried to light the lantern. It sputtered a couple of times, but soon she was rewarded with the steady hiss of the flame within the mantle.

"Like I said," Henry continued weakly, "you're a regular Girl Scout. Maybe I *did* make the right decision in bringing you along."

"I do my best," Abby said. She sighed and stretched out her legs, her muscles burning. She looked down at the silver matchbook in her hand and tilted it toward the lantern. *Carl & Gretchen* was printed in faint embossed script lettering on the front flap. Abby turned it over and looked inside the flap. Nothing. Probably from the plane. The bird probably found it when he was inside.

"Henry," Abby said, "You may not be so happy you brought me after I tell you what we should do next."

She pulled the metal piece out of the pile in the net. "I think we can use this to splint your leg. It's more stable than those sticks and will support it on three sides. But I know it's going to hurt to move it around."

Henry stared at the piece of metal from the storage box for a moment in the lantern light. "So, they did quite a job on the boat, I take it."

"It'll need some work when we get back," Abby said,

nodding. In her own ears it sounded like she was talking underwater. Her words came out warbly and out of rhythm. She simply could not remember a time in her life when she had felt this tired.

Henry heaved a great sigh. "You're right. It needs to be done. Can't say I'm looking forward to it though."

"Tell you what," she said, "when we're done, I'll make you up one of these delicious MREs in my pack. How's that sound?"

"How about those cans of soup? Did you bring those back?"

"Afraid not. They took them," Abby said. "The sleeping bags too."

"So, this little layover was definitely not part of their plan, otherwise they wouldn't need to steal supplies," Henry mused. "There were no provisions on the plane that I saw. What were they doing out here?" he asked, talking more to himself than to Abby. "Those little planes don't have that much range. Where were they headed? Who are they, and what are they up to?"

"The name is still bugging me," Abby said as she opened the first aid kit and started to organize the contents she thought she could use to make Henry's splint. "I know I've heard it or read it somewhere. The newspaper maybe, but I just can't remember where."

"Well, it wasn't on the sports page, that I can tell you," Henry said as he watched Abby, keeping a wary eye on the supplies she was setting out in a neat row. "That's the first section I go for."

"Mary reads the society page," Abby said, smiling.

"Thoroughly. She always wants to know what kinds of flowers people used in their weddings and things like that." Abby stopped, a roll of gauze held in midair. "That's it. That's where I've heard the name. From a wedding story. Atkinson. There was an article about it in the Seattle paper. It was a huge, splashy wedding. He and his bride were both big shot executives. Mary read it to me." She reached into her pocket and brought out the matches. "Carl and Gretchen. Yeah, I think that's right. Carl and Gretchen Atkinson."

"Do you remember any more about it?" Henry asked, pinching his lips together as he struggled to sit up straighter.

Abby frowned. "No, not really. I can tell you his bride carried a bouquet of red roses and baby's breath, which Mary thought was quite unimaginative—but that doesn't really help any, does it?" she said with a rueful smile.

"Not a whole lot," Henry said.

"And," Abby said, "I can tell you that I was very put off to hear that they used a live dove release at the end of the ceremony instead of throwing rice. I sure hope that doesn't become a trend. The people who do this keep those birds in deplorable conditions. Plus they have no idea what releasing them in an area where they don't normally range does to upset the balance of nature."

"I see your point about the birds," Henry said patiently, "but, Abby, can we get back to the people who may be after us right here on this island tonight? Hotshot executives, you say? Do you remember the company they worked for?"

Abby frowned again, willing her brain to bring up the information, but she got nothing. "No, Henry, I really don't. I'm surprised I even remember that much. I only remember because of the birds."

Henry endured the jostling of his leg into the new splint with a stoic determination. But when Abby was finished, he let out a big puff of air. "Well, that gives me a new perspective on what Mary has been through," he said.

Abby nodded. Mary never complained. She approached her life in the wheelchair as a new set of circumstances to be mastered. She had never wallowed in self-pity and still possessed a vibrant and infectious love for life. Abby admired her sister so much. But she knew Mary could also be prideful, and this business with Henry was an example. Mary thought she knew what was best for Henry. But Henry, as Abby had learned, was perfectly capable of being forthright and honest about what he wanted. She hoped Mary wouldn't do anything she would regret when they got back.

As Abby proceeded to arrange the things from her pack around their little bluff shelter, Henry teased, "This little place is taking on a woman's touch. You'll be measuring it for curtains any minute now."

"Keep giving me a bad time and I won't give you any dinner," she retorted. She took the two MREs and started to examine them. "Okay, we've got chili or beef stew. Take your pick."

"If it's food, it'll be fine with me," Henry said. "I'm long past being picky. I could eat tree bark by now."

"Okay," Abby said, reading the directions. "Beef stew for you then." She set off the water-activated, flameless heaters that came in each MRE and set them up to heat the pouch. "Dinner will be served in exactly twelve minutes," she said. "How's that for military precision?"

Abby continued to examine the MREs. The meal pouch was like a flexible can and, when the chemical heater had done its work, Abby opened Henry's up and handed it to him.

The smell of the food was enough to set her mouth watering. She opened her own pouch of chili and dug in. Abby slid over periodically to peer outside and they kept their voices low. Since the limbs and branches kept the lantern light from projecting out into the darkness, someone would have to be down in front of the bluff to see it.

"I can't believe I'm saying this, but I think this is the best thing I've ever tasted," Abby said, scraping the last vestiges of chili from the sides of the pouch.

"With the exception of your mother's cooking, I agree."

"Oh, don't remind me," Abby said. "That meal we left on the table seems like the stuff of dreams now."

"In more ways than one," Henry said, sighing. "I keep seeing the look on Mary's face. She was concerned about you coming out here with me. I should have heeded that. Look what I've gotten you into."

"Henry," Abby said firmly, "none of this is your fault. I came willingly. And anyway, strange as it sounds, I'm glad I'm here. Or I guess I should say, I'm glad you're not out here alone."

Henry tried to shift his leg and grimaced. "I can't argue with that," he said. "I just hope Mary doesn't hold it against me for putting you in danger. She seems a little distant lately. I don't know if I've done or said something wrong or what."

Abby was afraid to open her mouth. As exhausted as she was she wasn't sure what she was saying half the time. She didn't want to betray Mary's confidence, but she felt like she was being dishonest with Henry to pretend everything was okay.

"Mary's had a lot of adjustments to make, Henry," she finally said. "And you know how important it is to her that she doesn't cause anyone any inconvenience on account of her condition. She's trying to be very independent right now, but she'll come back around and realize it is okay to ask for help. It'll just take time."

"Well, I'm a patient man," Henry said, staring into the lantern flame. "If time is all it takes, then we'll be fine."

When they finished eating, Abby took inventory. She found the flares she'd stuffed into her backpack and muttered a grateful "yes." And the little camp coffeepot and pouch of coffee were a welcome sight. But she was dismayed to see they only had half of a small bottle of water left. With all the hard hiking they had done, they had needed to drink plenty of liquids to avoid getting dehydrated. And Abby's head cold only made her need for water that much greater.

They did have the little filtration pump and she knew where she could find fresh water. She'd seen a stream up near the wreckage.

She looked over at Henry, readying her argument for hiking back up for water, and saw that he was asleep. He had been perfectly lucid and his speech was clear so she decided she'd let him be. He'd be safe, hidden here. Sleep was probably the best thing for him.

Abby was bone tired, but she knew the longer she stayed still, the harder it would be to get moving again. She looked at her watch. Still a few hours until midnight. As quietly as she could, she put all the empty water bottles into her pack then grabbed up the fishnet and rope and stuffed it in as well. If she found anything usable at the crash site, she'd bring it back.

Forget evidence. This was survival.

MARY WAS JOLTED AWAKE by the twin yelps of Finnegan's barking and Zack's exclamations. "Mom, what in the world! Are you okay?"

"Zack, I'm fine," she told him, her voice raspy from sleep. "I was just a little careless when I transferred to my chair and I didn't check to make sure the brake was on."

Zack helped her up and got her into the chair. "You fell and you didn't call for help? Why didn't you call me?" he asked, digging his cell phone out of his pocket and looking at the display for missed calls.

"I wasn't hurt, Zack," she told him calmly. "I didn't fall. It was more of a slide. A slither, really. I couldn't sleep and I wanted a cup of tea. And I couldn't remember until I was down here on the floor whether you took the key. You did take it, right?"

"Yes I did. But why didn't you call me?"

"It wasn't necessary." She looked over to Finnegan, who stood looking back and forth from Mary to Zack as if watching a Ping-Pong match. "As you've been trying so hard to convince me, Finnegan here was all the help I needed. He was able to make me quite comfortable."

"Are you sure you're okay?" Zack asked again.

"Zack, I assure you, I'm fine," she said. "Toddlers take hundreds of worse falls learning to walk. I just got a little careless. I know this is a skill I just learned three months ago, but I'm usually very good at it."

"I have no doubt," Zack said, his shoulders relaxing.

Mary glanced at the clock. Almost midnight.

"Any word from Aunt Abby, or from the deputy?"

"No," Mary said, frowning. "Nothing. I had the phone right with me."

"They're probably on their way back in by now," Zack said offhandedly.

Mary forced her mouth into a smile. "Let's hope so. They're both going to be so exhausted when they get in. I'm thinking that they've probably found the plane by now. Else they'd be on the way to the next island already and would have called in by now. I hope they were able to help—I hope there were survivors to help."

"Me too," Zack said.

"Did you have a nice evening?" Mary asked, trying for a casual tone.

"We had a very nice time, Mom," Zack said, shaking his finger at her in a mock scold. "And don't even pretend you're not trying to be a matchmaker."

"Would that be so bad if I were?" Mary asked.

"Lily and I are friends, Mom. I like her a lot. And maybe it'll turn into something more serious, and maybe it won't. Right now I'm just enjoying spending time with her. I know her well enough already to know she's an honest person. She doesn't play games and she says what she means. It makes it easy just to hang out with her and enjoy my time with her without having to stress out about what comes next. Kind of like you and Henry, you know?"

"Yes, well that's nice, Zack," Mary said. She cleared her throat and rushed on. "So did you show her the lighthouse?"

"Yes, we drove all the way up Wayfarer Point Road to the lighthouse and back again. She really thinks it's beautiful here. I told her she ought to see it in the springtime."

"Well, maybe she will," Mary said, and immediately dipped her head and put up a hand. "I'm not matchmaking. I just meant maybe she'll have a chance to come back again in the spring. After all, she'll want to visit Finnegan."

"Visit him?" Zack asked, then turned back toward her abruptly, his eyes wide. "Okay, Mom, you can't let what I've said about Lily and me influence your decision about Finnegan. Honestly, one thing has nothing to do with the other. Lily and me, we'll still see each other, regardless. So, don't go factoring that in as part of your little plan."

"I know, Zack," Mary said, calmly. "This has got nothing to do with you and Lily." She looked over at Finnegan. "He was really with me tonight. And I realized during all this that his being here with me really did give me options I wouldn't have had without him." She felt her eyes tearing and blinked rapidly. "Anyway," she said lightly, "Blossom has gotten attached to him, so what am I going to do? She'd never forgive me if I sent him away."

"That's great," Zack said. He was smiling, but Mary still sensed some reservation. "But, remember what Lily said," he continued. "Finnegan has to choose you too. It's a two-way street."

Mary looked down at Finnegan, who sat patiently beside her chair. "Well, I'll just have to win him over then," she said, reaching out to stroke his head.

Chapter Fourteen

THE CLIMB BACK UP THE HILL was almost more than Abby's overtaxed thigh muscles could take. She continued her practice of stopping periodically to listen. She thought that was prudent, but then realized she had no choice in the matter. She had to rest her legs often just to keep from falling down.

Her turtleneck and the cardigan she had been so grateful for at Stanton Farm last night—*Was it really only last evening?*—were wet through and through underneath her coat and poncho. They had soaked up moisture from her overheated body. Her pants were caked with mud and her feet now actually made a squishing sound when she walked.

She finally emerged from the woods near where the underground stream fed into the larger one that ran out to the sea. She stared at the plane for a long time, making sure the couple hadn't come back for shelter or for some other reason that Abby couldn't even begin to guess. She saw no movement, no light and heard no unusual sounds. She walked out of the cover of the forest and over to the stream.

Water was a precious commodity in the San Juans. Eons ago the glaciers had filled the area with abundant groundwater, the meltwater percolating into cracks, crevices and pockets in the bedrock. All the resupply since came only from local rainfall. There were no rivers, no snowpack and no underground water table upon which to rely, so islanders tended not to take water for granted.

The trickle from the upper stream was slow, but Abby knew that because it was coming directly off sandstone, it would be purer than the water she'd get if she just dipped the bottles into the larger stream. With apologies to the salamanders, newts and other wigglies, she reached in and scooped out a spot where the bottles could sit upright and catch the drips coming off the moss-covered rocks.

She switched off her flashlight and glanced nervously around, her eyes becoming accustomed to the silver and black lace of the trees in the pale moonlight. She heard a rustle, ever so slight behind her, and froze. But something told her that whatever this was, it was part of the island and not a human interloper. Still, she was compelled to look, so she flicked on her flashlight and swung it in the direction of the sound. A small rabbit, maybe the very same one that had started the series of events that sent Henry tumbling downhill, was caught in her beam. After a momentary hesitation it bounded away.

Abby glanced back down at the water bottles and focused the light on them briefly.

This was going to take a while.

She turned off the flashlight and closed her eyes for a moment to let the last of the artificial light drain from her retinas. She then listened carefully, attuning herself to the hum of the island nightlife. She opened her eyes and gazed slowly around her. Her eyes came to rest on the wreckage of the plane, looking like some shed insect carapace in the eerie light.

She'd get that blanket Henry had seen. It would be warm and dry. Wonderfully dry. She squirmed in her damp clothing and tried to remember what fresh dry clothing, just off the line and smelling of sunshine, felt like when she was a child. It was a wonderful memory.

She shook her head realizing she'd almost fallen asleep, kneeling there by the stream. She got to her feet and headed for the plane.

She stepped gingerly around the wreckage and, remembering Henry's earlier demonstration, grabbed hold of the propeller and gave it a shake. Nothing even shuddered. She wasn't sure if the plane had settled or if her arms were so weak that the tug had been totally ineffectual. In any case, she decided it was safe to pick around.

She crawled to the hole in fuselage and switched on her flashlight. She put her arm just inside the opening and shined the light inside, half expecting the raven to come screaming out of the breech again. But all was silent. She peeked around the corner and then pulled her head back, losing her nerve. After a couple of more attempts, she had her whole upper body inside of the plane. She found the blanket right away. A corner was snagged under a broken seat, but she gave it a yank and it let go, leaving a strip of green behind. She put it in her pack and took another look inside. The briefcase Henry had mentioned was wedged underneath a broken seat. It was a fancy one, made of some kind of animal skin Abby was sure she'd disapprove of. She could only get it partway open. It looked as if it had been emptied, except for a few papers that were wrinkled up and caught in the underside of the seat. Abby reached in and pulled them loose, tearing the corners off in the process, and placed them in the backpack on top of the blanket. Maybe she'd be able to get some information about who these people were and what they were up to.

Further exploration turned up two individually wrapped restaurant mints, a pullover blouse awash with sequins, a man's polo shirt with one sleeve torn and a lacrosse stick. *Ah well*, Abby thought, *beggars could not be choosers*. She put everything but the stick into her pack.

She played the beam of her flashlight over the crushed compartment and could just make out where the couple had wriggled out of the front and maneuvered to the hole to get out of the wreckage. The blood smears had dried to a dark brown, but they made the path easy to trace.

Abby had a sudden thought. Had the couple even tried to use the radio? Maybe they'd been in shock. Or maybe it was of no use to them. If they were up to no good, whom would they call? Certainly not the authorities, and these radios weren't rigged for much else. The way they were avoiding her and Henry, they obviously had a plan that didn't involve being found.

Abby headed for the cockpit, bending her aching back into positions it did not appreciate until all that was between her and the pilot's seat was a collapsed ceiling panel. She peered around it and almost let out a scream. Sitting on the control panel was the raven again.

She ducked back around and covered her head with her arms, getting her body into as tight a ball as the space would permit, and waited for the bird to go swooping by.

But nothing happened. She waited for a long moment, holding her breath. Still nothing. She made a trilling noise and slapped on the panel a couple of times, but the bird still didn't move.

Finally, she tilted her head and slowly uncovered one eye. She peeked around the panel. The bird sat perfectly still—as would any plastic bird. Abby wanted to laugh, but was afraid she would dissolve into hysterics and never be able to get herself under control. The plastic statuette was bolted to the top of the control panel like some avian St. Christopher. Someone had hung a keychain around its neck.

"'And the Raven, never flitting, still is sitting, still is sitting,'" Abby said as she stared at the bird. "Henry was right. It is something out of Poe."

She worked her way into the front seat, but her hopes were deflated when she got a good look at the instrument panel. It had been practically folded up out of the nose and all the dials and buttons were broken and twisted.

Abby glanced over at the bird and took the keychain off his neck. On it there were a couple of keys and a whistle. Her boss Jerome back at Cornell had given her one just like this because he worried about her walking to the parking deck alone. She stuffed the keychain into her pocket.

She flicked her flashlight over the seats and the floor and noticed a rounded corner of plastic lodged in between the pilot's seat and the door. She grabbed hold and gave it a tug, but it didn't budge. Slowly she slid her hand down the outside to get a better grip. This time when she pulled it came out like a stopper out a bottle, almost making her slam her hand into the roof. It was a BlackBerry, one of those personal organizers everyone was always fiddling with these days. She shined her flashlight on it. It was pretty badly mangled and probably inoperable, but she took it anyway.

On the way out she found a couple of items that made her feel like she'd won the lottery. A small, travel-sized tissue box was lodged where a seat back had been twisted up against a window. Abby wrested it out and plucked one of the tissues from the crumpled box, placing its softness against her sore nose. Where the blanket had been caught she saw a small patch of white peeking out from under the torn scrap she'd left. She pushed it aside and found a large bottle of sunscreen and a tube of zinc oxide in a clear zip case.

This was a different kind of sign cutting altogether, Abby

mused. Now she knew someone—probably the woman, judging from the bikini top she'd seen in the debris in the tail section—was a sunbather, and that they had probably been headed for someplace warm and sunny.

The zinc oxide would come in handy to doctor her raw nose, she thought. She stuck the case into her pocket and made her way back to the opening in the fuselage, turning off the flashlight and taking the time to let her eyes and ears adjust.

As she grabbed at the edge of the plane to pull herself out, she felt a gritty residue. She shined her flashlight on her hand and saw flecks of black. She crawled out and swept her light over the outside of the plane. There she saw a duplicate of the sloppy paint job she'd seen on the other side. She rubbed at the spot with her coat sleeve and the cheap paint let go of the hard epoxy on the panel. Underneath was the silhouette of a bird similar to the model inside. The words *The Raven* appeared in script just below it. She was so tired, she thought maybe she was hallucinating, or dreaming. Ravens everywhere. Raven the helper or Raven the trickster?

When Abby got back to the stream, the water bottles had all filled to the top and were overflowing like some pop art fountain. She capped each one carefully and put them all back into her pack. Then she gathered up her lacrosse stick and started back for the bluff.

She was so tired now she'd almost passed the point of awareness. She still stopped often to listen, and she thought she was making a good attempt at stealth as she moved through the forest. However, she really couldn't tell if her perceptions were accurate. She could have been thrashing her way through like an angry bear for all she knew. She could no longer accurately judge the passing of time, and she had to stop twice as often going back down to put down her pack and rest for a moment. She was still frightened of who might be out there waiting in the woods. But at this point she was more afraid of slipping and ending up like Henry.

When Abby finally made it back to the bluff, she found Henry awake. He was none too happy about her having slipped away for a little night ops. But after he saw that she was okay, and he'd extracted a promise that she wouldn't go off again without telling him, he settled down. He showed great interest in the objects she'd brought back. He examined each item carefully while she pumped water through the filter.

If she was going to stay awake and functioning she would have to make coffee, which meant risking a small fire.

"I don't think it'll be a problem if we put it out by first light," Henry said. "The smoke is the thing I'd worry about. Unless they're on the south side of the island, the smell won't drift to them, and they'd have to be below us to see the light if we keep it under the bluff. Just make sure you build it close to the edge so the smoke doesn't blow back in on us," he told her, puffing out a breath as he repositioned his leg.

"I'll build it small," she told him. "It'll burn out quick."

Henry picked up the keychain and leaned over near the lantern to examine the fob. "*Hmm*, Raventech," he said.

"What? What's Raventech?" Abby asked, looking up from where she was kneeling.

Henry turned the lantern wick up enough so that she could make it out then dangled the keychain in front of her. The leather fob had a bronze plate on it with the same depiction of the bird statuette she'd seen in the plane and the one painted on the outside panel. Except, on the fob the bird had his wings spread and the whole frontal section of his chest was made up of some kind of circuitry, indicated by small inlaid stones.

"It's one of the dot-coms over in Seattle," Henry said. "I hear the big financial players talking over on San Juan Island all the time. You know the guys I mean, they're always gathered around the marina while somebody else takes care of their boats, talking about their investments and bragging about their coups. They like having money, they like making money and they like talking about money.

"I heard a couple of them in a lather about this outfit just a couple of weeks back. One said he'd heard some rumblings about the stock being about to tank and he was unloading his. The other one said he was thinking about it too. Said he'd heard they had management problems. I don't know why that stuck in my head, but it did. Probably the way the guys were talking. It was like they were talking code or something you know. Like with a wink and a nod."

"Yeah, high finance is a world of its own," Abby said. "Atkinson," she repeated slowly. "Yes, I think maybe that's the company he worked for. Raventech. Yeah, I remember now," she said, snapping her fingers. "Mary made some joke like it's a wonder they didn't release ravens at the wedding since the bride and groom both worked for Raventech."

"Yeah, according to the letterhead on these papers, he's the Chief Financial Officer and she's the Comptroller," Henry said, pointing to the papers Abby had torn away from under the seat. "Looks like it was a marriage made in the boardroom. Carl and Gretchen Atkinson, Raventech royalty. But these keys may not belong to either of them. The fob is engraved *WK* on the back."

"Well, all I know is something is definitely rotten in Denmark—or in Seattle in this case," Abby said. She stopped pumping and rested her arm for a minute. She looked in the bottle and decided she had enough water for coffee. She would never, she vowed, take water coming out of the faucet for granted again. She stepped outside and gathered a few sticks for the fire.

"What else can you tell from those?" she asked when she came back under the bluff, tipping her head in the direction of the sheaf of papers.

"Not a thing," Henry said. "My finances are not very complicated. I'm pretty good about balancing my checkbook and I keep a close eye on my retirement account and a couple of CDs. My biggest gamble is a little I've put in a conservative mutual fund. This stuff might as well be hieroglyphics."

Abby held out her hand. "Same for me, but I've got a pretty good grasp of institutional funding. Let me have a look."

She studied the papers for a moment, but couldn't make anything out of the rows and columns of numbers. She suspected she wouldn't have been able to even if her head weren't swimming and her sinuses weren't aching and her eyelids weren't feeling like they weighed five pounds apiece. "No, it's beyond me too," she said at last, putting the papers aside. "All I can see is that they're handling lots and lots of money."

She gathered several loose stones and constructed a tiny fire pit and then put the sticks inside. The wood was damp and she had to tend the reluctant flame, cupping her hand and blowing a gentle stream of air to get the fire to take. When she had it going, she placed two flat rocks on either side so that they supported the edges of the coffeepot. Within minutes the smell of coffee filled the little cavern. The aroma was enough to make her swoon.

"Now that might draw 'em," Henry said, only half kidding. "Best bring the pot back over this way. That'll overwhelm even the sea smells."

"I need about four cups of this to stay awake," Abby said, sipping the earthy brew. "But I'm not sure I have the energy to pump that much more water, and I don't think the grounds would yield that much anyway," she told him, handing over his travel mug.

"Thanks," he said taking the mug. "I can really use this." He ran his hand across the top of his head and then looked down at the ground. "I'm more than a little embarrassed about falling asleep earlier. Sleeping on the job, that's a first for me."

"I think you can be excused this one time, Henry," Abby said, pointing to his makeshift splint. "You'd better rest while you can. Like you said, we don't know how long it'll be before they come for us."

"Nor how they'll find us when they get here," Henry said. "Our dilemma is that we need to let the deputies know where we are without alerting the Atkinsons. Don't know how we're going to accomplish that, especially with me in this shape."

"I've been thinking about that," Abby told him. "We've got these," she said, holding up the flares. "I could hike up to the cliff and set them off, so at least they'd know they've got the right island. And if they come around the south end of the island, they're sure to see the boat."

A frown pleated Henry's forehead. "Except I don't want to bring my men in blind with us still having no idea what the Atkinsons are up to. And besides, if my men can see the flares, so can the Atkinsons. They might come after you."

"But I can get back down here quicker than they can hike up," Abby said. "And I'll still have the cover of darkness. As for your men, do you have any kind of signal we could give as they approach, like with the flashlights maybe?"

"How's your Morse code?" Henry said.

"I could do a serviceable *caution*," Abby said, running through the sequences in her head to make sure she could spell out the word in dots and dashes.

"Seriously?" Henry asked.

"Yes," Abby said. "When we were little, Mary and I used

to send one another signals with our little flashlights from our treehouse."

Henry shook his head. "Amazing," he said. "Well, it's a good plan. All except for the part where you hike up the cliff alone. I don't like that at all."

"But Henry, there's no point in setting them off anywhere else. Unless the boats are already on this side of the island, they'd never see them. They're just highway flares. We don't have a flare gun. And we have no idea how they'll approach. Setting them off on the cliff will at least get them down to this end."

"Truth is," Henry said, "we have no idea whether my deputies even know we're on this island. We don't know for sure that the last transmission got through."

"No, but we know the one before it did, and they knew this is where we were headed. Even if they backtrack our whole route, they'll be here before long."

"How are you holding up?" Henry asked.

"I've picked up a cold," Abby said, sniffing. "My nose is raw, but look what I found on the plane," she told him, holding up the tube of zinc oxide. She put a glob on her fingertip and rubbed it on her nose.

"You could set a whole new fashion trend," Henry said, grinning at her white nose.

"Speaking of fashion. I got these too," she said, scrambling around in the loot pile and holding up the articles of clothing. "Dry shirts. So if you'll excuse me, I'll retire to my dressing room, and leave you to change here. Put this on and then put your coat back on. I'll put our shirts by the fire to dry. No sense getting pneumonia on top of everything else."

"Yes, ma'am, I hear that," Henry said, looking at the lime green polo shirt. "I'm not one to wear these Popsicle-colored shirts, but dry is dry."

"You're lucky," Abby said, holding up her sequined number. "Get a load of this. It's not exactly *me* either."

Abby climbed up above the bluff and went behind a row of thimbleberry bushes to change. The sparkly shirt was ridiculous. It was made of some kind of stretchy material and the sequins interlocked across the whole front like some froufrou plate of armor. However, the dry fabric felt wonderful. She pulled her coat back on and instantly felt better. Warm and dry was much better than cold and wet, no matter what it looked like.

Back under the bluff she dragged some of the salal branches over near the remaining embers in the little fire pit and stretched out their shirts on them.

"The things that become important to us in times of hardship, eh? I wish I had a razor," Henry said, drawing his hand across the stubble on his chin.

Abby nodded. "Wish I could Morse code them to bring me a toothbrush. And maybe some sinus medicine," she said, her voice now twangy and breaking up every couple of words.

She brushed off her hands and spread the scraps of paper from her backpack out on the ground. She retrieved the electronic organizer from the pile of stuff she'd gotten from the wreckage. She turned the flame on the lantern a little higher and sat down. She carefully scrutinized each small piece.

"There are several partial receipts here, looks like from a marine supply store," she told Henry. "This is a lot of stuff. Somebody spent a bundle. Looks like it was sold to the WK Corporation. Isn't that what was on the keychain?"

"Yeah. I've never heard of it, you?" Henry asked.

"No," Abby said. "Could it be a subsidiary of Raventech, or something like that?"

"Could be," Henry said. "What else you got there?"

Abby held up the BlackBerry. "It's pretty smashed up, but cross your fingers."

She pushed the button to power it on and was more than a little surprised when it flickered and the screen lit. Well, partially anyway. It was cracked and about half the pixels didn't work. She pushed the buttons to navigate it. "That's what I figured," she said to Henry, her voice weary. "It's password protected."

"If it belongs to one of them on the plane, let's try the obvious. Maybe their names or initials," Henry said.

Abby ran through names and initials, but the device stubbornly refused her entreaties. She stared again at the matchbook, but couldn't make out the date. She tried to think back to when Mary had read her the article and tried the Friday and Saturday dates around that time. No go.

"Oh well, nice try," Henry said. "Guess he's not a romantic. Probably wouldn't tell us much that would help right now anyway. Save it and I'll let the lab guys at it. They'll crack the code."

Abby nodded and leaned her head back to rest. But she couldn't let it go. She tried to remember details of the article Mary had read to her. She remembered clearly they had been sitting out on the back deck with the Sunday paper on a sunny afternoon. She remembered Mary reading the detailed descriptions of the bride's dress, the flowers, the horse-drawn carriage delivering the bride to the church. The unfortunate release of those doves at the end of the ceremony. Abby was almost dozing when the thought came to her. Mary had laughed over the word they had used to describe the groom. A wunderkind.

Mary had repeated the word, rolling it off her tongue. In his youth Carl Atkinson had apparently been some kind of computer genius who had been wooed by and worked for numerous companies before Raventech snagged him. "How would you like to be known as that for the rest of your life?" Mary had asked.

Wunderkind. WK? That was the kind of tag people either fought against or totally embraced. Abby grabbed up the BlackBerry and punched it in. W-U-N-D-E-R-K-I-N-D. The device beeped and gave her a menu. There was a cell phone function and Abby's heart soared for a moment, but her hope was instantly dashed. It didn't work.

The address book function didn't work either and she couldn't access old e-mails, but she found a folder with more recent e-mails and it opened up.

"What have you got?" Henry wanted to know.

"Two e-mails. A puzzle and a riddle," Abby said with a sigh. "I can only see a word here and there where the screen's still intact. This one looks like a sell order for some stock. Can't tell what company, but it's certainly a lot of shares. Looks like it was about a week ago." Abby took a stick and drew on the ground. "From the spacing it looks like nine letters. Second letter is an A, fifth letter is N, last two letters are C-H. Raventech? Why would they be selling their stock in their own company?"

"Maybe they're cashing out. Quitting," Henry said. "Or maybe they've got insider information that it's about to tank."

She advanced to the next e-mail. "This is to someone named L-e-n, something," Abby said. "'Good job on' . . . something missing there," she mused skipping her finger across the screen. She moved over so that Henry could see, careful not to jiggle the device too much lest it quit altogether. "'VERY IM—' . . . something, something," Abby continued. "Letters and numbers. I know what this is!" she said suddenly. "It's a latitude and longitude notation, a waypoint."

"Yep, N48. That's the San Juans," Henry said. They puzzled over the rest of the numbers, trying to divine what the burned-out pixels refused to divulge. They tilted the BlackBerry and looked at it from every angle. Abby pulled the map from Henry's bag and used both fingers to trace the intersection using their best-guess coordinates. "That could be Castle Island," Abby said.

"Do you think that was their destination?" Henry frowned.

"Perhaps it was a rendezvous point maybe?" Abby said. She scrambled in her bag and brought out her notebook. "Every scientist who does fieldwork has a page somewhere in the back of the journal where they write down anomalies. Sometimes it helps to clarify what *does* fit if you look at what *doesn't*," she said.

"You better have a few pages for this set up. Nothing seems to fit," Henry said, rubbing his hand across his head.

"Okay," she said, writing industriously. "The plane being vandalized, painted over like that," she said. "Why? The couple surviving the crash, but trying to make it look as if they've perished. Why? It looks like they were going someplace warm and sunny based on the clothing, swimsuits and sunscreen. A floatplane doesn't seem like a likely mode of transport for a long trip. And if they're trying to get off the island to meet up with someone, why not take our boat instead of vandalizing it?"

"That one I can answer," he said. "They probably have their own boat."

"Oh yeah. Okay," Abby said. "But where is it? I'd say they were planning to meet up with someone, but what about the plane?" She frowned. "Maybe they were going to make a switch. They take a boat and whoever they're meeting switches to the plane."

"All good theories," Henry said. "But it still doesn't tell us the main thing we need to know. Are they dangerous?" He looked at his watch. "Tell you what, I had my nap. Why don't you catch a quick one while I keep watch? I don't think you'll be able to make it to the cliff if you don't rest a little. I'll wake you in about an hour and you can go set off the flares. That'll give you plenty of time to get back here before first light."

Abby reluctantly agreed to his plan, then sat down near the little fire pit with her back to the wall and wrapped the green blanket around her. She wanted to protest. She wanted to tell him she was good to go. But she was tired and things were getting fuzzy and faraway and sleep soon overtook her.

MARY SWITCHED ON THE LAMP and ran her fingers along the inside of the shade, popping out a little indentation it had suffered in its fall to the floor. Even though it was well past midnight, she still couldn't sleep.

Zack had helped her back to bed and retrieved all her scattered items. Then he'd replaced the bulb in her nightstand lamp before saying goodnight.

"Finnegan, if she tries to get out of bed again without me to spot her, give me a bark right out loud, okay?" he'd said to the dog from the doorway.

Finnegan had looked to Mary then got up and turned around and sat back down, his back toward Zack.

Mary had laughed softly. "He knows where his allegiance lies. All I'll promise is that I'll be more cautious, Zack," she had told him. "Sweet dreams, son."

"Sweet dreams to you too, Mom," Zack had said, the teasing tone gone. "Try not to worry, okay? Everything's going to be fine."

But Mary couldn't sleep. She kept thinking of Abby and

Henry and what could possibly have kept them out of communication for this long. And what of the people from the plane? The crash had happened over a day ago. Had help arrived? Was it in time? Were they beyond help? The worry got into her head and just kept repeating in a loop.

Mary found herself gently sobbing. Finnegan came padding over. He put his muzzle up along the edge of the mattress and bumped his nose gently against Mary's arm.

"It's okay, Finnegan," Mary said. "I'm just worried, that's all. People have been telling me all day not to worry, and I've been trying to pretend for all their sakes that I'm okay. But I can tell you, right? Finnegan, I'm worried and I'm upset."

She stroked the dog's head and he kept his eyes fixed on her face. "I feel better now, just being able to say that," she told him. She sniffled and pulled a tissue from the wicker dispenser on her nightstand.

"This is so unlike me," she said. "I'm normally a very positive person. You'll see. But right now I'm just a little down."

"Did you call?" Zack asked, appearing in the doorway. "I was just getting a glass of milk in the kitchen and I thought I heard you."

"No, no I didn't," Mary said, quickly wiping her eyes. "I was just talking to the dog."

"Oh, okay," he said. "Trying to work your charms on him, huh?"

"Something like that," Mary said.

As Zack said goodnight again Mary went to turn off the

lamp, but then noticed the literature Lily had given her sitting on the nightstand. She picked it up and browsed through it.

"I think I'll study this stuff so we can really wow Lily tomorrow," she whispered to Finnegan. "Might as well make good use of the time. I simply cannot sleep a wink."

Chapter Fifteen

It was a long swim up to consciousness. Abby wanted nothing more than to keep her eyes shut and continue to float in this liquid dreamless sleep. She could hear Henry whispering her name, but she couldn't seem to find where he was. She couldn't even tell if he was really there or just in a dream that was trying to drift in and intrude on her solitude.

"Abby, it's time to set off the flares," he said, adding a little breathy fake whistle to pierce the fog in her head. That brought her awake and she winced as the crick in her neck convinced her to move more slowly. Her leg muscles were knotted and she made a few slow experimental moves to test their limits. She was going to pay a high price for those few hours of sleep—Henry had definitely let her sleep longer than he said he would. Her muscles were now cold and she was stiff, but it had been worth every blissful second.

There was no sound under the bluff save the low hiss of the lantern, which Henry had turned down to its lowest flame. It cast ghostly shadows and Abby almost jumped when she glanced over and saw their shirts draped over the salal limbs. She reached over and grabbed the sleeve of her turtleneck. It was still damp.

She blinked and stared longingly at the little camp coffeepot, but knew it would take too long to pump the water and rebuild the little fire that had burned out hours ago. And anyway it probably wasn't possible to coerce another pot from the grounds that had given their all for the cups they'd had earlier. She settled for a few gulps of the water she'd pumped, which tasted of minerals and earth and moss, but was much appreciated by her dry, scratchy throat.

"I've got something for you," Henry said. "Sort of to express my apologies for getting you into this—"

"Henry," Abby interrupted, "I've told you—"

But Henry held out his hand and Abby stopped short. "Okay, to express my thanks then. How's that?" He handed over a chocolate bar. "Found it in the outside pocket of my backpack after you fell asleep."

Abby's face brightened as she reached for it. "Great, we'll split it."

"No," Henry said, waving it away. "I'm not expending energy. You are. It'll be light in a few hours. If you can get up to the top of the cliff while it's still dark, the flares can be seen from a long way off. Then come back here and we'll move out from under the bluff and listen for the engines. When they come within distance, we'll split apart and both try to signal them."

"You shouldn't try to move, Henry," Abby told him. "You could do worse damage to that leg."

"The pain's manageable. I can't put any weight on it, but I can hobble a little, thanks to this ingenious, but I must say very homely splint you've fashioned for me."

Abby looked down at Henry's leg. She didn't quite believe him about the pain's being manageable, but she knew the splint would hold. She had used everything she could find to cushion the leg against the side of the trough, including the strips of material she had cut from Henry's pants leg, all the cotton balls in the first aid kit and some moss she had gathered from the forest floor. Then she'd strapped the whole thing up with gauze and surgical tape—every bit in the kit. She'd have to admit, it looked a little ragtag. It reminded her of a barn swallow's messy nest, but it was getting the job done for now.

"But what if the Atkinsons spot you, Henry? Like you've said, they may be dangerous. We've got no way to know."

"For all we know the Atkinsons are long gone. Maybe someone had already taken them off the island before we even got here. They must have developed some kind of plan to get out of here. I don't think they're *Gilligan's Island* types."

"What about the sabotaged boat? That had to have been them."

"Well, now, that's the logical thought, I admit. But it *could* be totally unrelated. Could have been some other vandals. That's our problem. We just don't have a clear picture of what we're dealing with here. And I sure don't want anybody rushing headlong into it. Not while everything's this foggy."

"Speaking of which," Abby said, walking haltingly over to the edge of the overhang and peering out around the pile of limbs. She squinted out into the darkness, but couldn't make out anything. "I hope this day dawns a little clearer than yesterday so we have better visibility."

"That cuts both ways," Henry said. "They'd see better too. Anyway, with all the rain we had yesterday, I think you can count on another foggy day, at least in the early morning."

Henry pulled out the map. "Probably best to stay in the forest line on your way back up. But if you loop around here, just at the edge, it's flatter for longer and there's not likely to be so much undergrowth," he said, tracing the route with his finger.

Abby nodded. "I agree. Should take me maybe forty-five minutes to make it around. Another five to set off the flares, and maybe thirty to get back. I'll come back down the hill the way we came before. Well," she said, giving Henry a tired smile, "not the way *you* came, I hope."

"Me too," Henry said. "You be careful. Are you sure you don't want to take my service revolver?"

"We've been through this, Henry," she said firmly. "But, I'll take this," she said, hefting the lacrosse stick.

Henry rolled his eyes. "Great, so you go armed with the crosse?"

"Pardon me?" Abby asked.

"That's what the stick is called, a crosse," Henry answered.

"Well, I like to think that's how I face every day," Abby said. "Why should today, of all days, be any different?"

She set out, her body lodging complaints from several locations all at once. But as she started up the hill, the lacrosse stick proved to be a useful hiking aid. She was able to increase her stride, and her time, by using it to balance and test the terrain ahead. She made a mental note to give Henry a bad time for scoffing at it.

Again she kept her hand partially over her flashlight beam so as not to advertise her presence. She hoped Henry's speculation that the Atkinsons might have already left the island was right, but she couldn't shake the feeling that eyes were watching her from the woods.

She thought of Mary, her parents, Hugo and Bobby. They must all be frantic by now. She said a little prayer, asking for comfort for them.

As she skirted a small clearing and neared a mudflat, she thought she heard something. At first she thought it was just the calls of night birds. But as she tuned her ear to the sound, it was more like the low murmur of human speech, and this time she didn't think it was her imagination at work. Her "fevered imagination," as her mother called it when she was little. She put her wrist to her forehead. Yes, she was probably running a low fever, but no, she didn't think she was that far gone. She put the hood of her coat down and tilted her head, straining to make out the sounds. Definitely human voices.

Though every brain cell was telling her to move in the opposite direction, Abby felt drawn toward the sound. If she could just get close enough to allow the scattered tones to coalesce into words she might learn something she and Henry needed to know for their own survival. Or for that of Henry's deputies or the Coast Guard crew.

Step by careful step, Abby moved toward the sound, placing each foot deliberately and transferring her weight forward slowly so as not to cause rustles in the leaf bed or underbrush. When she got closer she crouched low to the ground and duckwalked for a few more steps, every move making her aching muscles sting.

After what seemed an eternity she came to a small berm studded with lodgepole pines. She got into a prone position and crawled up behind the berm. She took a quick peek over and could see the backs of two people in silhouette seated on the rocks just where woods gave over to a long stretch of soil. She could tell that it was a man and a woman, but couldn't make out their features from this distance. She also couldn't decipher the words in their conversation, even though they didn't seem to be making much of an effort to keep their voices down.

Abby got herself as flat to the ground as she could, but her bulky coat wouldn't let her hug it tight enough to move up the berm to where she could pick up what they were saying. She rolled onto her side and took a couple of long minutes to unzip the coat, tooth by tooth, using her fingers to insulate the noise. Now she was able to spread it out like birds' wings on either side and crawl up the berm to a spot near the top where the sound floated back to her unobstructed.

The woman was doing the talking. "I'm going to have to find a good dermatologist the minute we get to the islands. Some of those weeds we waded through up there in the woods have given me some kind of an allergic reaction. It feels like someone's poured acid on my face where I've touched my hands to it. It hurts," she said, her voice whiny.

"Don't you women *go* to the dermatologist to have acid poured on your face these days? What do they call it, a chemical peel? Think of the money you're saving," the man said, trying for a teasing tone, but coming off sarcastic.

"You stopped being funny about five hours ago, Carl," the woman said. "I should never have listened to you. This all sounded good when we were sitting in the condo back in Seattle, but out here in the backside of nowhere it seems like something Lucy and Ethel would have cooked up in one of those old black-and-white reruns. What if they find us before Lenny gets here? What are we going to say? We need to get our stories straight."

"They're not going to find us before he gets here," the man said, slapping his knee with his hand in frustration, as if this were a continuation of a long-running argument. "I told you, they'll think we've had a terrible accident and fallen off the edge of this miserable rock, that is if they've even found the plane. These local yokels aren't exactly masterminds you know."

"It's just that attitude that's going to get us into trouble, Carl," the woman said, hissing. "You underestimate people."

"On the contrary, Gretchen. I give people full credit. I know just what they're capable of, and I make it my business to stay two steps ahead of them. If, by some incredible *fluke* we are happened upon before Lenny gets here, we'll simply act relieved to be rescued. Our gratitude will know no bounds. We'll allow ourselves to be taken to whatever passes for civilization out here and checked out by the medical people. Then, at the first opportunity, I'll get on the phone and have Lenny come pick us up there. We are just an unfortunate couple who crashed on this island on a sightseeing trip. What is it people come here for? To look at the blue whales or something?"

"Orcas," Gretchen corrected. "And you know very well that explanation is not going to hold for long."

"Doesn't have to hold for long," Carl answered. "Only has to hold until we can get to our new boat and get out of U. S. waters. If Lenny's followed my instructions, which I can assure you he has, we're provisioned for at least a month. We'll be well clear of here by the time the auditors raise the alarm. There's no way they'll even know anything is wrong before Monday."

"That's still cutting it pretty close, if you ask me," Gretchen said.

"Which I didn't," Carl said curtly.

Ah, trouble in paradise, Abby thought. So these two were intent on getting away. But from what? What had they done? They didn't sound exactly like Bonnie and Clyde. Abby suspected they'd probably been involved in some financial shenanigans. Well, that was bad, but it wasn't life or death. They wouldn't have much of a head start, not with Henry's deputies on the way. They wouldn't get away.

She'd about made up her mind to slip away and go about her business of setting off the flares, but decided to listen awhile longer and see if she could pick up something specific that might help the authorities when they nabbed them.

"What's that awful smell, anyway?" Gretchen asked.

"How should I know? It's like island smells or something," Carl said. "It's nature. You think nature always smells like flowers?"

Abby smiled. Next time maybe they shouldn't choose a mudflat for a rendezvous with this cohort of theirs. What had Gretchen called him? Lenny? The smell was gasses from anaerobic bacteria that get energy from sulfur compounds. It was a stinky brew, but it nourished lots of food for the birds, so Abby tried to think of it as a good thing and kept her breathing shallow.

"But the plane," Gretchen said, her voice again becoming whiny. "They're going to find the plane and then they'll start asking questions. They'll call Raventech. I'm telling you, they'll put it together."

Carl stood up abruptly and Abby quickly put her head flat down on the leaves and pine needles and stayed very still. She wasn't confident that the darkness of the woods would completely cloak her. She could hear Carl pacing and realized if she stayed here much longer she'd be trapped until this Lenny person came for them and they all left.

Which, the more she thought about it, seemed like the best-case scenario. If they were off the island there was no danger to Henry's men or anyone else coming to evacuate them. Abby could be back on Sparrow Island soaking in a hot tub by noon. Whatever this couple had done would catch up to them sooner or later, and Abby would be able to get a good look at any boat that came for them, so she'd be able to put the proper authorities on their trail almost immediately.

Hunkering down seemed a good option. She reached over and pulled pine needles and leaves over her head, then raised up ever so slowly until she could see the couple again through the openings in her makeshift ghillie suit.

"I'm telling you, Gretchen. They're not going to trace this back," Carl said, turning to look down at her. "Not until it's too late. I took the registration papers out of the plane and the tail numbers aren't legible."

"Yeah, and you don't think they're going to be curious about *that*?" Gretchen hissed.

Carl shrugged. "No one's going to have reported a plane stolen. They don't have anything to check against."

"You don't know that. Suppose someone from the company was planning to use the plane this weekend. They could have already discovered we've taken it."

Abby could just make out the man's features and carriage

now. He looked like just what he was—a wealthy executive *very* out of place on an isolated island.

"First of all, Gretchen," the man said, his voice tight and irritable, "we didn't take it. We checked it out, just like we always do when we're going somewhere for business."

"We have never taken the floatplane, Carl. Not without a pilot. You're not certified on the floatplane. We sure found out the hard way what a mistake it is to let someone fly it who doesn't know what he's *doing*," she said, the words coming out like so many little icicles.

"So it turned out to be harder to land the thing than I thought. This is better anyway. Will you give it a rest, Gretchen? You're giving me a headache. I'm injured you know. This cut on my head is killing me."

"Oh please," she protested. "You've cut yourself worse shaving."

"What are you talking about? You saw how much it bled."

"Yes," she said, not willing to give ground. "All head cuts bleed a lot. And lucky too. You were able to use it in your little over-the-cliff tableau."

"It did add a touch of the dramatic," Carl allowed. "And you'll thank me when we sail away while they're still down there searching among the rocks for our bodies," he told her with a strange little laugh. "I'm telling you, this is better. We'll be long gone by the time they figure out we haven't gone off that cliff—if they ever do."

"What if Lenny isn't coming? What if he can't find us?"

Gretchen demanded. "You know you're leaving a big part of your genius plan in Lenny's hands. He's just a kid."

"And why wouldn't I? He's the most talented intern I've ever had. And he has never failed in anything I've given him to do."

"That may be, but he can still make mistakes. And he has no idea what's riding on this. What if he can't find us?"

"Relax, Gretchen. That's what this GPS is for," he said, holding up a small global positioning device. "Despite how little faith in me you seem to have, I've thought of every contingency, even this little setback. Lenny was anchored off that little island, Castle Island, right where we were supposed to meet him. When I radioed him from that sheriff's boat, I told him we'd had engine trouble and we'd had a change of plans. He'll follow this transmitter and he can pull right up to get us. It's like whistling for a cab."

"Yeah? Well I hope Lenny's better with the boat than you were with the plane," Gretchen said.

"Sarcasm does not become you, my bride," Carl said. "And as you well know, Lenny grew up on one of these specks of land around here. That's one of the reasons I picked him for my intern. Well, that and the fact that his old man's a boat broker. Plus the kid worships me and would do anything I asked him to without questioning me. Eager beaver, that one. Really wants to get ahead. And I've got him completely buying into the company line. He'd do anything for the good of Raventech, and as far as he's concerned, I *am* Raventech. He didn't even bat an eye when I told him I was sending him on this special mission to buy and provision the boat for us."

"Wasn't he the least bit suspicious about our planning such an extended vacation? That's a long time to be away from our jobs."

"Not at all. After all, we're due for a long postponed honeymoon. And with the world wired up the way it is these days, we could do business from any port. Lenny understands that—the global village and all that."

Abby glanced up at the horizon line, which was just starting to divide into murky dark and hazy light. If she was going to change her mind about whether to stay or go, now was the time. Soon it would be full light and she wouldn't have a choice but to stay.

"All that may be true," Gretchen said, "but he's going to spill everything when they ask him. If we leave him here they'll question him. And if we take him with us, where will we drop him off? You said we're not going to port until we clear U.S. jurisdiction. Are we going to take him all the way to the Caymans with us?"

"Oh, we're going to drop him off. Just not in a port."

"What are you talking about?" Gretchen said, her voice tired. "Where else is there?"

"Let's put it this way. He'll probably wash up somewhere down in California. I understand that's how the currents move," Carl said, his voice steely.

Gretchen's head jerked up. "What are you saying?" she asked, her voice going high and tight. "You're not thinking of hurting that boy."

"Not at all," Carl said, and gave another strange, hollow laugh. "I'm just going to evict him from the boat. If he's a good enough swimmer, he'll be fine. If he's not—well, he should have spent more time playing sports and less time on the computer."

"Wait a minute, Carl," Gretchen said, now jumping to her feet. She was tall and very slender in build. Abby thought, judging by her clothes and manner, that her idea of hardship would be missing her Saturday morning manicure. "I didn't agree to anything like this. We take the money, that's fine. But no one's supposed to get hurt."

"No one *was* supposed to get hurt, but there's a little kink in the plan now, Gretchen. Would you rather go to jail? How long do you think we'd get for embezzling this kind of money? You'd be an old woman when you got out. We didn't just dip our quill in the company inkpot, darling. We stole the whole inkwell. We can't be leaving loose ends."

Abby pinched her lips together to keep from gasping. So maybe Lenny wasn't an accomplice. It sounded as if he was a pawn in Carl's plan.

"But we've got the money, Carl. It's not traceable," Gretchen said. "That's what we wanted."

"True," Carl said. "I've been thinking about that. It would probably be a good idea for both of us to have the numbers for the accounts. Just in case we get separated, you know?"

"Yeah, sure Carl," Gretchen said. "So I can end up with Lenny? I'm not that good a swimmer."

"Don't be ridiculous," Carl said. "I just think as a fail-safe we should both be able to get to the money."

"Fine," Gretchen said. "We'll both get to it, together. And in case you have any ideas, remember, the account numbers are right up here," she said tapping her temple. "They aren't written down anywhere."

"You don't trust me?" Carl asked, putting both hands to his chest.

"Of course I do," Gretchen answered. "Just like Lenny does." She balled up her fists and paced. "Isn't there any other way? Can't we just leave him here? It would take them a while to find him."

"Not long enough," Carl said, hammering each word. "Look," he said, his voice softer, "when the time comes, you'll just go below. I'll take care of it. Try not to think about it. But one way or the other, it's got to be done. Lenny knows too much. We've got to take him out of the picture."

Chapter Sixteen

WHEN MARY AWOKE it was full light and the booklet Lily had given her was resting on her pillow. For a split second she wondered if Abby had come in during the night and elected not to wake her, but the thought quickly evaporated. Abby would never do that. She had to know how worried Mary was by now.

Mary put the booklet back on the nightstand and Finnegan picked up his head as if waiting for a command. "Good morning, Finnegan," she told him, her voice thick with sleep. "I've done my homework and we're ready for our final exam. Aren't we, boy?"

The dog got up, stretched and yawned, then shook himself. Then he came over to stand by the bed where Mary could reach down to pat his head. Abby was going to be crazy about this dog, Mary thought. She couldn't wait to show her all that she and Finnegan could do. Today's training session would be a serious one. Mary was no longer simply going through the motions; she was out to *earn* her half of this special partnership.

"Always best to channel our worries into an activity," she told Finnegan. "That's what Abby always says. So today I'll put all my pent-up anxieties into our training. You with me on that?"

Finnegan continued to look at Mary and she had the strangest sensation he knew what she was saying. Not the actual words, but that at some primal level, he understood.

Mary looked over at the wheelchair and up at the transfer bar. "You know, Finnegan, I've never been one to let a little adversity defeat me. Why should I start now? What do you do if you fall off a horse?" she asked him, then looked around remembering how Zack had caught her talking to the dog last night. She lowered her voice. "I know, you're a dog, you've probably never been on a horse. It's just an expression anyway," she told him. "You get right back on, that's what!"

She looked down at the brake and made doubly sure that it was locked, and even grabbed the arm of the chair and tried to push it back. It held firmly. When she looked back up at the transfer bar, Finnegan moved over and sat alongside the wheelchair without Mary even giving him a command.

"A big part of this is attitude," Mary said, continuing to talk aloud to the dog—or to herself maybe—in a very soft voice. "Abby's got a favorite saying about this. It's from a man named Barrie who wrote a story called *Peter Pan*. Anyway," she said, continuing to eye the transfer bar, "he said, 'The reason birds can fly and we can't is simply that they have perfect faith, for to have faith is to have wings.'" She grabbed the bar and sucked in a breath. "I need to have faith that I can do this," she said, taking a moment to pray for just that.

She took her time and tested her strength at each step along the way. She wasn't going to make the mistake of getting overconfident again, but she was determined not to let one mishap stymie her progress.

This time all went smoothly, her best transfer so far. Yet another thing she couldn't wait to show Abby. So much had happened in the last couple of days, it seemed Abby and Henry had been away for a long time. Mary realized that she wasn't just worried about them, she missed them—both of them—very much.

She went to the kitchen and made coffee, then went straight to her morning devotional, fully expecting to find what she needed to face the day.

She was not disappointed. The reading was from Philippians, Paul's letters to those early, struggling Christians in Philippi:

> Do not be anxious about anything, but in everything,
> by prayer and petition, with thanksgiving, present
> your requests to God. And the peace of God, which
> transcends all understanding, will guard your hearts
> and your minds (Philippians 4:6–7).

MARY LOOKED OUT THE WINDOW. The sun was up, but had not yet begun to burn away the morning fog. Out on her back deck a freshening breeze had set the wicker rocking chair into gentle movement. It reminded her of her mother's more home-spun homily on worry. She always said worrying was like rock-ing in a rocking chair. It gives you something to do, but doesn't get you anywhere.

Well, it certainly hadn't gotten Mary anywhere in the last couple of days, except flat on the floor as a result of her restlessness.

Zack had asked Mary to wake him if he wasn't down by nine. He was trying to reach a happy compromise between keeping his regular hours and being able to spend time with the family in the daylight hours. Ordinarily Mary might have demurred, let-ting him sleep longer, but today she had so much nervous energy, she was keeping a close eye on the clock.

She called Candace to let her know she would not be coming in to work at the shop as she'd planned, then put in a call to Ana Dominguez to let her know she'd be absent from the crafting group in the afternoon. Each encouraged her to enjoy her time with Zack, so she now had a cleared calendar.

The ringing of the doorbell caused Finnegan to let out three sharp barks and come over to nuzzle at Mary's arm.

"It's okay boy. I've been getting a lot of early morning visi-tors lately." Mary fluffed her hair and checked to make sure she was presentable. She had on the lovely embroidered bed jacket Nancy had sent her, so all she needed to do was grab a lap blanket from the couch in the living room and spread it across her legs.

She found Hugo Baron and Bobby McDonald waiting on her front doorstep. Hugo looked as dignified as always and was his usual ebullient self as he greeted Mary. But she could tell by the slight crease in his forehead that she wasn't the only one who'd been worrying.

She invited them in and Bobby went straight for the dog. "So this is Finnegan?" he asked. "I heard about him. May I pet him, Mary?"

"Thank you for asking, Bobby," Mary told him. "That's exactly the right thing to do. He's off duty right now, so yes, you may. But when he has his cape or his harness on, it's not a good idea." She offered the explanation she'd heard Lily make over and over to people who had asked and that she'd read about in the booklet last night.

"Cool," he said. "So, are you going to keep him?"

"I hope so, Bobby," Mary said, and meant it wholeheartedly. "I think the choice is all up to Finnegan now, but I'd like to."

Hugo stood looking on, stroking his mustache. "Beautiful animal," he said. "And he really appears to be as smart as advertised." He gave a sidelong glance in Bobby's direction. "I don't suppose you've heard from our Abby this morning," he said, his voice carrying a forced cheer.

"Not yet," Mary answered. "I expect I'll hear from Henry's deputy soon. He's been very good about keeping me updated."

"Well, I'm sure she'll be in soon. In the meantime, Bobby's mother went in early this morning. Her class is going on a field trip today. Bobby and I had breakfast together and we've made a decision. We wanted to come by and ask you to tell Abby we've postponed the release ceremony for the falcons that we had scheduled for tomorrow morning. We felt she'd need a couple of days to rest up when she gets back."

"Well, she'll appreciate that, I'm sure," Mary told them. "What do you think she's going to make of Finnegan?" she asked Bobby. "She doesn't know anything about him yet."

"Really?" he asked, his hazel eyes twinkling. "She'll be so surprised. And she'll like him a lot. I know she will."

"I think so too," Mary told him.

"Well, I must get our young scholar here to school," Hugo said, giving her a wink. "He just wanted to come by and check in on you and meet this Finnegan, who is, I must tell you, taking the island by storm."

"He has that way about him," Mary said.

After Hugo and Bobby left, Mary called the substation and talked to Deputy Washburn. "We sent a boat out to pick them up a few hours ago, Mrs. Reynolds," he said. "We're not one hundred percent sure about their exact position, but we'll find them, I promise you that. And I'll let you know the minute I hear something."

Mary noticed he no longer bothered to tell her not to worry.

ABBY'S HEART WAS BEATING WILDLY. They were going to kill an innocent young man. Once they got away from the island the authorities might not be able to find them in time to save him. She had to stop them from leaving the island. But how?

A thousand thoughts moved to the forefront of her mind as she glanced frantically around the shoreline and the woods. How could she stop that boat?

Then she heard it, and so did Carl. "Listen. I think I hear a boat engine," he said. "Keep out of sight until we make sure it's him," he warned, pushing Gretchen back toward the woods on the opposite side of the mudflat.

"If you hadn't lost that other walkie-talkie we'd be able to communicate with him, but now we'll have to depend on the GPS until he gets close enough to signal," Carl said as he prodded her along.

"*I* didn't lose it, Carl," Gretchen snapped. "It was in the briefcase. It fell out somewhere in the plane *you* crashed, so get off my case. Besides, that thing was a toy, lot of good it would do."

"It wasn't a toy. It had a two-mile range," Carl said. "Don't talk about things you know nothing about. It was exactly the right thing for the job. Limited range. No one else could pick up the signal. Get it?"

Gretchen made no reply as she slumped down beside a tree and craned her neck to look out into the channel.

Abby was looking too, but she had the benefit of binoculars. The boat was just coming into view with a handsome golden-haired man—a boy really—at the helm. He was probably in his early twenties and positively radiated innocence. Seeing the flesh-and-blood young man Carl Atkinson had just been casually planning to harm made Abby's blood run cold.

"Hey, where's he going?" she heard Carl say. She took the binoculars down and saw that the boat was veering off on a southward course. She frowned and then remembered. The reef. Thank God for the wicked reef. A native of the San Juans would certainly be on the lookout for them and wouldn't try to come any closer to shore with the boss's spankin' new boat.

"Looks like maybe he's got to anchor off and bring the dingy in for us," Carl said. "Here, get your stuff together. We'll go out to the shore and signal him. The sooner we get out of here the better."

Gretchen grabbed up a battered suitcase and Carl snagged a gym bag. They started across the mudflat heading for shore and straining to try to see the boat around the bend in the land. Unlike Abby, they seemed unconcerned about being quiet. She doubted very seriously that they understood how sound carries on the water. They snarled at one another as they made their way across the terrain.

Abby took that opportunity to crab-walk back from the berm and slip into the woods. There were no buoy anchorages on this side of the island, so Lenny would have to swing at anchor. She closed her eyes and tried to remember the features of the shoreline she and Henry had searched. If she could guess the right spot maybe she could get close enough to talk to him, to warn him.

Carl and Gretchen, thankfully, seemed oblivious. Abby heard Carl grumbling about why Lenny was going so far away to anchor when the GPS should clearly show him where they were. It made Abby wonder how this man ever expected to make it out of U.S. waters and all the way to the Cayman Islands in a seagoing vessel. He seemed to know as little about boats as he did about floatplanes.

She made her way through the woods as quickly as she dared, trying to think of how to get Lenny close enough to have a conversation. She couldn't just shout out to him. Carl and Gretchen were too close. She needed a way to communicate with him, quickly and quietly—and convincingly.

Then she remembered the walkie-talkie. Carl had indicated that they were supposed to communicate that way once Lenny got to the island. She had a single one in her backpack. If luck was with her, Lenny's half would be tuned to one of the frequencies hers could pick up. She stopped and rummaged in the bag for it. She was relieved to see the battery still had life, though not much.

She moved faster toward the spot where she thought Lenny would choose to anchor. All the while she was thinking, planning and moving quicker and quicker. The fact that this young man's very life was hanging in the balance did wonders to clarify her thoughts.

When she was in place she saw the boat moving toward shore, just about where she'd thought it would be. She made her hasty preparations and then settled down to wait. She could still hear Carl and Gretchen, their voices faint now, moving through the woods toward the shore. They still seemed to be operating under the delusion that this was as easy as hailing a cab.

She watched through the binoculars until she saw Lenny lower the dingy and start rowing in. She then switched on the walkie-talkie. "Lenny?" she said, cupping her hand around the mouthpiece and keeping her voice low. "Lenny, can you hear me?"

The young man went about his business as if nothing had happened and Abby hummed in frustration and flipped the switch to another frequency and tried again. "Lenny?"

The young man threw up both hands as if to say *finally* and dug a walkie-talkie from his jacket pocket. "I'd about given up on you two. Mrs. Atkinson, is that you? You don't sound like yourself."

"I have a cold," Abby said, which was the truth—just not the whole truth.

"Oh well, listen. I can't get in at your GPS location. You'll either have to hike down here or I'll have to bring the dingy down to you. Which do you want me to do, Mrs. Atkinson?"

"We need your help with something. Can you come to us, please?" Abby said, doing her best to imitate Gretchen's voice. "But don't go by the GPS, we dropped it in the muck and lost it. We can see you. Just come on in to shore right where you are, okay?

"Sure," Lenny answered. "I can do that. Hey where's the plane?"

"We had some trouble," Abby said. "Don't worry about that now. Just come and pick us up, please."

"I'll be right there. Where are you?"

"Just come straight to shore and I'll talk you in," Abby told him and got into position.

She waited patiently while Lenny rowed to the shore. He got out of the dingy and tied it up, then started up through the woods. She watched, holding her breath, for him to step just where she wanted him to. But he missed the mark and walked on, craning his neck and squinting into the palely lit forest.

"Back over this way, Lenny," Abby said into the walkie-talkie, keeping her voice very low. She knew this would be the last chance she'd get at this. He turned and when he put his sneakered foot into just the right spot, she gave a mighty yank. The fishnet she had laid out on the trail and covered with leaves caught his foot and pulled it skyward. Lenny landed flat on his back.

He let out a guttural grunt and Abby sprung at him. She placed the lacrosse stick across his chest holding his arms pinned down.

"Listen to me, Lenny," she told him, bending over him, her voice low and rapid. "Carl and Gretchen are going to try to kill you. They've embezzled a lot of money from the company—from Raventech—and the boat is for a getaway, not a honeymoon. You've been duped. You're in danger. You've got to get away from here."

The boy was at first dazed, then wild-eyed. He started to make noises and Abby made shushing sounds and put her hand over his mouth.

As he looked at her in terror, now in the half-light of dawn, she realized what a picture she must have made. Her hair was bedraggled and hanging in her face and accessorized with pine needles and leaves. Her nose was white with smeared zinc oxide and she had little pieces of leaf and dirt sticking to her face. And she was wearing a sparkling evening top and mud-caked pants. She had lain in wait with a primitive trap and a lacrosse stick. Her voice was raspy and she was talking very, very fast. He had to believe he'd been set upon by a mad-woman from the wilds.

"Listen to me," she said again, more calmly. "I know you think I'm crazy, but I'm trying to save you. Carl and Gretchen want to hurt you. I overheard them plotting. You've got to get away from them."

The boy was thin, but scrappy, and he gave a mighty heave and scrambled away from Abby, clawing at his shoe to pull free of the net. He got to his feet and started to back away fast.

Voices came from the direction of the mudflat. "Lenny? Where are you, man? We're down here. Stop fooling around, okay? Come on. Me and Gretchen have waited a long time for this trip. We want to get going."

There were heavy footfalls and rustling through the forest. The Atkinsons were on the move, coming toward them.

Lenny glanced quickly in the direction of the sound and cupped both hands around his mouth as if to call out an answer, keeping a wary eye on Abby. He hesitated and frowned, look-ing Abby up and down, then fixed his eyes on hers.

Chapter Seventeen

"LET'S GO OVER TO THE FARM," Mary said to Zack after she had delivered his requested wake-up call at nine. "I'm eager to show off Finnegan, and it will help to occupy Mom and Dad and keep them from worrying so much about Abby," she told him as he sipped his morning coffee. She didn't add that it would be a good distraction for her as well. She was trying her best to be heedful of the morning's devotional reading, but sitting around at home wasn't helping. She needed to be doing something.

They picked Lily up at The Bird Nest and both Martin and Terza Choi came out to greet Finnegan like he was an old friend. "We missed him last night," Terza said. "Did you enjoy having him at your house?" she asked Mary.

"Oh yes, yes I did indeed," Mary answered, exchanging a look with Zack.

Lily said she had hoped to visit the ferry landing with Mary and the dog to see how Finnegan reacted. "That's an environment he's unfamiliar with, and I want to make sure the new noises and smells don't throw him," she told Mary. "Would it be okay if we go by there for just a few minutes before we go to the farm?"

Mary hesitated for a moment. If Finnegan did get distracted, would this influence Lily's decision about whether she and Finnegan had bonded properly? But when Mary looked over at the dog, her doubts were erased. She had absolute confidence Finnegan was up to any task put before him.

As they drove to the ferry slip, Mary observed the easy interaction between Zack and Lily. She thought of what Zack had said the night before about them trusting one another and enjoying their time together as friends. If only things could be that simple for her and Henry. But the accident had changed everything. It was complicated now.

Neil McDonald, Bobby's father, who worked on the ferry, greeted them at the dock. After Mary explained why they were there, he let them go onto the ferry and back off again a couple of times while it was loading.

"Anything for the famous Finnegan," he said. "I've been hearing about this dog from just about everyone in town. Especially Bobby. It's been all we can do to keep him off your doorstep."

Mary told him about Hugo's bringing Bobby by earlier. "I hope he'll come by often. I'll need someone to romp with Finnegan in the backyard," Mary said. "Assuming I get to keep him," she added, smiling up at Lily.

"Well, Bobby's your guy," Neil said. "You know how he

loves animals. Mr. Baron has been really nice about keeping him busy while Abby's off the island."

"Is Bobby worried about Abby?" Mary asked.

"Not one bit," Neil answered decisively. "He thinks Abby can do anything. And you know, far as I can tell, he's got it about right."

Zack laughed. "That's what I think too." He turned to Lily. "Wait until you meet Aunt Abby. She's sweet and kind, but she's strong on the inside. Just like her sister," he said, patting Mary's shoulder.

Mary smiled. "Well, one thing she's going to be when she gets back is tired and I would imagine hungry for a decent meal. Mom and I are going to whip up a little soup pot and some homemade bread when we get to the farm."

"Maybe they'll be there in time for lunch," Neil said. "I heard they sent out two more boats a little over an hour ago. They've got practically a fleet going out to help them."

"We'd better get a move on then," Mary said. "That bread's not going to make itself."

Finnegan passed the ferry test with flying colors. He kept looking over at Mary as if for his cue—or for reassurance. She tried to give him both.

As they were leaving, William Jansen, the editor of the local paper, came bustling up. His bushy brown hair was blown back in the breeze and he had his usual serious scowl. "Mary, glad I found you. This dog here is what you'd call hot news. Can I get a picture of you two for *The Birdcall*?" he asked.

Mary and Finnegan posed for the picture and William looked the dog over. "This is a nice human interest story. I'd like to come by and talk to you when you've got a minute."

Mary looked at Lily whose smile gave away nothing. "Check back with me in a couple of days. I've got a lot I can tell you about service dogs. And yes, it's a very interesting story."

"Big story of the week is this plane crash business, of course," William said. "Don't suppose you've had any word from your sister?"

"Not directly, no," Mary told him.

"Well, whatever they've found, I'm betting they'll have some story to tell when they get back." He started to move away. "And that is a good-looking dog, I guess. I'm not much into dogs myself."

As he walked away Mary reached over to pet Finnegan. "Don't you worry, Finnegan. He will be before you're done with him."

As they returned to the van, William's words echoed in Mary's ears, "They'll have some story to tell." Mary just hoped it had a happy ending.

LENNY STOOD STOCK STILL, staring wide-eyed at Abby. Then he tore his eyes away and glanced back in the direction of the voices. He was poised to run, every muscle taut. The question was, in which direction?

"Look," Abby said, her voice low and calm. "I know I look like a lunatic. But I'm not. I'm with the search party that came to look for the survivors of the plane, the Raventech plane. Carl crashed it. Did he tell you that?" She watched the reaction on the young man's face. "No, I didn't think so. They've sabotaged our boat and disabled our radio. And they mean to do you harm. You've *got* to believe me."

Lenny took a couple of practice bounces, like a runner in the starting block, but couldn't seem to make up his mind.

"But Mr. Atkinson . . . ," he said, his voice trailing off.

"Is *not* a good man," Abby finished for him. "He's using you, Lenny. We've got to get out of here right now."

"O—okay," he said at last, still glancing over at the sound of the Atkinsons' noisy approach. "What do we do?"

"This way," Abby said. "And be as quiet as you can." She led him back toward the crash site.

Carl's voice grew fainter but decidedly more agitated as they moved away.

"I don't understand," Lenny said, when they were far enough away to risk talking quietly.

Abby told him everything as best she could about what she'd overheard about their embezzlement and their plan for escape.

At first Lenny challenged her, but gradually he was convinced. "I thought he was a business genius. I wanted to be just like him. Man, I must be the biggest dope in the world."

"No, Lenny. You're not. They apparently fooled a lot of people. In fact, from what I heard they don't expect people to be on to their scheme yet, so nobody's looking for them right now."

She motioned for him to stop and they stood still, listening.

The voices had stopped. "Maybe they'll just take the boat and leave," she said. "At least then we'd be safe from them. The authorities can catch up with them later."

Lenny shook his head. "Can't. The boat's got a security system. You've got to have the code to unlock it. I didn't give him the code. I haven't been able to talk to them. I was just going by the GPS signal like he told me to and they never answered on the walkie-talkie."

"They lost it in the crash," she told him. "Okay, we need to keep moving quickly. Reinforcements are on the way, but I need to get up to the top of the cliff to set off these flares to let the deputies know where we are."

"I can do it," Lenny said. "No offense, but you look like you're about on your last legs." For the first time he smiled a nervous smile.

"I can't argue with you there," Abby told him. She hesitated a moment, assessing the young man. She prided herself on being a good judge of character. She wouldn't tell him about Henry, she decided, but she'd trust him with the flares. "I know you grew up on these islands. I heard Carl say that. Did you spend much time outdoors? It's a pretty rough climb."

"I'm tougher than I look," Lenny said. "I'm a mountain goat. Just point the way."

He proved to be as tough as he'd claimed. Abby was having a hard time keeping up with him. Of course he had also been right about her being exhausted. When they came upon the crashed plane, Lenny stopped and stared. "So he stole one of the company planes too? Look at what he's done to it! What a hypocrite. He was always going on about how he believed in the company and how important it was to be a team player. He snookered me right in. There's nothing worth believing in anymore."

"People aren't always what they seem, Lenny," Abby told him. "But there are plenty of things in this world worth believing in."

She described the route he would need to take to get to the top of the cliff. "Set off both flares and then come back as fast as you can. We'll go down to the shore when we hear the engines approach to warn them. There's a bluff near there we can hide under."

"Why don't you go on down now?" Lenny asked. "I'll be all right."

"Not on your life," she said then wished she'd used another phrase. "I'll wait here for you and we'll both go down together. You'll never be able to find it on your own."

Lenny set off and Abby moved behind the wreckage to keep vigil. She was incredibly tired, but a good deal of adrenaline was also coursing through her body so she was edgy and fidgety. Her head was throbbing and her eyes burned.

Abby had no concept of time anymore. A minute seemed the same as an hour. She wasn't sure how long she waited there before the walkie-talkie in her coat pocket squawked. "Done," Lenny reported. "I can see the boats coming. There's three of them. Looks like they may be planning to loop around to the west side. I'll be back down as quick as I can."

"Great," Abby told him in a hoarse whisper. "I don't think we'd better risk using these anymore. Noises carry. Let's turn them off and you come right back down."

Abby leaned against a tree. She wasn't sure how long she'd stood like that. Maybe she'd actually fallen asleep standing up, she thought vaguely. But when her awareness sharpened, she realized she heard movement and it was coming in her direction. She stiffened.

As she looked around she saw Lenny moving quickly, almost at a trot. He looked relieved to see her.

"Lenny," a voice rang out. "Lenny, we've been looking for you. Why'd you run off, buddy?"

It was Carl Atkinson's voice. Abby couldn't see him. He was on the other side of the wreckage. But she certainly recognized the voice. The voice of evil.

Lenny turned and veered off, moving away at an angle, then glanced quickly over at Abby. "I was just . . . I saw the plane and thought maybe you were hurt or something," Lenny said.

"Hey, no, we're fine," Carl said. "Didn't you hear us calling back there? Way back there in the woods?" he asked, his voice singsongy. "We were back there waiting for you to come and get us, Lenny. Depending on you."

Abby moved slowly to the back of the plane and peeked around the tailpiece. Gretchen and Carl were both coming across the open expanse of land toward Lenny. Lenny didn't look back in Abby's direction, but started moving slowly toward the trees on the opposite side of the clearing. He was leading them away from her, Abby realized. Protecting her. Doing his own killdeer imitation.

"We're pretty eager to get out of here, Lenny," Carl said, his voice now steely. "But I think you know that. We need the code for the boat, though, and we'd kind of like you to come with us," he said evenly as he continued to move in Lenny's direction.

"Thr—three's a crowd," Lenny stammered. "I mean, this is your honeymoon. You two go on. The code is 4221. You can punch that in and be right on your way," he said, giving Abby a fleeting sidelong glance as he continued to move one sidling step after another.

"I'm afraid we can't leave without you, Lenny," Carl said, bringing an ugly-looking gun out from behind his back. "Now come on with us and everything will be fine. I don't want to hurt you, but I will."

Abby's hand closed into a fist in her pocket and she felt the keychain she'd taken from the plane. She pulled it out and made a decision. Lenny was totally in the open. She at least had the cover of the plane. She put the whistle to her lips and let out a short shrill blast then ducked back behind the plane. Carl swung around toward the sound and started to move toward Abby with the gun raised.

Thistledown floated on the easy breeze and caught the rays of the sun as it broke through the clouds. Time seemed to stand still.

Chapter Eighteen

LILY WAS ENCHANTED with everything about the farm. Zack took her out to show her the lavender fields.

"She seems like such a nice young lady," Ellen said, as their footfalls on the porch died away.

"I really like her," Mary said. "She and Zack seem to have a special friendship. And Mom, I want more than anything now to keep Finnegan," she said, the words tumbling out with an urgency Mary didn't even know she was feeling. "I see now what Nancy and Zack had in mind for me. He's wonderful."

She stopped and looked up at her mother. "How do you feel about having him in your house? I know how you used to feel about our pets being inside when Abby and I were young."

"Oh posh," Ellen said. "This is entirely different. Finnegan's welcome anywhere in this house if he helps you, Mary. Did you even need to ask?"

"I can't wait for Abby to see him," George said. "She's going to be impressed with all this animal can do."

"I know," Mary said. "As well she should be. I'm still amazed."

Mary had reported to her parents as soon as she'd arrived on the farm what everyone was predicting about Abby's return, making it sound perhaps a bit more imminent and definite than the bald facts supported. Her mother was now intent on a humble version of the killing of the fatted calf. She was industriously kneading dough for her famous sourdough bread while Mary chopped vegetables for a hearty chicken stew.

"I hear they've spotted the plane," George said. "Search plane was able to go out again at first light. That was on the news a little bit ago."

"Still no word about survivors, though," Ellen said. "I just hope everyone is okay."

Mary realized that she had become so fixated on Abby and Henry's safety it had been a long while since she'd given much thought to the victims of the plane crash. She said a silent prayer for their survival.

"I think I'll go out and join Zack and Lily for some fresh air," George said, grabbing his coat and hat from the rack beside the door.

Mary glanced over at the silent television set in the sitting room off of the kitchen. "I think I'll turn on the set and catch the local news update," she said. "There might be something about the crash."

Ellen continued to turn and fold the dough, with perhaps

a little more vigor than was necessary. "Okay, but if it's bad, I don't want to see it."

Mary found the remote and flipped on the set. The weather report matched perfectly with what they could see outside the window. Fair, with the temperature approaching balmy. The sports report droned on for a while with neither woman interested, and then something caught Mary's ear. The financial report was breaking news about the Raventech Corporation. She looked up and saw a familiar photograph on the screen. "That's the article Abby and I saw about that big wedding over in Seattle. They went all out, let me tell you," Mary told Ellen. "Every extravagance you can think of."

She quieted and listened as the reporter recounted the discovery of what company officials were calling "gross irregularities" in the auditors' report ordered by the corporation's board of directors. The auditors, the reporter continued, had worked with "some sense of urgency over the past two days. Two top officers of the company, Carl and Gretchen Atkinson, could not be located to answer the auditors' questions."

"That's them. That's the couple that got married," Mary said, pointing to the set.

"Sounds to me like maybe all that money for the fancy wedding may have been ill-gotten gains," Ellen said. "Doesn't bode well for the marriage, I would think."

"No, it doesn't," Mary said.

They shaped the bread dough into loaves, and Ellen put them into the pans and set them in the warm oven to rise.

Mary flipped the set to the home and garden channel and the two women watched a short segment on crafting fall wreaths, then flipped back to the news.

The stewpot was simmering and the bread rising by the time they heard the others out in the backyard.

Mary kept thinking she was hearing a car drive up. Wishful thinking. Her father padded into the kitchen in his stocking feet followed by Lily and Zack, who went straight for the television set. "Ellen, it smells like heaven in here," George said. "I hope Abby's not too tired to eat."

"If she's too tired when she gets in, it'll keep," Ellen said. "All I care about is that she gets in safe and sound—and soon. I just want to see her face and count all her fingers and toes and make sure she's okay. Guess that's an instinct that never goes away for a mother," she said, reaching down to rub Mary's shoulders.

"Listen up," Zack said, putting his head around the doorway, "there's something on about the plane."

Everyone went into the sitting room and gathered around the set. The bulletin crawler was moving across the bottom of the screen. "Again, this just in," the anchorwoman intoned gravely. "A plane reported to have crashed over the San Juan Islands is thought to be a Cessna 180 belonging to the Raventech Corporation. As reported earlier, auditors have discovered financial irregularities in the company's records and two high-ranking company officers are being sought for questioning. It is thought that the two were aboard the plane. No news yet on whether they survived the crash."

There was a cutaway to an aerial view of the downed plane. "This footage just in," came the voice-over of the anchorwoman. "The plane is down on what is reported to be an uninhabited island in the southern reaches of the San Juan Islands. Authorities in the area have been notified and a search is on for survivors. The two people aboard the plane, Carl and Gretchen Atkinson, are now considered fugitives."

There was silence in the room as they all continued to stare at the television screen, then looked at one another.

A plaintive "oh" escaped Ellen's lips, and she put her hand to her mouth and sat down heavily in a chair.

Lenny took off running toward the trees. Carl looked from him to the plane, and then turned back to Lenny. While he was suffering his moment of indecision, Abby had one of pure clarity.

Back in biblical times when birds were captured to be sacrificed or used as caged pets, the fowlers had lots of methods for capturing them—almost all of them now seemed reprehensible to Abby's way of thinking. But desperate times called for desperate measures. One method was using a throw stick. These were hurled in a rotary motion at the legs of the running ground birds such as partridge or quail to bring them down. She glanced down at the lacrosse stick and thought it was just about the right dimensions.

She grasped the stick and pictured the motion in her mind. Lenny was in the open. She had to do something.

Carl made his decision and started to run after Lenny. Abby stood up and aimed. She gave one practice heft, then gave the stick as much wrist motion as she could generate. At first she thought she had overshot him, but then he put his out-stretched leg right into the whirling stick and went sprawling. The gun flew out of his hand and landed in the grass just a few feet in front of Gretchen, who was dancing back and forth and screaming. She picked it up and waved it at Abby, then turned it toward Lenny. "Stop!" she yelled, her voice high and shrill. "Everybody just stop. I am sick of this. I want off this island and I'm telling you right now, I don't care how I have to do it."

"It's over, Gretchen," Abby said, with as much calm as she could manage with a gun being waved around in her direction. "The whole thing has come unraveled. You're not going to get away. People know. Lots of people know."

"Don't listen to her, Gretchen," Carl said, trying to get to his feet and hold his shin both at the same time. "Just hold the gun on them till I can get up." He struggled to disentangle himself from the stick and the clump of Scotch broom he'd landed in. "Who *are* you anyway?" Carl asked, staring in Abby's direction with both hatred and curiosity.

"I'm with the search team," Abby called, trying to make it sound bigger than just her and Henry. "Looking for survivors from the crash," she said, cutting her eyes to see that Lenny was moving inch by inch toward the trees and cover.

"Search crew," Carl sniffed. "I saw you. There's only two of you. Where's the guy?"

"I'm right here," called a deep voice from the edge of the clearing. Abby's head snapped around and there was Henry, his rustic crutch in one hand and his service revolver in the other. He was using a large cedar for cover. "Everybody just stay right where you are till we get this sorted out. My name is Sergeant Henry Cobb. I'm with the San Juan County Sheriff's Department. Now I'd like you to put down that gun please, ma'am," he said to Gretchen.

"Don't do it, Gretchen," Carl said, his tone cagey. "He's not going to shoot you. And he's sure not going to run you down, not with that leg." He finally got to a standing position and began to move slowly toward Gretchen. "And he's not going to shoot me. I'm unarmed. There are witnesses. I don't have a weapon," he said, holding his arms high and speaking loudly.

Henry held the gun steady, but Abby could tell by the strain on his face that it was all he could do to remain standing.

"Here's what we're going to do," Carl said. "Me and Gretchen are just going to back on out of here, and you all are going to stay right where you are. We got no beef with any of you. We just want to leave." He reached Gretchen and started to urge her backward.

"Stop right where you are," came a voice from the edge of the woods about twenty feet down from Henry. Abby looked up to see Deputy Mike Bennett peer out from behind a boulder. He, too, had a gun trained on the couple.

Carl's head jerked around. "You don't want to do that," he called. "Gretchen's not so good with a gun. She starts shooting there's no telling who she might hit."

"Stop right there," boomed another voice from the other side of the meadow. Abby looked around to see two more men standing in the tree line.

Gretchen stopped abruptly and drew back and tossed the gun on the ground. "Oh shut up for once in your life, Carl," she said, turning toward him. "I'm not going to *shoot* anybody. It's over."

Carl looked desperately toward the gun, then turned and took off running down the hill back toward the mudflat. Suddenly a raven flew into the clearing, a solid line of black cutting the blue sky. It let out a deafening *caw-caw*, and swooped within inches of Carl's head. He ducked and swatted at it, and it flew skyward, then flipped and went into another power dive. Carl tripped on a tangle of juniper roots and went sprawling. The bird let out another raucous cry and made one more looping dive before flying off toward the cliff. Carl continued to swipe at the air as he struggled to his feet.

Deputy Bennett moved forward with amazing speed and had his knee on Carl's back before he could disentangle himself. In less than thirty seconds the deputy had him secured in handcuffs.

By then one of the officers from the opposite side of the meadow had gotten into position in front of Gretchen. "Stay right where you are," he warned her. "And you, keep your hands where I can see them," he called out to Lenny, who immediately put his hands to the sky.

"No, no," Abby said, coming out from behind the plane and blurting out the story. "They were after him too. He hasn't done anything wrong," she said. "He's with us."

"All right, come on over here," Deputy Bennett called. "We'll sort it all out at the station." Lenny did as he was told, but kept his arms up. Abby shot him a reassuring smile.

"Boy are we glad to see you both," Deputy Bennett said as he got Carl to his feet and tugged him over toward where Gretchen stood. Henry tossed him his set of handcuffs and Deputy Bennett clasped them on her. Ever the gentleman, he asked, "Are those comfortable, you need me to adjust them?"

"Comfortable?" Gretchen snarled. "Comfortable?"

"Good then," he said, cutting her off. He turned to Henry. "You two had us worried. We've had a lot of folks out looking for you."

"I'm glad you got worried. And that you got worried just in time," Henry said. "Well done, Mike." He leaned against a tree and sighed.

"This is all a misunderstanding," Carl protested, giving them a smarmy smile. "I can explain. Boy, are we glad to see you guys. We crashed. We've been wandering around this island for hours, days maybe. I don't know. I've lost track of time. I think we may be delirious, right Gretchen? We're a little crazed. We didn't know what we were doing."

Gretchen frowned at him, then rolled her eyes. "You're pathetic," she said finally.

"Oh, you'll have your chance to explain everything," Henry said. "In the meantime, Deputy Bennett, would you read these two their rights?"

"Be happy to, Sarge," he said, and proceeded with the formal recitation as the two glared at him.

A man in a uniform only slightly different from Henry's wandered over, and Henry greeted him. "Earl," he said, with a tip of his head, "good to see Skagit County's got our back."

"You don't look so good, Henry. Broken?" Earl said, nodding toward the leg.

"Probably," Henry answered.

Earl turned around and looked toward the small meadow. "I think they can land the medevac chopper here. We'll have you out in no time. Just get as comfortable as you can."

"No offense, Miss Stanton, but you don't look so good either," Deputy Bennett said.

"So everyone keeps telling me," Abby said. "I've picked up a cold. I feel about the way I look, I imagine."

"I know exactly what you mean. I'm still on the mend myself. We'll have you out of here as quick as we can. You're quite a trooper."

Abby looked at his red nose and bloodshot eyes and gave him a grateful smile. "Same to you, Deputy."

As they were leading Gretchen away she looked over at Abby and her eyebrows shot up. "Is that my *blouse*?" she asked. "That's a designer blouse. I paid four hundred dollars for that!"

Abby looked down at the top. It was soiled and ripped and random sequins had been pulled away and were hanging by threads. The color looked garish in the bright morning sun. "I'd say that was one in a long line of bad decisions," she told Gretchen, her voice gentle.

Gretchen opened her mouth to reply, but then looked down at the ground and nodded slowly.

OUTSIDE THE STANTON FARMHOUSE, life continued apace. The cows grazed, the birds sang and far off a ferry horn announced that people were coming and going on their daily business. But inside, nothing moved.

Everyone continued to stare at the television screen, long after the anchorwoman had moved on to a story about the latest political controversy in the state legislature.

Finally Zack broke the silence. "I'm sure Henry and Abby are fine. Even if they found those two, white-collar criminals are hardly ever violent." He turned to Lily and in a stage whisper, asked, "Are they?"

"Let's not go borrowing trouble," George said, but Mary could see that the color had drained from his ruddy face.

"I just wish that phone would ring," Ellen said, then pressed her fingers tightly to her lips.

As if on cue the phone let out a loud jangle. Everyone turned to stare at it, but no one moved. Finnegan barked sharply, then went and picked up the handset and delivered it to Mary's lap.

Everyone moved around in front of her and watched as her face went through a series of expressions, then finally broke into a smile that mirrored the sunshine outside.

"They're okay," she said, fighting back tears of joy and relief. "They're okay and they're coming home!"

Chapter Nineteen

FINNEGAN GRABBED THE STRAP Lily had attached to the refrigerator door in Ellen's kitchen and pulled it open following Mary's command. It seemed almost impossible to Mary that she had been in this same place just four short days ago, doing this very same chore. So many things had changed since Wednesday night when Abby and Henry went out to look for the plane. But one thing had stayed the same—she was still in a quandary over what to do about Henry.

She gathered the makings for a gigantic salad to go with the rest of the dishes that were threatening to collapse the sideboard in her mother's dining room. They were all gathered for Sunday dinner, just as planned. Only now it was a real celebration.

"Good boy," Mary said. "Now close."

Lily, who had come in to collect more bowls to bring to the sideboard stopped and clapped her hands together. "That's a new one. I've never seen him do that!"

Mary beamed. "He and I invented that one last night. After two days of plying Abby with orange juice and water to fight that awful cold, we've had plenty of practice with the refrigerator door."

She wheeled over and reached out a hand to take Lily's wrist. "I promise you, Lily. I will take very good care of Finnegan. And I will appreciate him every day. And you as well, for bringing him to me. I hope you'll come out again soon to visit."

"I hope so too, Mary." She and Mary entered the dining room. "I'd love to come and see how you two are getting on. And anyway, I have to come back to see all those wildflowers you told me about that bloom in the spring, right?"

"Absolutely," Ellen said, setting the table. "And again in summer to see the lavender."

"And I need to take you birding," Abby said, coming into the room, her hair slightly mussed.

"You're supposed to be taking a nap," Ellen said.

"I'm fine, Mom," Abby said. "Even my Rudolph nose is almost gone. I've done nothing *but* rest for the last two days. Not that I'm complaining. It's been heavenly."

"Well, okay then, come help me with the salad," Mary said, gesturing toward the kitchen. "Henry will be here any minute, and Zack and Lily have a plane to catch later. Dinner needs to be on time."

"I wasn't kidding, Lily," Abby said, as they entered the kitchen. She got the big wooden salad bowl down out of the cupboard. "You've got to come back and let me take you birding. You know we've got well over two hundred different species here at one time of the year or another."

"Well, I have a little confession to make, Abby," Lily said. "I don't know very much about birds. I know a robin when I see it, and a cardinal, but that's about the extent of it. I've been too busy with my four-legged friends to learn. But I'd love it if you could teach me."

"Ah, just what I like," Abby said. "A blank slate."

"Did you hear Zack's new piece?" Lily asked.

They could hear the piano music drifting in from the living room and a moment of stillness came over the kitchen as the women stopped to listen.

"He's calling it 'Blue-Eyed Mary,'" Mary said softly. "I choose to think he was inspired by me and not our island's wildflower of the same name. Either way, I love it. It really is a beautiful piece of music."

"Henry's here," George announced, putting his head in the kitchen door.

Mary's heart jumped, but then became heavy in her chest. Ever since Abby and Henry had returned from their ordeal she had thought of little else than how she would tell Henry her decision. She had thought once her mind was made up she would have peace about it. It seemed so obvious this was the right thing to do yet she was still in constant turmoil about it.

Henry came on crutches more finely crafted than Abby's tree limb. A fiberglass cast covered one leg from ankle to thigh, and his cuts and bruises had faded. He was in good spirits. Mary was so happy to see him, yet so filled with dread at the same time.

"How's the leg?" Abby asked him.

"It's going to be fine. Simple fracture. I'm going to be in this thing for a while, but I'm getting around okay with these, no offense to your more stylized maple limb."

Mary felt a familiar, but very unwelcome, pang of what could only be called jealousy. Abby and Henry had shared an experience—albeit a very unpleasant one. The point was that it was an experience only for the able-bodied. She was ashamed of herself, but there it was. Didn't that only prove that she had to break it off with Henry?

ABBY HAD NEVER BEEN SO HAPPY to come back to normal life on Sparrow Island, though normal had shifted considerably since she'd left with Henry to go look for the plane just a few short days ago.

The idea of a service dog for Mary had never once crossed Abby's mind. And if it had, she would never, not in a million years, have expected Mary to go for the idea. But here they were, and Abby was awed by how many tasks Mary and Finnegan could already perform together. And more than that, she was pleased to see that Mary had a true affection for the animal.

She watched as the dog circled Mary's chair at the table and laid down beside her on her command.

Abby bowed her head as her father said the blessing over the food and lifted a prayer of thanksgiving for her safe return, as well as Henry's and young Lenny's. Then, in true Stanton spirit, he added a prayer for the Atkinsons that they would find redemption and reconciliation.

All the questions that everyone had been holding back came tumbling out as they started to pass the myriad bowls and platters.

She and Henry had been taken straight from the island for medical treatment. Henry had been kept overnight and she'd been sent home, too exhausted to even speak. Now they were on the mend and rested.

"How long are you going to be in that cast, Henry?" George asked. "That's going to cut in on your fishing, wouldn't you say?"

"I would imagine so," Henry said. "Several weeks anyway. Maybe I'll take up golf—or lacrosse," he said, giving Abby a grin.

"What was this big scheme those two had in mind anyway?" George Stanton asked. "Surely they didn't think they could just clean practically the whole company out and nobody would notice."

"Actually, I think that's exactly what they thought they could do," Henry said, ladling gravy onto his mashed potatoes. "And if they hadn't gotten a couple of insomniac auditors— and more importantly if Carl Atkinson had gotten a few hours of instruction with floatplanes—they might have pulled it off. Now all they'll be pulling is a nice stiff sentence, I think."

"That must have been a scary experience," Lily said. "I understand that island is pretty isolated. Scary for them too. It sounds like they weren't the outdoor types."

"I think it's safe to say that," Henry said. "I think before this, their idea of enjoying the great outdoors was drinking a latte in a Seattle city park."

"I'm just glad it's all over," Abby said. "For me the scariest part was losing our communication. We didn't know if help was coming in time or not. There were some pretty dark moments," she said, exchanging a knowing look with Mary. "But now that we're all safe and sound back here, I can look back on it and some of it strikes me as kind of funny."

"Like when you captured Lenny!" Henry said. "You scared the kid half to death. He said he was walking along and the next thing he knew his foot was up in the air, his back was flat on the ground and some woman from an ancient, undiscovered primitive tribe had a stick across his chest. She had a white nose and some kind of shield that made her sparkle and glow and she was right in his face speaking in a foreign tongue."

Abby shrugged. "The cold," she said, her voice still nasal. "And I guess I was a little frantic by then. I was probably talking pretty fast."

"I don't imagine the wardrobe helped, either," Henry said. "Or the fact that we'd been hiking around the island in the pouring rain for hours on end and didn't exactly look our best. My deputies found me in a lime green polo shirt at least a size too small. Don't think I'll ever hear the end of that one."

"Maybe that's what's giving you the urge to take up golf," Zack said, which provoked laughter around the table.

For the rest of the meal, the atmosphere was festive.

Everyone—almost everyone—was in good spirits. Abby noticed that Mary was subdued. She smiled and laughed in all the right places, but Abby knew her well enough to see that something was bothering her. Maybe the fact that Zack was leaving. She hoped that's all it was. Mary hadn't said anything else about breaking up with Henry, but Abby sensed she was still thinking about it.

Abby looked across to Henry. His face lit up when Ellen started bringing out the dessert. He'd finally have a chance to get a piece of Ellen's lemon meringue pie.

"I dreamt about this pie when I was down under that bluff," he said, a faraway look in his eyes. "I could almost taste it. The very thought of it inspired me to keep going," he gave Mary a quick glance. "That and all the other good things back here on the island."

"I think I'll take Finnegan out for a few minutes," Mary said as the table was being cleared of dinner dishes. Abby opened her mouth to volunteer to do it for her then clamped it shut. Mary needed space. Whatever was bothering her would come out in its own good time.

MARY LED FINNEGAN OUT onto the back porch and down the ramp into the backyard. She reached down and took off his harness and cape. "Off the clock," she said and he pranced away to explore the backyard with his nose.

It was a glorious day. The sun was shining. The air had turned clear and brisk and there was a light breeze blowing in from the sea. Abby and Henry were back safe. Finnegan would be staying with her and together they would begin a new phase of life. Her children and grandchildren were all happy and healthy. But still a dark cloud hovered. Henry.

Mary heard the porch door open and looked up to see Henry backing through. He did a rough, three-point turn with his crutches and worked his way clumsily down the ramp, a knitted throw draped over his shoulder. "Your mom was afraid you'd be getting chilly out here. The sun's deceptive," he said, handing her the colorful throw.

She took it and put it over her lap. "Thanks. It is cooler than it looks."

Finnegan looked up and watched the two for a moment, as if checking to see if Mary needed him to come over and fend off this intruder. "It's okay, Finnegan," she repeated. "Off the clock, boy."

Henry laughed. "Does he punch in when it's time to go back to work?"

Mary smiled. "I don't think he's ever really *not* working. He's devoted to me already. It's quite remarkable."

"Yes, it is. Ah, Mary, this is going to be a good thing for you. What a gift."

"Yes, I feel that way too," Mary said. "I feel like I'm getting stronger all the time."

Henry smiled down at her. "I know you are."

"Henry, I have something I want to say . . . ," she began.

"I can see that something's clearly troubling you," Henry

said. "And I think I know what it is. It's the fact that I'm on these things, isn't it?" he asked, picking up a crutch and waving it around. "I know I'm not going to be able to do a lot of things over the next few weeks. That's going to be a drag for you. I suppose you're going to tell me you don't want to see me anymore because of that."

"I would *never* do that," Mary protested. "What kind of person do you think I am? I would never want to stop seeing you for something—"

She stopped abruptly and looked up into Henry's smiling face. He raised his eyebrows. "Pretty simple when you think about it, isn't it? I hope you don't think I'm that kind of person either."

"But Henry," she said, sighing, "in a few weeks you'll be off those crutches. You'll want to go fishing and hiking and dancing again. I'll still be in this chair."

"Mary, how many times did you go fishing with me before the accident?"

"Well, I never did. You never asked, but . . ."

"That's because fishing is a solitary activity for me. It's what I do to get away by myself. And if I wanted company, there are plenty of guys to go along with me. As for hiking, we're blessed around here with parks that have lots of trails that can handle your chair, especially with Wonder Dog over there coming along with us. And as for dancing, all I care about is that my heart dances whenever I see you. It doesn't matter to me whether my feet do or not."

"Henry, I—" Mary began again, but he held up a hand. He turned himself around and got settled in the garden chair near Mary and leaned toward her, seeming to gather his thoughts.

"Mary, I've had a lot of time to think about this the last few days. I've turned it over in my mind a hundred times what I want to say and just how I want to say it, but all of that has disappeared from my head."

He squirmed a little in his chair and put the crutch underneath his cast to support it. "Here's the deal. You're a beautiful woman. And if what *you* want is for us to stop seeing one another, then I respect that and we'll still be friends as far as I'm concerned. I can accept that. But if what's troubling you is something you *think* might be happening in my mind, or in my life, then I want you to reconsider. I pride myself on being an honest man, Mary. And I make you this pledge right now: I'll always be honest with you. And I expect you to always be honest with me. I'm happy spending time with you. I'm not asking for anything else. I'm happy to live in the now, especially after the last few days."

"You sound like Zack," Mary said, thinking of what he had said about Lily.

"Well, Zack is a smart guy," Henry said. "Now just one more thing and then I'll hush and listen to whatever you have to say. I'm a grown man, Mary. Way grown. I've been making my own decisions for a long time. I don't need or want anyone making them for me, even if they think it's for my own good. Even you. Now I'm asking you plain, do you *want* to continue to go out with me, or would you rather I didn't call on you anymore?"

Mary fought tears that threatened to spill out. "Henry, I . . ."

Finnegan seemed to sense her distress and came over, placing his head in her lap. He glanced over at Henry, then back at Mary and gave one sharp bark.

"I guess he wants me to fess up," Mary said. "I have over-reached a little I think. I've been trying to decide what's best for you without ever consulting you about it. That's pretty presumptuous, isn't it? I guess that's why I've been so troubled. I even had the answer put right in front of me, literally, but I ignored it still. 'Trust in the Lord with all your heart and lean not on your own understanding,'" she said, her voice faint and bemused. "No wonder I could never get any peace.

"Henry, I enjoy going out with you," she said, sitting up straighter and cocking her head to one side. "I am a grown woman—way grown—and I too have been making decisions for myself for a long time. I *do* promise to be honest with you. I don't want your life to be limited because of me. But if you tell me you want to continue to see me, despite everything, I'll believe you. And I'll trust you to tell me so if those feelings ever change."

"I do and I will." He took her hand and kissed it. "So, are we good?"

"Yes, we're good," Mary said with a wide smile. "But I *will* be taking you up on that offer to take Finnegan and go hiking in the park, maybe even *before* you get off those crutches."

Henry called Finnegan over and scratched around his ears. "What do you say about it, boy? Are you good with that?" Finnegan looked from Henry to Mary then let out another sharp bark and went off again to explore the yard.

ABBY LOOKED ON FROM THE DOORWAY, every muscle tensed. Then she heard her sister laugh. A real, genuine Mary-laugh, coming from all the way down in her toes. Abby let out the breath she didn't even realize she'd been holding and smiled.

She leaned against the door frame and watched the bright orange orb of the sun floating above the blue expanse of the sea. She was near tears at the sheer beauty of it. It might have been tragedy that brought her back home, but it was the every-day gladness filling her heart that made her want to stay here.

"Aunt Abby, come look," Zack called. He was standing in front of the kitchen window pointing toward a madrone tree about halfway down the hillside, its russet bark standing out in sharp contrast to the sparkling blue waters. "Look at that. Isn't that a raven? He's perched right up on the very top of the tree. Isn't that strange?"

Abby saw the bird slowly turn his head and survey the sur-rounding land. Then he pushed off the limb and flew away, silent and blue-black in the afternoon sunlight. In the Bible a raven fed the prophet Elijah when God told him to hide out in the desert. Maybe the one on the island had been sent too. Raven the helper.

Chapter Twenty

ABBY POURED PANCAKE BATTER onto the griddle as Mary rolled toward the refrigerator Finnegan already had open for her. "Close it, boy," she said automatically as she wheeled back to the counter with a dozen eggs in one hand.

It had been two weeks since Abby and Henry's ordeal on the island. Hugo, Bobby and Henry were coming for breakfast at Mary and Abby's house before they all decamped to the Sparrow Island Nature Conservatory for the delayed release ceremony for the peregrine falcons.

Abby breathed in the aroma of the freshly perked coffee and was once again grateful for all the amenities of home. Being out in the wilderness had made her appreciate each and every day how wonderful it was to have food readily available in the kitchen, a hot shower just a few steps from her bedroom and access to a toothbrush anytime she felt the need for one. She had added each to the ever-growing list of things in her gratitude journal.

Mary hummed softly as she broke the eggs into a bowl.

She added a bit of cream and went at the mixture with a whisk. She was happier than Abby had ever seen her since the accident. Abby attributed this change to several things. First of all, there was Finnegan. They were shaping up to be quite a team. Mary had her van, which she drove with her usual aplomb. That brought her a new level of independence. And of course, it didn't hurt that both Nancy's family and Zack and Lily were planning to all come for a visit together soon. But more than any of those things, Mary seemed at peace. She and Henry were having a wonderful time and both seemed relaxed and perfectly themselves these days.

Mary finished whipping the eggs and pulled a piece of plastic wrap over the top of the bowl. "I'm going to put this back in the fridge. I've got to run down to the ferry and pick up Henry."

"Would you like me to go?" Abby asked, already knowing the answer.

"No, Finnegan and I will go get him," Mary said. "Henry's still a pedestrian, you know. Can't drive with that awkward cast. I'm enjoying being his chauffeur."

Abby thought back to the time she and Henry had searched for that plane, and of all the confusing and conflicting events that followed. Despite the hardships, she felt she had been in the right place at just the right time. Through their efforts and the grace of God, young Lenny Bascom had escaped the fowlers' snare—though not Abby's.

Lenny had called Abby just yesterday to let her know that

he would be returning to work at Raventech. The CEO of the company had learned the whole story and called him in and asked him to stay. "He seems like a good guy who really believes the company can do good things for people," Lenny had told her. "But from now on, I'll be looking at what people do and not just what they say."

"Always a good practice," Abby had told him.

She smiled, remembering the conversation. There was no telling what this young man would bring to the world. And to think it could have been lost because of someone's greed.

AFTER A HEARTY BREAKFAST, the party set off for the conservatory. Mary deferred to Abby to drive so she could sit with Henry in the back of the van where he had his cast resting across the seat. When they arrived, Abby and Bobby got out and Mary wheeled her chair onto the lift.

Abby overheard her say to Henry, who was still in the van, "Don't worry, I'll wait for you."

Finnegan turned toward Henry and reinforced that with a couple of short chuffs before turning to leap down out of the van.

"I appreciate it," Henry said, looking over to Mary with a smile playing around his lips, "but I surely don't want to hold you back."

Mary returned the smile. "I'm a grown woman—way grown—remember?"

Abby realized this represented something private and

understood between the two of them. Whatever it was, she was very happy for it.

To Abby's surprise, the parking lot was almost full. Lots of islanders had braved the sharp wind and nippy temperature to come out for the ceremony. As people walked down the pathway toward the observation platform, they made up a sort of ad hoc parade. The mood was joyful and there was a feeling of solidarity and camaraderie. It made Abby's heart swell.

Only one of the falcons was still occasionally spotted around the grounds. Abby viewed that as a good sign. If they survived the first danger-fraught year, they'd probably be back again to nest. The urge to return home was strong, as Abby had certainly come to appreciate.

Bobby had decided that the one remaining was Shadrach. And in Bobby's imagination the birds had all gotten together and designated one to stay behind and say thank you before flying off to find his way in the world. He fully expected the falcon to make an appearance today and Abby had been trying, gently, to tamp down his expectations.

Bobby did his part of the presentation with enthusiasm and with a stage presence any Hollywood actor would envy. Then Abby did her spiel about the falcons. "We had hoped we might see one of them today," she concluded, "so that we can all say good-bye and wish them Godspeed, but . . ."

"There," Bobby said, pulling on her coattail. "It's Shadrach. Over there."

Abby looked to where he was pointing and sure enough,

one of the falcons was flying above the cliff. He flapped his great wings, then, in a movement that was spare and elegant, he swooped and lifted. He then wheeled and turned and lifted again.

There were smiles and murmurings and much scrambling for binoculars, but the bird was in no hurry. He lingered, doing his aerial acrobatics as if to say, "Look at what all your efforts have wrought—wasn't it worth it?"

Abby felt tears sting her eyes. What a gift it was to be back in such a place as this after so many years. She looked from the bird to the people on the observation platform. Almost all had played some role in helping raise the falcons. People had made sacrifices; they'd cared enough to put aside their daily concerns and help.

That was the nature of Sparrow Island, as Abby had known it as a child and knew it now. Changing, yet unchanged.

Abby looked up at the bird floating against the crystal blue sky and her heart was glad for so many reasons, she couldn't begin to count them. There were hardships in life, and sometimes people gave in to their baser instincts. But there was also great beauty, and more often than not, people did the human race proud.

More than anything, Abby was glad that she had listened to that small voice that had led her back here. She felt she was just where she needed to be. She had come home. Home to Sparrow Island.

Flight of the Raven
by Ellen Harris

Whispers through the Trees
by Susan Plunkett & Krysteen Seelen

Meet Abigail Stanton, an ornithologist, bird watcher and keen observer who brings a sharp eye to bear on the secrets that lie hidden on Sparrow Island, a place of extraordinary natural beauty in the San Juan Islands. Fate has brought Abby back to the island—and the life she thought she had said farewell to forever. But Abby, inspired by hope and faith, soon discovers that life on Sparrow Island is full of intrigue and excitement when she opens her eyes to the mysterious ways God works in our lives.

Ellen Harris is a Southern writer whose short stories have been featured in numerous mystery anthologies and in publications under the name Brynn Bonner. Harris was born in Alabama, spent a number of years in Michigan, and now lives with her husband and three children in North Carolina.